FIFTEEN-SIXTEENTHS

An American Historical Novel
by Renae Weight Mackley

ISBN: 978-1-7346258-0-6

ACKNOWLEDGEMENTS:

The support of my husband is priceless; I could not do this without it. He takes me to various Civil War sites and lets me spend endless hours on the computer.

Thank you to my dedicated critique group—Rebecca H. Jamison, Janice Sperry, and Carolyn Twede Frank. Thank you to readers Reo Mackley, Jennifer Mackley, Tammy Holt, and Lisa Mackley. I appreciate the written record others have made, especially Ralph Happel for his valuable article titled "The Chancellors of Chancellorsville, published in *The Virginia Magazine of History and Biography,* July 1963, Vol. 71, No. 3. Thank you to my supporters and fans. You're the best!

DEDICATION:

This book is dedicated to Krista, Cathy, Kate, and all my Piedmont friends, and to lovers of freedom everywhere.

AUTHOR'S HISTORICAL NOTE:

I became interested in exploring the lives of the Chancellor household after visiting the Chancellorsville Battlefield Visitor Center in Spotsylvania County, Virginia. Among various displays, there is a marvelous model of what the mansion looked like, a photo of a slave named Hester Lewis—who would have been twelve in 1863, and an informative film. I knew there was an interesting story to be told beyond the brief depiction in the film. I imagined the harrowing events of witnessing a battle and being trapped in a cellar, becoming inspired to retell their story.

Though nearly all the characters surrounding Mary really existed, her character needed to be fictionalized, the representation of a slave girl. The things that happen to Mary are imagined or inspired by the accounts of others. Surrounding characters generally follow true events during Mary's time period. However, this is a work of fiction, and some storytelling is inevitable.

Thank you for taking this trip back into history with me. Please enjoy!

CHAPTER ONE

Charlotte, August 1963, South Carolina

I WASN'T TAKING ANY CHANCES that I couldn't get into Oakmont—the all-white high school, so I dragged Dad along with me to register. Mom passed for a tanned Caucasian. Dad, however, was as pale as they came. I put on a Sunday dress instead of an everyday one, going for that first good impression. It couldn't hurt, though the notary only required my birth certificate and me swearing to the truth. That I needed a notary at all, told me my new town would do things by the book, making it harder on me.

As we got into the Dodge Dart, I justified the truth that I would swear to. "Fifteen-sixteenths is practically the whole pie." I smiled at him when he glanced from the driver's seat. "Lots of students have mixed blood. I just happen to know about my ancestry. It's not fair that I have to hide it and others don't, but my future depends on it."

"I know." He smiled back. "It's not me you need to convince. I would have married your mother even if the one-drop rule were in force. I'd support you attending the other school if you wanted, but I reckoned you wouldn't be happy with a mediocre drama program. The students at Oakmont will be different than at your last school."

Yep. He knew me well. We shared more than his angular jawline and above average height. We could both be stubborn. He was a pain when we didn't agree, but battling with him or my brother gave me great practice for the stage. More often than not, Dad's good heart and good ideas had saved my hide. Mom was more easy-going.

"We're all the same in God's eyes," he continued, "but here in the South, people are stuck in old traditions—including Jim Crow laws, and their own notions of what's right, false or not. It's best not to rock the boat."

I almost laughed. Didn't he understand that I needed to blend in? Maybe he thought my flair for acting would make me get dramatic at the wrong time. *That* I could see.

He took my silence for needing more of a lecture. "I'm not asking you to change who you are, but don't go looking for trouble where none is meant to be found. Remember the Golden Rule."

I rolled my eyes. "Dad, you're preaching to the choir. I have to blend in at Oakmont."

"How can you blend in when God gave you such beauty?" He glanced at me with a serious face, like he expected an answer.

I snorted. Dad was biased, but I loved him for saying it anyway. What God had given me was a certain amount of talent for acting. I'd worked hard to develop it and I wasn't going to throw that away. I didn't go to the movies solely for entertainment. I noticed ways that actors got emotion across. I looked for lines to repeat in my bedroom at night in different ways. I would honor that talent by taking advantage of the best drama program available, but I couldn't risk standing out off stage.

I spotted a couple of cute boys walking down the sidewalk, my eyes following them as we passed. I had yet to go on my first date and hoped for some real possibilities here, but these two were too dark to attend Oakmont. I couldn't help wondering if I was giving up some good dates by going to an all-white school. I bit my bottom lip. Oakmont's drama program better be all it had been advertised to be. Surely there would be cute boys at my school too. And new friends.

I didn't want to get sad over the friends I was leaving behind in Maryland. That was something I reserved for time alone in my bedroom. So I glanced again at the boys on the sidewalk.

One of the boys was lighter-skinned, like how Gran's skin tones reminded me of milk chocolate with extra cream. She was one-quarter colored. Her dark hair with streaks of gray felt wiry and her nose looked broad, pointing toward her African heritage, if anyone should be in doubt.

If we had to move at all, I was happy that Dad's job transfer took us closer to Gran. She was a good cook and the best storyteller I'd ever heard—not only her word choice but her voice nuances and facial expressions. She was the one who inspired me to act. Her, Grace Kelly, and Lucille Ball.

Acting was my identity back in Maryland. I'd had a supporting role as a freshman last year. One side of my mouth lifted as I envisioned the stage and me as Mrs. Webb in *Our Town*. I daydreamed for a moment of what the school auditorium might look like and me bowing before the audience in a major roll until my cheeks warmed with the vanity of it.

I stared out the window, seeing a corner drug store and movie house as we entered the downtown area. I checked for the current flicks. Palmetto Peaks didn't look much different than my old city, except for the 'whites only' signs. I made friends with anyone I wanted back there, and our school was desegregated.

Here in South Carolina, it felt like I had to choose sides. I hoped the kids at the white high school were nice. I had no problem testifying to being white to get there. I was white and lived white. Having to hide that one-sixteenth wasn't right. I still knew who I was, even if the rule-makers didn't need every last detail.

You'd think that this modern day would have progressed away from prejudice, what with all the hippie talk of peace and love going on. Maybe the march on Washington this week with Dr. Martin Luther King would do some good.

We parked and walked the cement path to the notary public office, where a lady sat at a desk and asked, "May I help you?" in a slow, Southern drawl.

I handed her my birth certificate, standing straight and tall. "Yes, ma'am. We recently moved here. I need to register for school."

"Welcome." She smiled. "It's nice you arrived in time to start with the other students. You wish to attend Oakmont High?" Her accent remained strong. "There are extra fees associated with that high school. Understood?" She glanced at Dad, taking in his brown hair and light complexion.

Dad nodded, his dimpled smile greeting her.

She looked at the certificate and then eyed me through her rhinestone-studded cat-eye glasses. "This is your father, I assume?"

"Yes, ma'am."

Another smile. "I see that you're nearly sixteen, so no other ID yet?"

"No, ma'am, just a learner's permit." Maybe dad would let me drive home now that I knew the way.

"Of course." She held the certificate between two fingers and gave it a shake. "You swear that you are Charlotte Ann Rogers and you are Caucasian? Raise your right hand."

I confidently did as directed. "I do."

She had me sign a form, stamped it, and applied her signature as well. "Take this to the school district office and y'all will be set. Welcome to Palmetto Peaks."

I thanked her and off we went. I only hoped that passing the State of South Carolina driving exams would be as easy.

I glanced at my brother as we walked the half a mile to school on Monday morning. "Hey, when did you pass me in height?" I lightly punched his arm. Mark only shrugged and continued in silence. Ignoring his opportunity to gloat left no question that he was nervous. We stopped at the corner where he would turn off toward the Junior High. I gave him a half-smile, saying, "Hang loose."

Mark practically whispered, "You too." Neither of us moved.

Junior high—ugh. I felt for him. We both had new school worries, so why hadn't we talked about it before today? It was different here in South Carolina. Mark could make friends with white kids and colored, like in Maryland. I didn't know how it would go in this place for me, but I knew the first day would be rough for us both.

The junior high was one of two secondary schools in the county that had complied with the desegregation laws. I supposed mine would be the last. White parents didn't want the school's rank or accreditation to fall. Nor did they want their students developing romantic relationships with other races.

"Maybe it won't be such a drag," I said. "Some cute chick will probably dig the new guy." He was cute, for a thirteen-year-old brother, that is. His brown eyes were warm and friendly, and so was his smile— when he let it show.

He squinted sideways at me before taking a step.

4

"Good luck." I watched him go, suddenly feeling the chill of being on my own.

I could see my school on the next block over, two stories tall. Oakmont High stood stately with its wide cement steps leading to the columned porch of a creamy-yellow bricked building. Students streamed toward the tall double doors, laughing and meeting friends they may or may not have seen all summer. It gave me a pang that I couldn't return to my old school.

There was nobody familiar for me to greet here. At least the skirt and blouse I wore looked similar to what other girls had on. I'd put my hair in one braid at the back so it would stay in control all day. It made me look younger, but it was better than frizzy hair. My first impression couldn't raise any suspicion.

Once inside, I stopped the nearest person. "Excuse me." A gorgeous boy with bright blue eyes turned toward me. "Um, can you tell me where the office is?" I asked.

"Sure. Are you new?" His smile warmed me.

"Yeah, I'm Charlotte Rogers."

"Jake Notley. It's right over there." He pointed. "See the big glass window? Let me walk you over."

"Oh, Ja-ake!" A sing-song female voice summoned him from across the entryway.

"That's okay," I said. "I see it. Thanks."

"No problem."

Jake stared after me as I glanced back to give him a grateful smile. A friendly face, not a suspicious one. The girl reached him, took him by the elbow, and shot me a glare as she bounded away, her bracelets jangling together.

I stopped at the office—practically holding my breath—and picked up my class schedule, a school map, and my locker combo without any trouble. There wasn't anything to put in the locker yet, but I should have enough time to find it and try out the combo. It opened. Not a bad start so far.

American History in room 209 was listed first. I climbed the stairs, feeling jostled by the boisterous crowd. A bell rang. My heart pounded. I would end up tardy, making a grand entrance after the bell. By the next breath, I knew it couldn't mean that class had started. Too many students filled the halls. They had some kind of warning bell.

Finding room 209 wasn't hard. Now to find a seat in a nearly full classroom. A few empty desks had backpacks on them like they were being saved for friends. Also, kids stood in the aisle so I couldn't tell which seat they had picked. I saw one lone desk with nothing on it and headed there, then remembered to show the teacher my schedule because I was added after her class roll was typed up. "Hi. I'm new," I said. *And I'm white enough to be here so please, please don't think otherwise.*

"Hello. I'm Mrs. Burkhart," the pretty, young teacher said. "Welcome."

I liked her smile and her curly strawberry-blonde hair.

She held out her hand for the schedule and wrote down my name in her roll book. I turned toward the class and the empty desk now had a body in the chair. "Okay, Charlotte, why don't you have a seat right there next to Ellen for today? Ellen, please remove your backpack. Whomever you're saving it for should get here on time." She pointed at a desk in the second row farthest from the door. The blonde girl frowned and removed her backpack from it. I sat down, grateful not to sit on the front row but still feeling a classful of eyes on me.

A girl with straight, chestnut hair strode in right as the bell rang, multiple gold and silver bangles on her left arm. Her expression brightened when she spotted her friend and fell when she saw me sitting next to Ellen. We recognized one another from the front entryway only minutes ago. She took the only seat left—center front, and turned back to glower at me. She pointed at my desk and mouthed, "Mine tomorrow."

Mrs. Burkhart came around and leaned on the front of her desk, tucking her copper curls behind her hears. "Welcome back, students. And welcome to our new student, Charlotte Rogers."

All eyes were on me again. One boy greeted me with a, "Hey, baby", and my cheeks further enflamed. Mrs. Burkhart sent him a glare. A girl nearby said, "Can I call you North Carolina, Charlotte?" The reference of my name as a city got a few chuckles.

Mrs. Burkhart cleared her throat. "Okay, that's enough." She called roll, where I learned the name of the girl in center front was Melanie. The teacher steam-rolled right into what we would study this semester. "Last year you had the history of our country's birth and the Revolutionary War. This year we will advance into the eighteen hundreds with the War of 1812, the Mexican-American War, and the American Civil War. You will pick one of these war time periods from which to write an essay, give an oral report, or dramatic reading at mid-term that will be a third of your grade. You may work alone or in small groups." The moans dominated over scanty gasps of enthusiasm.

Now that the attention was off me, I felt a prickle of excitement. A dramatic reading was right up my alley. Gran had instilled in me a love for the Civil War time period, telling me true stories of an ancestor who lived near the Battle of Chancellorsville. I could bring out the details from everyday life instead of the boring facts about how many soldiers marched with which army. I might even show up Melanie, who seemed like the queen bee of the girls. I pursed my lips. The ancestor happened to be a slave for the Chancellor family, and I couldn't risk someone connecting the dots.

Melanie turned her head and glanced at me, as if she had heard her name in my mind. Her look, which I saw out of the corner of my eye, sent a challenge, but I ignored it, not giving her the satisfaction of a reaction. What was the big deal? It was a desk, not her boyfriend.

When Mrs. Burkhart dismissed us at the bell, I grabbed my map to see where my next class would be. Melanie stepped from her seat into my direct line toward the door. She bumped hard into me with the textbook she had just received, making me stumble and drop my own book with a loud thud that called attention to my flailing arms. I hadn't been watching where I was going, but it seemed awfully convenient to be an accident.

"Oops. Sorry." She gave me a fake smile and strolled out the door.

My mouth hung open as I stared after her, stopping the flow of traffic before I could retrieve my book.

"What's the holdup? Go around her," a boy from the back suggested when the exit line halted.

My entire row waited behind me as others skirted me. My cheeks flushed again. Never mind a hundred years ago, I reckoned Miss Melanie had started a new civil war.

CHAPTER TWO

I CROUCHED TO PICK UP my book and saw a hand grabbing it before I could. I stood and looked across at a face I'd actually seen before. A pleasant face with a kindly smile and greenish blue eyes.

"Here you go." It was one of the boys from Brother Mike's Sunday school class. "I'm Brad, if you don't remember from yesterday."

He smiled, and I recognized a tender mercy in answer to my prayers. "Thank you, Brad, and I remember."

He shrugged. "No problem."

He walked with me out the door. "What class do you have next?"

I checked my schedule. "Math."

"Not your favorite, I take it."

"I always struggle with math. Can't wait for drama third period though."

He nodded. "Math's not my bag either. I've got debate next. Do you know where you're going?"

"Yeah. Thanks again."

He smiled and we parted at the doorway.

Math featured a quiz review to see what we remembered from last year. Most of it looked familiar, though I didn't do so well. At least this school wasn't ahead of the material I'd studied as a freshman. I kept anticipating my next class and hoping drama would meet my expectations. The bell finally rang and I shot from my seat.

I found the classroom downstairs, across the hallway from the stage. First, I peeked into the nice-looking theater with about five-hundred seats. I took in the padded cushioning, two sets of curtains, lots of track lighting above the stage, and some panels that likely held the sound system. Far out!

I entered the classroom, shoulders squared, feeling jazzed by what I'd seen. The drama teacher looked retirement age, but perhaps that meant lots of experience. I showed him my schedule and took a seat, spacing myself from the next girl.

A boy sat right between us, looked at me and said, "Don't I know you? Wait. Elizabeth Taylor, right?"

"Psh. Not hardly." My brown eyes were far from violet, but he'd made me smile. His coloring was closer to Elizabeth Taylor's than mine, with his black hair and dark eyes contrasting his pale skin. My cheeks warmed but I didn't look away. The weird introduction seemed fitting in a class like this. "Charlotte Rogers."

"That was my next guess, I'm John Hagley. A name you will see in lights one day." His hands stretched out a rectangle, bringing the marquee to life. He chuckled.

I smiled back. "I'll have to remember it then."

The teacher, Mr. Dodd, soon had us playing a pantomime game where we acted out three things about us that we liked to do, so we could get familiar with one another. For my turn, I ran two-handed arpeggios up and down an imaginary piano keyboard. Next, I tuned a radio dial, bobbed to the beat, and mouthed the words of a Beach Boys song. They got that one fast. For the last clue I rode a bicycle. It was tricky pedaling with one leg. The students got it as soon as I rang the bell on the handle bars.

"Not bad, Charlotte," John said. "We'll see what you've got when we get past the easy stuff."

The twinkle in his eye let me know his teasing was friendly, yet I sensed a challenge underneath that could push us both toward greater potential. A true thespian. I returned his grin, feeling an instant draw toward him.

My English, Chemistry, and Health classes went by fairly painlessly with no other prima donnas who bothered me. Until PE. My school day started and ended with Melanie. I could see other bumps and trips in my future, sprawling me onto the floor of the basketball court or soccer field. Living that Golden Rule would test me hard.

Melanie mostly ignored me until the very end. In the locker room we were trying out the locker combos newly given when she and another girl came up behind me.

"Oh, there's something in your hair," she said, pointing at the back of my head as I sat on the narrow bench. "A bug? Oo!" She recoiled like I was the bug.

I slapped at my neck and the elastic band broke, releasing my braid.

"Cut it out, Melanie. There's no bug," the girl on my left scolded.

Melanie turned to me with a bored look on her face. "Huh. I could have sworn something wasn't right with that hair of yours." As she stared at my partially unraveled braid her eyes got bigger and her face grimaced. Was she guessing my lineage from my hair?

I reached back and touched the pouf of increased volume. The braid had frayed to a mass of waviness up to where it held together by another elastic at my shoulder blades. I undid the elastic and finger-combed the braid apart.

"Oh, my! Did you ever see such unruly hair?" Melanie asked louder than needful, drawing more attention my way.

The girl next to her chortled and fluffed her hair. "Who needs that problem?"

I shrugged, aiming at indifference. "It's the extra humidity you have here. My hair hasn't adjusted." It was partly true.

The two girls walked off together, sniggering and leaving me with a pit in my stomach. How many had seen the frizz in my hair and might connect it to me not belonging? Maybe I should wait in the locker room until after the busses left.

"Don't mind Melanie," the girl to my left said. "She can be a brat sometimes. I'm Patty, by the way." She sent me a grin.

I clutched the lifeline as if I had been drowning. "Hi Patty. I'm Charlotte."

"You should wear your hair loose tomorrow to spite her." Her eyes twinkled. "You're lucky that it's so thick. You can do a lot with that, you know, even in this humidity."

I wasn't big on spite, but I liked Patty's suggestion.

"I can get some hair relaxer samples from my sister that I could bring tomorrow, if you want to try some."

"Really? Thanks." I didn't know there was such a thing. Patty's hair—a soft, wavy ash blonde—looked like she used some kind of conditioner.

"My oldest sister is a beautician. She gives me stuff all the time."

"Cool."

"I gotta catch the bus. See you tomorrow."

"Yeah. Thanks." I watched Patty go, observing how gracefully she moved. I stepped over to the mirror. Melanie had called my hair unruly, but she hadn't accused me of having African hair. Patty hadn't seemed suspicious either. It wasn't the perfect first day of school that I'd prayed for, but it could have been a lot worse.

When I reached home, the front door was locked. I went around to the back and snatched the hidden key under the flower pot. Opening the back door to the kitchen, I called out, "Mom? Mark?" Nobody was home. There was a note on the kitchen table. *At the hospital with Gran—Mom.*

Mark came into the kitchen a few minutes later and found me pacing, worry showing on my face. "Look at this!" I thrust the note at him.

He looked up after reading it. "Oh no! What do you think happened?"

"Who knows?" I'd been picturing a car accident, a seizure, a kitchen fire burning her hand. "Poor Gran."

"Yeah, I hope it's nothing too bad." He opened the fridge and peered in. "We both survived day one, I see."

"Right." My main goal of getting through the day without someone questioning if I belonged there had gone smoothly enough, so I didn't dwell on the awkward stuff that happened. "The auditorium is fab. How was your day?"

"Fine." He bit into an apple. I supposed there was awkward stuff he didn't want to dwell on either. Day one was now in the past.

The kitchen phone rang. I got to it first, but Mark ran to the extension in the den.

"Well, Granny broke her leg," Mom explained. "I'm still at the hospital, using a pay phone. Gran fell taking her garbage can in from the street. A neighbor called an ambulance and then the hospital called me. At least it wasn't her hip."

"So she'll be alright?" I asked.

"She'll be in a cast for six to eight weeks, but yes. They'll watch her overnight and probably release her tomorrow. She'll need help. Dad and I have already discussed having her move into the guest room. Could you see if I left some boxes on the bed and put them in the closet—tidy up a bit?"

Mark and I both said yes.

"There's enough leftover casserole for you two and Dad to have for supper. Make a salad to go with it. I'll grab something here and be home about eight o'clock. That's when they'll kick me out."

"Okay. Tell her we love her." I hung up, realizing Mom hadn't asked about our first day of school. She must really be worried. It made me uneasy. A new worry appeared. My not-so-Caucasian-looking grandmother was moving in with us.

CHAPTER THREE

GRAN WAS SETTLED IN THE guest bedroom when I returned from school. I peered through the crack in the door to find her sleeping. She would be on pain meds for a few days. My heart felt as if someone were squeezing it like a lemon to get the last drops of juice. Her pain was mine.

Later, when her supper tray was ready, I volunteered to take it to her. "Hi, Meemaw... I mean Gran." I hadn't called her Meemaw since I was little. Maybe I wished she could still take care of me instead of the other way around. "I have some homemade chicken noodle soup for you."

"You know by now, child, that you can call me anything as long as you don't call me late to supper." Her arms strained to scoot to a sit. "Did y'all already eat? Chicken soup. What does your mother think, that I'm sick or something?"

Her gruffness didn't fool anybody. It was good to see a little spunk in her again. "Yes, she thinks you're helpless, so I'll spoon feed you every bite."

She harrumphed, and the smile came out.

I set the tray on the nightstand and stacked pillows behind her back. Then I set the tray on her lap. "I can sit with you while you eat. Would you like some company?"

"Of course, dear." She blew on the soup to cool it. "Did I hear Christmas music?" she asked.

I smiled. "I don't think so. It's September."

"I was dreaming then. Right before you came in."

Though she was raised in the North, Gran had lived in South Carolina for several years—long enough to follow the Southern habit of leaving off the end sound off certain words, especially the ing ending, drawing out her vowels, and slipping in yuh for you. With her deep mellow voice, I found it charming.

"Ah, yes," she continued. "Dreaming about the Chancellor House at Christmas time." She took a few bites of soup. "This is good. I like the little carrots in it."

I brightened. "Do you want to tell me your dream?" Gran loved Christmas. She loved talking about the Chancellor family and the stately mansion they lived in. It would give her something to think about other than her painful leg.

"Not yet. I'm eating." She picked up the slice of buttered bread and took a big bite.

"How about I start? You can see how much I remember."

She nodded and picked up her spoon.

I cleared my throat. "The Chancellor house was an inn twelve miles west of Fredericksburg, Virginia along the Orange Plank Road. Waggoneers bumped along the heavy planks laid over the red clay road to prevent wheels from getting stuck. The inn stood in a heavily wooded area at a crossroads to and from the city. Travelers and merchants used to come to the two-story brick tavern for food and lodging before the Chancellor family inherited it in 1861.

"Mrs. Chancellor was left with six unmarried daughters and a young son when her husband passed away. She often extended her hospitality to neighbors and the Confederate soldiers in the area, but not for profit."

My intention of setting the scene was quickly rejected when Gran rotated her wrist. "Yes, yes. Get on to it being Christmas." She continued to eat.

I knew the specific Christmas scene Gran was interested in—the one from 1862. "Miss Sue, the fourteen-year-old, was busy stringing a popped corn garland to circle about the Virginia pine. Her little brother kept snatching popcorn from the bowl in her lap." I pantomimed sewing through the popcorn and then whisking away an imaginary bowl out of the boy's reach.

Gran chuckled, encouraging me to continue.

"A fire roared in the fireplace on this cold December day. Fannie sat at the piano playing Christmas carols and Abbie sang along." I was rather pleased with myself for remembering two of Sue's sisters' names, probably because of the double consonant and similar ending. There was another name like that. Bettie? I pretended to play the piano.

A sparkle lit Gran's eye. "That's how it was in my dream. Christmas carols at the piano." She set the empty bowl down on the tray and picked up her remaining bread.

"There was a knock at the door." I mimicked the action and clicked my tongue. "Miss Fannie whirled her legs around the bench to see who had arrived. Mary opened the door, getting a blast of frigid air in her face."

Gran chuckled. "Hester probably pushed Mary to the door, not wanting to get a chill herself."

"Both girls were about Sue's age, right—with Hester being the younger one?"

"Right. Mary was fifteen and Hester only twelve."

"I remember Mary best because she is our ancestor. I wonder if she remembered her mother before she was sold to the Chancellors as a young child. Do you want any more soup?"

"No, I'm fine." Gran batted the air and huffed. "Oh, let me tell it. You're getting distracted."

I gladly conceded, half expecting this. The pink was returning to her cheeks along with a little of her feistiness. That was Gran—always the storyteller, even with a broken leg. There were few details she didn't know, and the story had been passed on to her by her own mother.

I set her tray on the nightstand and put my hand over hers, making certain she was warm enough so I could give her my full attention.

Gran took one last swallow of water. "So Mary opens the door to a porch full of people."

CHAPTER FOUR

Mary, December 1862, Virginia

THREE FAMILIES STOOD ON THE porch and Mary took a step back, a bit overwhelmed with whose hat or coat to take first. This didn't seem like typical travelers stopping to stay the night. She backed away from the daunting group and let Mrs. Chancellor welcome the party.

Both Abbie and Fannie rushed from the piano, pushed past Mary and threw their arms around the friends from Fredericksburg. Mary recognized the Williams family now, but the other two families were unfamiliar.

Mrs. Chancellor turned on her Southern charm as she beckoned them in with her hand. "Come in. Come in from the cold." The mistress peeked out the door and looked for a carriage. "Did all y'all walk the whole way?"

"All twelve miles? Heavens no," Mrs. Williams said.

"There's a winter campaign going on—" her husband explained, "—between the Army of Northern Virginia and the Army of the Potomac, of all things. Why they couldn't wait until spring I'll never know." He shook his head. "We made preparations to leave the city as soon as we heard the artillery start up somethin' fierce. Your groomsman has seen to our carriage. I know you're not running this as an inn anymore, but we hope you have room for us."

"Of course. We have several rooms," Mrs. Chancellor said, taking off her apron, thrusting it toward Mary without a glance, and giving the Williamses a kiss on both cheeks. Mary stood by, waiting for her next instructions while the other two families were introduced. Her gaze rested on the large colored woman coming through the door, holding the hand of a white girl about ten years of age. The child looked ill from the journey.

Mary wondered if the slave of the Forbes family would be treated as a guest as well, or if she, Hester, and Hester's mama would have to make room for such a large woman to sleep with them in their cramped cabin. They rarely had overnight guests.

Mrs. Williams unbuttoned the coat hiding her trim, corset-tight figure and hooped skirt. She let the coat slide off her arms for Hester to take. The woman went to stand by the fire. Her face pinched as she spoke of the ordeal. "It was so awful. Both armies had been there for weeks, waiting to kill one another." She shuddered. "We couldn't stand not knowing when we'd be in danger, so we prepared to leave. Then the cannons started firing and that decided that. You might be getting more refugees soon."

Mrs. Chancellor smiled. "Well, now. They'd be welcome too."

Mary thought of the extra work that would involve—more linens to wash, more food to prepare, and frequent cleaning of the chamber pots. *Ugh!* She kept her thoughts to herself through her well-practiced stony look, not that they would pay her no never mind anyway.

Hearing the commotion, the other Chancellor daughters came down the stairs.

Mr. Williams continued with the news. "The armies are facing one another across the Rappahannock as we speak. The Union wants to set planks atop pontoon boats for bridges across the river. Our Northern Virginia Army is sheltering in Fredericksburg, hoping those Yanks won't fire upon citizens, but we can't trust the Union not to destroy our beloved city. We don't know if it will all be rubble when we return."

Mary took a woman's proffered fur bonnet as she absent-mindedly listened to more talk about how their guests were afraid they'd run into a brigade of soldiers along the way and get shot at. It wasn't until Joshua Williams spoke that she paid them any mind.

"Yes, we've seen soldiers aplenty," Joshua said. "But the most unusual sight was the hot air balloons the Union sent up. It was a glorious thing to watch, all for the purpose of reconnaissance."

Mary wondered what a hot air balloon looked like. She lifted her eyes to the handsome young man, thinking he must be quite knowledgeable, and studied his features for a full five seconds before returning her eyes to the floor. Right before she did, he caught her gaze and hid a smile. Her cheeks burned, and she scolded herself for looking.

Mrs. Chancellor broke into her thoughts. "Mary, take these suitcases upstairs. Hester, go put on some tea and tell your mother how many we have for supper." The mistress turned to her guests, her grace and politeness on display. "Y'all must be cold and starving. Please, come sit by the fire and the Christmas tree. We'll have supper shortly."

☆ ☆ ☆

Gran hummed a line or two from an old Christmas Carol. I wondered if she was trying to remember the next part. She took a sip of water and plowed back into the story.

☆ ☆ ☆

Mary, December 1862 to April 1863, Virginia
The Chancellor mansion filled with refugees over the next few days, and they stayed and stayed. Mary grew tired of hearing the women fret over where it might or might not be safe. "Whatever shall we do?" became a common phrase. They had it good right where they were, and on Mrs. Chancellor's generosity, no less. No wonder nobody left.

Mary about wore herself out going up and down the stairs, making beds, bringing this and that to the rooms, and cleaning. Oh the cleaning! At least the Chancellor girls were used to helping out since most their slaves done run off. Helping a little. When they weren't enjoying the company of others. Miss Sue helped the most because her older sisters sometimes left her out.

Mary and Hester helped Hester's mama, Sally, who was the head cook, prepare a huge Christmas feast of roast goose, rolls, and root vegetables. Every seat at the long mahogany table was filled plus the settee and a few scattered chairs so the white folks could all sit down at once. Mary and Hester would get to eat after their work was done. Mrs. Chancellor had promised them a real treat of the leftovers in the kitchen, once the tables were cleared.

Mary listened in on the conversation about the Confederate victory in Fredericksburg as she hugged the wall. She stood at attention or refilled the basket of rolls and wine goblets. Joshua Williams smirked at her like he knew about her listening trick. She ignored him and continued her duties, practically salivating the whole time with how good it smelled and looked.

Just after the new year, a truce of sorts began between the armies. Several guests waited for a mild day and made the trek homeward to get on with their lives. Things still weren't back to normal for Mary. Mrs. Chancellor had extended her generosity to the Williams family when they learned that Mr. Williams' printing business had been destroyed. They stayed another three, long months, testing Mary's patience.

"I swear, Hester," Mary told her friend one day as they washed dishes in the kitchen. "Where did all these dishes come from? We's going to run outta food before too long if these dishes is any indication."

"I know. We still got to feed them Williamses and Miss Kate and her mammy. Too bad the Forbes' couldn't take them home too. Aunt Nancy sure like eatin'."

"Yeah, but I like Aunt Nancy. She makes me laugh. And she don't mind helping out when Miss Kate ain't too sickly."

Hester nodded. "I expect we'll have more soldiers to feed too. They's getting restless with no fighting going on, and bound to come visiting."

Mary learned that Confederate troops had made their way into the area to guard the river. She overheard Abbie, Joshua, and his sister talking about it. A few of the soldiers started dropping by, like Hester predicted. Then came the day when Miss Sue asked her mother if Mary could accompany her on a walk because everyone else was busy. That's when she saw one of the army camps for herself.

They strolled into the woods for a bit until out of sight from the mansion's windows. Suddenly, Sue grabbed Mary's hand like old times. "Come on," she said, rushing Mary along. "Let's go spy on the army camp."

The thrill of something new shivered over Mary's spine. She almost felt their former closeness return. Almost. Sue hadn't taken Mary on a walk since the war began, and they hadn't played together for several years. Mary figured Sue's sisters were too old to be interested in spying with Sue when they had company nearer their ages. All the better for Mary. She, only a year older, once again became the perfect companion.

With a breeze in their faces and Sue's hand in hers, the two invented their own path, dodging tree trunks as their laughter carried away on the wind. Mary felt that taste of freedom teasing her all over again. All too soon they would return to the house where Mary would be expected to catch up with her work, even without the Chancellors having an overseer. Still, Mary was grateful for this experience, and she would enjoy it while it lasted.

The girls lay on their stomachs atop a wooded knoll. Canvas tents were set up between trees. Men in grey or tan butternut uniforms moved in lines where the trees were thinnest. The stale aroma of tobacco filled the girls' noses as a group of men drilled over and over to the shouts of leaders in command, the call of a bugle, and beat of a drum. They watched long enough that Mary reckoned she had learned what some of the calls meant. Miss Sue must have too. Suddenly she sat up and waved her fists up and down in front of her as if holding imaginary drum sticks.

"Drum ba-da rum pum pum," she said rhythmically. "What does that mean?"

"Continue forward," Mary answered. "The soldiers march in step together."

"Right. How about this one?" Sue lifted her hands near her mouth and wiggled her fingers while trumpeting out a pattern.

The imitation bugle sound made Mary laugh. "One quarter turn to the right."

"Good!" Sue laughed in delight, then sent Mary a pointed look.

Unsure, Mary waited to be told.

"Go on. You try one," Sue suggested.

A wave of emotion caught Mary off guard. It sounded friendly and reminded her of when Miss Sue truly thought of her as a friend, an equal— back before they learned the difference between their places. It should feel like that now instead of Mary being used as company when Sue was desperate. It would do Mary no good to get upset. The outing would end and Mary would go back to less pleasant tasks. She pushed down the feelings that vexed her and came up with a new drum pattern instead. The game continued for a few minutes until they lay back, Sue laughing into the sky and Mary playing along.

They rolled onto their stomachs, chins propped up in their hands, and the soft spring grass tickling their wrists. They watched the soldiers perform a more complicated drill. The men stood in a long row of four or five men deep. The soldier in front aimed his gun, pretending to take a shot. He made a right quarter turn, dropping his weapon to his side while the man behind came forward and aimed. The first soldier made another turn and stuffed a long metal rod down the barrel of his rifle while he marched toward the back to the beat of the drum. He fiddled with something in a case on his belt and loaded it into the rifle as he made another quarter turn. By the time he made it back to the front of the row, he was supposed to be ready to take aim again. Not all the soldiers had the rhythm down of cleaning the gun and reloading as fast as the commander wished. They repeated the maneuver over and over again.

When a bugle blew and the men were given a break, it became quiet for a moment. The girls heard the moans of sick men in their tents. Someone retched. Army life surely wasn't glamorous.

All too soon, Miss Sue said, "We should be getting back." Mary quietly obeyed, wishing she were free to come and go on a whim.

When Mary returned, Aunt Nancy came up to her, "May I speaks with you a moment?"

Mary looked around but they were alone. Sue had run up the stairs. Even so, Nancy led her into the kitchen and used a low voice.

"You saw the army camp? What was they doing?"

"Drills and more drills. Why?"

Nancy pointed a finger at Mary in the small distance between them. "You needs to use those opportunities to be our eyes and ears. We gotta work together. We need you, girl."

Mary wrinkled her brow. "Need me for what?"

"To get us to freedom, a course."

Mary's eyes widened. "How's I's 'sposed to do that?"

"Find out all you can and I'll do the same. That northern army is coming, and one a these days we going to join over to the free side. You wants that, don't you?"

24

"I…" Mary guessed she did but needed to think harder about it, so she simply nodded.

Nancy firmly dipped her kerchiefed head once, as if making a pact. "We gots to be ready."

☆

Over the next few weeks, on several occasions, army officers came to the mansion for some home cooking or a cup of ale. The unmarried daughters enjoyed the attention of the soldiers, learning to play cards, much to the chagrin of Mrs. Chancellor. Mary stayed invisible while serving them, but she longed for a time when she would be free to do such carefree things.

Each time a new soldier visited the mansion, the Chancellor girls would get out their memory books and ask, "Will you please sign my book?"

"Why I'd be glad to." The officer scrawled his signature into a couple of the books and took a moment to thumb through the previous pages of the third one. "I see one of these men wrote you some poetry and left a lock of his hair. It's mighty dangerous getting sweet on a soldier, if you ask me."

Miss Abbie smiled and fanned herself with her fan. "Well, I didn't, but I thank you for the advice just the same."

Collecting signatures from men seemed silly to Mary, yet she envied the daughters who laughed and conversed with the soldiers. She told herself to remember that her life here was better than most slaves had it. Much better. She'd heard stories after church. Some had overseers that whipped them for little things. A woman Mary knew had her husband sold off to work another plantation and she hadn't seen him in ten months.

Two evenings later, a soldier named Lamar from South Carolina gave Miss Sue a better gift than a signature in a book. "How would you like a pet?" he asked.

"Oh, yes!"

Unlike a memory book, this was something useful. Mary secretly shared in Sue's excitement, wishing she could have one too. All the animals on their acreage were used for survival, not like a pet she could cuddle and treat as her own. It would never happen.

The soldier went to the drover of sheep and picked out a nice white lamb for Miss Sue. She loved it immediately and named it after the soldier. Miss Sue let Mary hold little Lamar a few times, but it wasn't the same as owning a pet herself and taking charge of it however she wished.

On the first nice day after several spring rains, the sheep were shorn. After the wool had been carded and spun, Mary was near the out buildings behind the house dying the skeins in a big hot vat over a fire. It was quiet and peaceful with a gentle breeze. She didn't her Miss Sue outside frolicking with her lamb or anything. The solitude felt good. Or was it being out in the sunshine?

"How come they have you doing that?" Joshua Williams asked, startling her. "Don't they keep you by the front door on account of visitors needing a pretty face to greet them?"

Mary stiffened. He knew very well what kind of work she did. This was sweet talk… coming from a white man. He better not come any closer or she might be tempted to use the long wooden paddle in her hands on him, but then she'd get a whipping for sure. Why was he speaking to her? Did he need a favor? She continued submersing the yarn with her paddle, hoping if she ignored him he would go away.

"You know you have a pretty face, don't you Mary?"

His tone was kind but he was teasing her now for sure. He'd used her name. That wasn't right but she politely answered him. "No, sir."

"Well, the way I see it, you should know that. You're a pretty girl."

She waited for him to add 'for a Negro' but it didn't come. She stirred the pot again.

"A woman, actually," he added, alerting her senses further. "You've grown into a woman since the last time we were here. I've seen you reading too. Where did you learn that?"

She chided herself for not being careful. Could she trust him not to turn her in? Of course not; she barely knew him. Something about him made the hair on the back of her neck stand up.

She realized that turning her in would have consequences for Mrs. Chancellor, and she doubted he would do that—not after all her generosity. She breathed a little easier. "The mas'er let his daughters teach me before he died. They was practicing to be teachers and I was 'round for them to teach. Not teaching like an assemblage or anything. Just harmless little ol' me out here in the middle a nothing."

He smiled at her with yellowed teeth and an intense look that made her ramble on. "I can write too. Sometimes I read recipes to the cook or sneak a look at the newspaper. The mas'er said I's smart." She neglected to add what the master had: for a colored.

"He ever whip you?"

Mary swallowed. The steamy pot suddenly felt a lot hotter. She hadn't been whipped but she'd seen it done a couple times and heard grown men yelp out in suffering. Those awful screams and groans were forever burned into her memory. "You asks a lot a questions."

"Fair enough. You ask *me* a question."

Mary cocked her head and narrowed her eyes at him. He didn't seem quite so handsome when he was acting like this. "That's the silliest thing I ever did hear."

"No, really. I don't mind. Ask me something. Go on."

Mary blinked in surprise, stepped back, and set a fist on her hip. White folk didn't want chit chat or opinions from slaves. She never heard a white man talk or act like that. "Huh," she grunted at his crazy request. There was something she had been wondering though. She glanced around and found that they were still alone; maybe it wouldn't hurt to ask. He hadn't laughed at her. "How come you's not in the army? You looks old enough. A little older than me."

It was his turn to look around. He lowered his voice. "I'm hoping the war is over before I turn eighteen in the fall and they draft me. If the Feds had to go and destroy Fredericksburg, they should have won the damn battle instead of getting slaughtered. Then this war could be over sooner. This is a rich man's war in a poor man's fight.

"I'm proud to be a Virginian but I don't believe we should have seceded from the Union, though I keep that information to myself."

"Huh." Why was he telling her his secrets? He must've taken her grunt as interest because he prattled on like he was nervous.

"I happen to like Lincoln's way of thinking. As for abolishing slavery, I know it will change the Southern way of life and ruin the economy for the rich plantation owners, but most of us could get by with a few changes. Slaves should be free. Especially ones as smart and pretty as you." He gave her a sly smile and outlined her jaw with his finger.

Mary froze, debating on whether to hit him with the paddle if he did anything else. She backed away. "I'm not your property. Missus Chancellor owns me, and she wouldn't like what you's doin—Awk!" Mary stumbled over a rock behind her. She dropped the paddle and slumped onto her backside.

All at once, Joshua pulled her up, scooped her into his arms and headed to the shed.

"Put me down!" Mary flailed and then beat her fists against him. Only when he opened the shed door did she think to yell. "Help! Miss Sue!" She prayed Miss Sue was outside with her lamb. Or anybody. Then Joshua's fingers tightened around her neck so she quit speaking altogether.

"Mrs. Chancellor likes her guests to be pleased, and I am pleased with you."

Tears leaked from her eyes. "No, sir. Please, no."

But Joshua was stronger than Mary.

My stomach instantly soured and I shrank back. "Granny! You never told me that part before."

"No, I guess I didn't. Maybe it's my pain pills wearing off that let that slip. My leg is hurting again and I was feeling Mary's pain too. But I guess you're old enough to know." She looked at her watch, and automatically twisted its winder. "I've got thirty minutes before I can take another pill."

"I'm sorry. Can I do anything to help?" I preferred turning my attention to Gran than dwelling on Mary's troubles at the moment.

Gran got a mischievous look on her face. "Can you find me a piece of chocolate?"

I laughed. "I'll sure try."

I left to rummage through the cupboard where Mom might have a stash. Nothing. I found Mom and Dad watching *The Rifleman* in the living room. "Gran needs some chocolate," I announced.

Mom picked up her purse from off the floor next to her arm chair and pulled out a Hershey bar.

"So that's where you hide them now. We're going to need more, by the way."

She nodded. "How's Gran?"

"Her pain pills are wearing off. She's being strong. No junkies in this house." I sent a weak smile, but Mom didn't find it funny.

"Tell her I'll be in with a pill as soon as this show ends."

"Is your homework done?" Dad asked.

"Yeah. Not much on the first few days of school." Luckily math was still a review. "I have a parent note you need to sign. I'll say goodnight to Gran and get it for you."

As I gave Gran the chocolate bar, my heart went out to Mary and all the slaves with their hard work and restrictions. Why did people have to be afraid of someone different from them? My growing interest stretched beyond enjoying time with Gran and her storytelling. This was my heritage. I appreciated not having to live back then, and being able to enjoy the benefits of the white world. Was that being selfish?

If I recalled history correctly, after slavery came peonage. Debt servitude, where charges were often drummed up so that a colored person would have to work off the so-called debt without payment. It wasn't much of a step up from slavery. Even today, dark-skinned people were generally poor and treated poorly, especially in the South. They craved freedom as much as Mary had. It was a basic human need. The movement toward civil rights for all needed to make greater progress in my lifetime than the snail's pace of the past.

Gran gave a little groan of pleasure as she chewed, and then one of pain.

I frowned. "Mom said she would come give you your pill after their TV show."

"Don't go feeling sorry for me. We each have our own troubles, and I'll get through this." She attempted a smile. "But I'm afraid we'll have to continue our story-telling another time. Keep me in your prayers."

"I will. And I look forward to the next time. I'm getting some papers for Mom or Dad to sign and then I'll be back."

"Nah, you go on and leave me be. I want to rest."

"You sure?"

She nodded.

"Okay. Goodnight." I kissed her soft cheek and slipped out the door.

Despite what Gran had said, I did feel sorry for her. She was hanging on until her next pain pill. My troubles didn't compare to hers. Or Mary's.

Things were better living in 1963 than what my ancestors had gone through. I sat on my bed, pondering if people like Mary were innately stronger and therefore could handle bigger burdens or if they were stronger because of their burdens. I knew life was a test and it took faith to endure, but having fewer or more opportunities because of one's race wasn't right.

I didn't blame God; people had made this situation. Stupid people. Fearful people. Selfish people. God gives us the strength to get through our situations. Sometimes when we don't ask for help.

If I could do something to ease another's burdens, I should. But what? There wasn't anyone whose freedom I was restricting. How could I help?

Could I do more good if I went to the desegregated high school? I didn't know what that would be. I was only a sophomore in high school and new in town, for goodness sake. Plus I wouldn't get to be in a quality school play put on for the community in a 500 seat auditorium. I'd have to take the bus and Mark would have to walk alone. I'd made my choice— the only choice I could really make.

I still felt concern about what might happen because of Gran staying with us. If someone with authority and narrow mindedness decided I was attending the wrong school then it would no longer be my choice. I would have to comply. The very idea put an ache in my stomach.

I gave myself a talking to. Don't be a baby, Charlotte.

Mary had pushed through worse things than I might face. I could use her courage for any situation that came along—including leaving Oakmont. No, there wasn't going to be a situation like that. Not if I could help it.

Part of me harbored relief that Gran couldn't get out and about for a while. Nobody would know she was my grandmother. I couldn't see a single reason why Gran would need to show up at my school.

A fat lot of courage I had.

I knelt beside my bed, feeling a little lost. "Dear Heavenly Father, what would you have me do?" I stayed there for several minutes. No peace or comfort came, only more questions and worries. Perhaps it was too broad a question for an immediate answer.

CHAPTER FIVE

ON THURSDAY, WHEN WE WERE all supposed to have purchased our PE clothes, I walked to the gym with Patty. Two volleyball nets were set up. "Oh, good. I like volleyball."

"Me too, except when the ball is really hard and it hurts my arms."

Miss Zindle, a rather athletic woman pushing forty, took roll. She explained the rules and had us practice serving. After a few minutes of that, she blew her whistle. We all gathered around her. "Let's try a game. We'll need four teams. Team A's captain will be Amanda. Team B, Bethany. Team C, Charlotte. And team D, Diane."

"Ha!" It was a half laugh, half surprised sound from Patty. She socked me lightly on the shoulder. I noticed Melanie roll her eyes and sigh heavily.

Miss Zindle motioned with her arm. "You four come up front and pick someone to join your team. Amanda, you'll start."

On my turn, the first pick was easy. "Patty." I didn't know hardly any names or who was athletic, but Patty and I had made a connection. After that, I looked around, hating that it felt like a popularity contest. I could ask her for a suggestion.

What would Jesus do? The thought came into my head without warning. It was my turn again. I looked for a girl who watched the floor. "You," I said, pointing.

Somebody elbowed her and she looked up. "Me?"

"Yeah," I said confidently and motioned with my hand. A timid smile appeared and I returned a solid one. Melanie slapped her forehead to tell me how stupid I was. I noticed she hadn't been picked yet. Would picking her be a way to start over? I didn't know how she would take it, but I called out, "Melanie" on my next turn. She tilted her head at me but bounded my way.

Patty raised an eyebrow, but said nothing. When my turn came around again, half the girls were left and I suspected the best players were already chosen. It wouldn't make a big difference who I picked at this point. Again I looked for someone who expected last pick.

Melanie stepped closer and whispered, "Go for Josie. Say Josie."

"You." I pointed at another.

"Ugh. Not her," Melanie complained under her breath.

Melanie told me another name to call, but Patty whispered, "You're doing fine." I continued with my own plan, liking that Patty approved "You."

Melanie set a fist on her hip. "What are you, stupid? We'll never win."

This wasn't a competition team, but obviously Melanie didn't understand that. She could think what she wanted. We ended up with seven on our team. "I'm Charlotte. And you are?" I looked to the girl next to Patty.

Before she could open her mouth, Melanie went around the circle, quickly naming the four girls I didn't know, then said, "Let's get on with it. I'll serve first."

Patty folded her arms. "You're not the captain."

She huffed. "Fine. I'm just trying to help us win."

Miss Zindle tossed me a ball and pointed to one side of the court. I bounce-passed it to Melanie. "Go ahead and serve, Melanie. Let's see whatcha got."

I assigned places on the court and chose myself to rotate in. Melanie could serve, but we couldn't always return the other team's hits. The game progressed and I learned that one of the girls was timid about returning the ball, another tried but couldn't control the direction of her hit, and the rest of us were decent. We scored a few points here and there, but it was a long shot that we would ever win. Patty had joined me in saying things like, "Good try," or "You'll get it next time." Melanie finally gave up her complaining. I smirked to myself, having shown that I wouldn't let her get to me.

When we were dismissed, Melanie spoke into my ear again. "You should have listened to me." I could hear the sneer in her voice. She rushed ahead to the locker room.

"Good game," I called to our team, loud enough for her to hear. "Better luck tomorrow," though I knew tomorrow would be no different. I was happy to have learned four new names.

When I entered the locker room on Friday, there was a small mound of mud on the bench in front of my locker. "Watch out," my neighbor warned, but luckily I had seen it. I inwardly groaned, yet it was an easy fix. I sniffed to make sure it wasn't something worse, then took a towel and wiped it away. I dialed the combination, careful of where to sit on the bench. The door opened and a pile of leaves, dirt, and small twigs dumped onto the cement floor. Ugh! Someone had stuffed them through the air slits, covering my PE clothes and filling my tennis shoes. My cheeks flamed. If I had three guesses they would be Melanie, Melanie, and Melanie. I looked around, scowling. Now I'd be late because I couldn't put the dress I wore in there until I had cleaned the locker out.

"Oh, man. Somebody's got it in for you." the girl next to me said. Each tsk of her tongue deepened my embarrassment. Several others looked over their shoulders at me but no offers for help. Nice.

Patty rushed into our row, taking in the scene as she arrived late. "Yikes!" she said, squatting next to me with her eyes smoldering. "Here, let me help. Don't let her get to you."

I waved Patty off. "You're already late getting here, but you have a chance of not being tardy. Go on. I can do this."

I took my shoes and PE clothes over to a garbage can and shook them out. When I returned Patty had grabbed two towels, wetting one of them, and left them on the bench as she changed. "Thanks, Patty."

"What are friends for?"

I wiped out my locker and changed, arriving at the gym tardy. Melanie had the team on the court, with her in serving position. Patty lifted one shoulder and sent me a what-could-I-do look.

I put on a confident expression and clapped my hands together. "Okay, team. Let's go!" I glanced beyond Melanie to look at the others. I was cool. Everything was groovy. I wouldn't give her one pinch of satisfaction, though I still felt rattled.

Melanie was smooth too, pretty much ignoring all of us and focusing on herself. Much better than her complaining. She had to be acting too. I was good with that. Without Melanie's intimidation and complaining, the girls were more relaxed. We actually had a decent score today. We didn't win, but that was okay. Six of the seven of us seemed to be having fun.

Thankfully, no surprises awaited me in the locker room, but that didn't mean another day might be different.

"So," Patty said. "What are you doing this weekend?"

I shrugged. "Not much. My family and I planned to explore the area but my grandma broke her leg and is staying with us so I doubt we'll go anywhere…except for church on Sunday."

Melanie walked past and looked right at me. "What a drag." She rolled her eyes as she walked, getting the last word on my pathetic social life.

Patty didn't seem bothered by her or my boring lifestyle one bit. "I have my niece's birthday party out of town tomorrow, but maybe we could hang out next weekend."

Was she a natural friend-maker or did she need me like I needed her? A heartfelt smile came to me. "I'd like that."

CHAPTER SIX

ON SATURDAY MORNING I STARED into the mirror above the sink after I washed my face, examining which of my features looked like Gran's. "Who are you?" I whispered. The answer came instantly, the training from my youth well-engrained. A child of God. My lips quirked into a smile. Knowing of my divine nature might be the only thing that got me through things like leaves in my locker and nobody to hang out with on the weekend.

What had Mary looked like? I mulled the question as I pulled my thick hair into a ponytail, enjoying the smoother feel of my hair after using Patty's sample. Having a sliver of African ancestry and this whole thing with Oakmont's rules inspired me to learn more about myself and my family history. I'd survived a week at Oakmont without any objection to my being there. Melanie didn't count; she had picked me to hate from the moment Jake spoke to me.

I remembered where the story of Mary was heading, but Gran hadn't given as detailed an account of her life after the war. Granny usually summarized the rest of her life. Why was that? I determined to get more out of her this time. The desire to know more about my family tree flared inside me like a sparkler on Independence Day. I headed to the kitchen. Hopefully Gran felt up to telling me more about her grandmother today.

The kitchen smelled of bacon. Gran's favorite. Mom stood over an electric griddle with a fork in her hand, wearing an apron over her day dress. How her hair looked so well-styled first thing on a Saturday morning was beyond me. "Hi Mom," I said.

"Good morning, Charlotte."

"So how is Gran today?"

"She slept much better. She actually has an appetite for bacon today." We both smiled. "I know you want her to tell you Mary's story, but don't forget your chores first."

Was there a motherhood code or something that made moms say stuff like that? "I know. I won't. Should I take a tray to her?"

"She's already eaten. The rest is for us. Go get your brother and Dad."

"Yes, ma'am." I did and then hurried through breakfast. Maybe I could get my chores done early enough for Gran to still feel well. Mornings might be better for her.

Mark had a friend coming over later today. I was happy for him. Though Patty was busy today, I wondered if I could ever invite her over. Wouldn't I need to keep her from seeing Gran? I made a face, wishing I could introduce my granny to any friend I made. She was wonderful inside and out. Unfortunately, knowledge of her could get me kicked out of Oakmont.

I finished cleaning the bathroom in record time, anxious to hear more about Mary. I washed my hands and knocked at Gran's bedroom door. "How's the leg today?"

"Ah, Charlotte. I've been expecting you." She fluffed a pillow and set it behind her back. "This bulky cast is no fun, but I'm doing a little better every day." A sparkle came to her eye and she patted a spot on the bed beside her. "Are you ready for more of the story?"

"You bet!"

$$\star \; \stackrel{\star}{\bigstar} \; \stackrel{\star}{\bigstar}_\star$$

Mary, April 1863, Virginia

The Williams family left dreariness in their wake for the Chancellor household when they went back to Fredericksburg. The sisters missed the gaiety of a full house and having Joshua's company. But Mary was happy to see Joshua Williams go. Perhaps her fear and the repulsion in her heart could begin to dissipate. At least she wouldn't have his constant reminder at every meal.

Nobody but Hester's mama knew what had happened to Mary. Sally had been the one to find her after calling her name when she couldn't see her near the dye kettle. She'd heard sobbing coming from the shed and found Mary distraught and bleeding after having her virtue stolen. There was no law against what Joshua had done. Sally, for all the strength it took her, told Mrs. Chancellor only that Mary had taken ill and asked for a day for her to recover. She stayed in their little cabin curled up in a ball on her bed for the rest of the day. This was Mary's trial alone to bear.

In those first days afterward, not even Aunt Nancy could get Mary to crack a smile. Spring had done little to invigorate Mary. Eventually she took some comfort from the mammy's nurturing care that extended beyond Miss Kate Forbes, her charge in delicate health. Nancy hummed soothingly as she worked, told funny stories, and gave out more hugs than scoldings.

Wishing for a festive mood, the Chancellors decided to throw a party set for Sunday after church, the day most of the officers had off.

"I don't mind not getting all of Sunday off if the reason has to do with a party," Hester told Mary when the event had finally arrived.

Mary shrugged. She felt a new wariness for the soldiers, skittish of them coming around. Her sense of whom she could trust among white men had proved inaccurate so she made sure she was never alone. With Hester working in the kitchen with her and Sally nearby, Mary pushed that worry aside and concentrated on her duties.

The young slaves set out the silver tea service, hot cornbread, and finger foods down the center of the long, mahogany table in a help-yourself-style. Bettie sat at the grand piano, playing *Dixie* for the officers who came. Everyone sang along—all the white folk, that is. Mary had a lovely voice and might have liked joining in, but she was never invited. Yet, there was something about that tune that perked her up too. Miss Kate Forbes and the rest of her family enjoyed the festivities for a while until Aunt Nancy could see that Kate had tired. Mary hoped she would return to help her wash the dishes or tell one of her stories.

"Miss Bettie, can you play *Home Sweet Home*?" one of the officers requested.

"Why certainly."

Fannie clasped her hands to her bosom. "How I love that song and the romance of a soldier longing to be home."

"It won't be long now, Miss Fannie," a tall lieutenant said. "We whooped them in Fredericksburg and General Hooker won't be any better than Burnsides was—just you wait and see."

General Posey stroked his dark beard. "Maybe Burnsides would have had more luck if he'd let the hair on his chin grow out." Fannie laughed but Mary could see nothing amusing in his remark.

"We'll see who has the luck tonight when we start playing cards. Hmm?" Fannie raised an eyebrow at him.

Mary couldn't complain. Fannie's light mood, despite her favorite soldier's absence, and everyone else's in the household helped things go better overall.

Across the sitting room, Mary heard Abbie speaking to major general Jeb Stuart, a favorite of the Chancellor girls on account of him being so nice. Mary thought he might be one of the few she could trust if she had to. "May I have a lock of your hair for my memory book, General Stuart?" Abbie asked, batting her eyelashes.

Fannie glanced their way and Stuart jokingly answered, "As long as your sisters don't all have the same idea on the same night. My horse might not recognize me with a new haircut."

Mary returned to the kitchen, where the servants spoke in hushed tones as they arranged a few more trays of food.

"Y'all are lucky that Mrs. Chancellor is so nice to you," Aunt Nancy said. "The Forbes is decent mas'ers too."

Mary nodded her head. Mrs. Chancellor was not affectionate toward her but gave occasional praise, provided shoes every year, and had kept Mary's stomach mostly filled. She allowed Sue to keep some company with Mary because her daughter had few occasions to be with girls her age. It was the best she could hope for.

The plump woman swayed in place. "But how I'd love to be out there, free to mingle and speak my mind. Um-hmm."

"So you're still set on getting free?"

"A course. You best be too, if'n you knows what's good for you. I dreams of freedom every day."

Though tired, Mary fully opened her eyes. Free to sing, to read dozens of one's own books, and buy fancy dresses and eat fancy foods? Those desires formed so quickly that she knew Aunt Nancy hadn't exactly put such wishes in her head, though the mammy's words tugged at and teased her. Mary quickly dismissed the notion and frowned. They were slaves.

Nancy continued speaking just above a whisper. "I been blessed to sleep in the same room as Miss Kate so's I can watch out for her, but y'all must go to your tiny damp cabin at night."

Aunt Nancy was right. Mary, Hester, and Sally shared a one-room cabin, and it was cold and damp. They had quilts but no fireplace. Some nights they heated rocks by the fire in the mansion and set them near their feet in bed. The privy was far away too. She looked forward to morning when she could stoke the fires in the house, but that meant getting up early while the Chancellors slept in a bit longer. That's how it had always been, but the way Aunt Nancy said it, these circumstances didn't sit right with Mary. Not at all. More things disturbed her lately. She stomped a foot. Nancy gave her a stern look and shushed her.

Sally spoke next. "The Greenfield Plantation had a bunch a our people run away last June and the nearby Bullock farm had the same. It's easier to do from households where the mas'er done gone off to war or passed on like ours has. I been thinking about it but I's scared. I got my daughter to consider. I couldn't stand it if'n she got caught. Or you neither, Mary." She glanced at Mary and then Hester, who looked back with wide eyes, and shook a finger. "Don't y'all say a word to no one."

"She's right," Nancy affirmed. "You got to hush about this. You got to be smart. If Mr. Forbes hadn't a brung us here, me and a few others was seeking an opportunity to get to Union lines 'cause they was so close to us."

Escape? Where would Aunt Nancy go? Mary had seen headlines about freed slaves being sent off to colonize some far away island. Nobody wanted them or knew what to do with them once they was free. Besides, who would look after Miss Kate?

Mary found it interesting that someone else who had better conditions than most slaves still wanted freedom. Maybe Mrs. Chancellor was nice because she felt sorry for Mary being sold away from her mama as a young child, but that didn't mean she would set her free. Perhaps her desire to be free from the mistress wasn't so wrong.

"I'm wondering if the Yankees will come 'round *here*," Sally said. Mary had pondered the same, though she hadn't planned an escape.

"They might." Nancy lifted the coarse fabric of her full skirt, showing her petticoat. "I done sewed deep pockets into my petticoat to hide supplies in if I's gets the chance. See?"

Sally nodded. "Menservants I knows about are scared too—not about running away but fighting in the war. President Davis has talked about using slaves to fight in the army."

"He's gathering support too. I saw it in the paper," Mary added. "The Union has a lot more soldiers than we do. Some say coloreds can't fight worth a darn. Humph. That sounds stupid if you asks me." Her resentment was blossoming. Mr. Chancellor had said she was smart. Why didn't other white folk know the same thing?

Aunt Nancy pointed a finger at Mary. "That's right. You can read. Girl, you got to pay more attention to them newspapers and tell us what's going on. Be our eyes and ears. I don't have the sources here that I did back home to keep me knowing things. We could be missing something important."

Mary nodded. She had a job now. A secret mission toward freedom. Her spirits instantly perked up, and it was about time. She'd been so tired lately, but now, life held meaning again.

When Mary and Hester brought the food trays to the table, Mary glanced around at the singing and laughter, the ability to be entertained with company of one's choosing, the luscious foods out on display. If that's what being free meant, then she would do whatever it took to make it happen.

☆ ☆ ☆

Gran paused for a few sips of water.

I knew what Mary felt like a tiny bit. Patty had perked me up after that stupid prank in the locker room, but I still wanted to be free to have her over, to not worry about what others thought or the stupid rules the school board and others had made. I had more freedom than most people with ancestors who were slaves, but I shouldn't have to hide one-sixteenth of myself to follow my dreams, as if my heritage was something to be ashamed of.

Gran brought me from my musings. "This is Mary's story, obviously, but don't forget that Sue has her own perspective. Sue is being raised to become a Southern belle. The two had been friends as children, but their eyes are being opened to the course laid before them. Their separate stations were taught by example more than anything. It's how things were."

"Okay." I leaned forward a bit more, took one of her hands in mine, and squeezed. "I'm glad you're telling it to me again. I'm really ready for it this time."

"So it seems." Gran gazed at me with love in her eyes, making me feel all warm inside.

I hadn't realized Gran could see all the sides to this story. Those two contrasting character voices—one from a slave's point of view and one from a Southerner would make a great dramatic reading for my history project. Then it wouldn't be so obvious who I favored. It was tempting, but could I pull it off? Would my dominant interest in Mary shine through? I frowned. The risk was too great. It also wouldn't stay Mary's story that way. It might turn into something else altogether.

I had to preserve this the way Gran told it. I should write down everything Gran said—for a family story that future generations would have.

I'd have to do something else for my history project. But what?

Gran's warm voice saved me from answering.

CHAPTER SEVEN

Mary, April 1863, Virginia

THE WARM SPRING DAY BECKONED Mary outside, so she grabbed a broom and went to sweep the porch. The air smelled fresh after yesterday's rain, and the sky looked clear and blue. All the bulb flowers Mrs. Chancellor had planted were in bloom. Lamar had started nibbling the new grasses out in the yard, and seemed to be growing bigger every day.

Horse hooves drew Mary's gaze. She recognized the short man coming up the porch with another soldier as General Mahoney. The general had taken a room at the Chancellor's inn on and off for several weeks, preferring this headquarters to a tent, she supposed. She didn't blame him. She'd take a room here too if she could. It reminded her of years back when Sue had asked her mother if she could have a slumber outing with Mary in her little cabin. Mrs. Chancellor grew red-faced and said no, asking whose idea this was, and carrying on about Sue's foolishness. That was the first time they noticed their differences.

Sue rushed out the front door and smacked into General Mahoney coming up the steps. "Sorry, sir."

"What's the rush, child?" the general asked in his high-pitched voice.

"Excuse me, sir. My lamb is waiting for me."

"Well, don't let me keep you from him then." He tipped his hat and smiled at her.

Sue curtsied and ran to Lamar, who baaed when she hugged him. Mary shook her head, knowing she'd get little help with chores until after Mrs. Chancellor called Sue in for her studies.

The general stayed on the porch for a moment, took out a handkerchief, and wiped his forehead and neck before putting his hat back on.

The lazy clop of horse hooves drew their attention.

To their left, Mr. and Mrs. Forbes had settled in their carriage to return to Fredericksburg. Mary remembered hearing them tell Mrs. Chancellor something about urgent business and leaving right after breakfast. She didn't see their daughter Kate or her mammy. She supposed that Miss Kate, with her delicate constitution, wasn't up to traveling and Aunt Nancy would take care of her here.

Mary didn't want to stir up any dust with the general still there, so she backed into a corner and watched Sue play with Lamar.

The sound of horse hooves turned her head again, though this time it went clippity-clip. Three soldiers dismounted and one rushed toward General Mahoney in a state.

"General!" the breathless soldier called.

General Mahoney trotted down the steps to meet them. Mary sensed it must be important.

"We've spotted Federal infantry coming into Germanna and Ely's fords."

The general gave a grunt but his high voice range made it sound more alarmed than angered. "Then our position at U.S. ford will soon be untenable too. Anything more?"

"General Posey is on his way, sir. He'll have the numbers and exact position for you."

"Thank you, sergeant."

It sounded like the enemy was getting closer. Mary held in a breath, staring after them as the informers turned and rode off. When she remembered to breathe, she'd forgotten all about this fine day and went inside to tell Hester and Sally the news.

The air felt different to Mary that day—like the tingle of change coming, making bumps form on her smooth arms. Generals Stuart and Anderson arrived, and neither of them took relaxed strides as they came and went. The northern soldiers must be here as well. Her heart pounded with excitement and her hands shivered when she considered what it all might mean. Were nerves the cause of her tender stomach?

She passed General Mahoney's closed door several times as she dusted but couldn't hear what they were fussing about. Something serious was brewing. Though she'd been told not to disturb them, Mary hoped to find out and tell Aunt Nancy and Sally something that would help them all gain freedom. She wished there was more news to tell.

The next morning when Mary went through the open door to make the general's bed, she could tell that Mahoney hadn't slept in his room. She smoothed the spread and looked around. He'd taken his hat from the chair post and his pack from off the floor. Unfortunately, no papers remained on the bedside table either. A peek into the dresser confirmed her suspicion that he didn't expect to be returning right away. It was empty.

Mary told of her findings as she and Hester scrubbed the soft potatoes and the last of the withering carrots from the cellar. They didn't know how far the soup they were making for the noon meal would need to stretch. The general and several officers might be back tonight or gone for several days. In either case, Mrs. Chancellor's generosity would extend until there was nothing left. Mary admired her mistress for that but also knew that the extra soldiers and refugees from Fredericksburg had taken their toll. The food portions given to the coloreds were the first to be cut. Mary didn't mind so much in the morning but by evening she was famished.

The peas had poked through the red clay soil but the rest of the garden wouldn't start producing for another couple months. Would the household finally know what it was like to get by on cornmeal mush and bitter dandelion greens like some of the slaves at church said they did?

Sally chopped another onion. "I wish Nancy were in here helping us so I's could get her opinion a what all this means," she said. "I don't know what to do."

The girls nodded. Mary also hoped they could find some privacy to speak with Nancy later on. Outside noises surfaced over their hushed conversation. Somebody was pounding something outside.

"Hester, go peek and see what's going on."

Hester came back with eyes as big as the onions. "Federal soldiers are setting up tents where the land's been cleared. They's fixing to camp here right close!"

"And fight, I reckon," her mama added.

A shiver ran down Mary's spine. Would they die before ever having a chance at freedom?

The household stayed inside all day, spending more time looking out the windows than getting anything done. "Why do *they* have to come here?" Abbie asked, her nose pressed against the window.

"I wish General Stuart were here instead," Fannie complained.

Aunt Nancy watched over Miss Kate right there in the sitting room with no chance to discuss anything privately. Mary ached to know what they should do. It appeared nothing would be sorted out before bedtime. She frowned again that Sue had taken Lamar into the house for her pet's protection. Mrs. Chancellor didn't have the heart to turn him out, but Mary knew who would have to clean up after him.

About dusk, while Mary was stirring some cornbread batter to go with the leftover soup, General Hooker of the Union came and claimed the room that the Confederate generals had met in only yesterday. He marched right up the stairs, picking the favored room and leaving another officer to explain to them that they would confiscate the mansion and plantation property. Mary took it to mean that the mansion would become Union headquarters. She thought that might be a good thing for the slaves, but with a dozen soldiers standing before them with rifles in hand, she wasn't sure. The one thing she was sure of was that she wouldn't even go to the privy alone.

An officer, tall and handsome for a man twice Mary's age, stood in front of the other soldiers. His rifle remained slung over his shoulder and his eyes held a kindly expression. He removed his hat and dipped his head toward the mistress. "Ma'am. We're not here to hurt you," he gently said, but it did little to make Mary relax. "I am lieutenant colonel Joseph Dickinson. You will be under guard for your own protection as much as ours." He turned and nodded to a man diagonally behind him. "Take good care of them, Sergeant."

"That won't be necessary, lieutenant colonel," Mrs. Chancellor said. "We'll stay out of the way."

"I must follow certain conventions, Ma'am. The army needs the use of your home. Your cooperation is greatly appreciated."

"But—"

"Carry on, Sergeant." Dickinson replaced his hat and made his way up the stairs to the general.

The stout sergeant casually pointed the way for the household to go with his short rifle. "Everyone to the back room," he ordered in a tone that sounded firm but without malice.

"Mother!"

Mary heard complaints and whimpering, yet she couldn't help wondering if this sergeant would be the one Nancy might get a chance to speak with about freedom. They were now behind northern lines, were they not?

"Come on, girls," Mrs. Chancellor encouraged in a defiant tone. She carried young George and lifted her chin as she passed the guards. Her Southern hospitality had come to an end.

Sue gathered Lamar in her arms, Miss Kate began crying, and Mary's elation shrank. A small hope in her heart lingered yet she knew the slaves still had to be submissive to both the Chancellors and the guards until the moment was right. How would they know when that moment arrived?

Glances from several guards lingered upon Miss Fannie and Miss Abbie as they stepped past and into the informal gathering room. Miss Fannie stuck her tongue out at the guards, making Miss Kate stop her sniffling and giggle. She stuck out her tongue too. Aunt Nancy had her young charge firmly by the hand and hurried her along. Three visiting neighbors, now stuck in this predicament, filed in after the Chancellor family, and then the slaves.

Mary hurried past, looking for a corner to shrink into as she noticed the admiring looks given to the Chancellor girls. If Joshua Williams had thought her pretty, perhaps one of these soldiers would too. At least she wouldn't be left alone. She kept her head down and followed closely behind Sally and Hester. That Dickinson fellow might talk nice but these Yanks were the ones with guns and taking them as prisoners in their own house. How could Nancy have thought that Union troops would welcome them into freedom?

The room felt crowded with the sixteen of them all together. One small window afforded a limited view into the back yard, and the guards wouldn't let them past the cased opening to see into the front parlor windows where all the action took place.

Within the hour, two soldiers brought in teacups full of soup, small pieces of cornbread that someone had cooked, and a pitcher of water. Mary noticed that the soup had been watered down, but nobody said anything. The guards must have watered their portion down too, as they would find little already prepared or on the shelves.

Though given some blankets from the bedrooms and a couple chamber pots, there was no sense of privacy. The sisters took turns holding up a tablecloth against the corner with the pots. Mary briefly considered dumping one of those chamber pots over the heads of the two guards at the room's opening. She soon repented of her frustration and hoped that this temporary prison would eventually lead to freedom. Would they offer it? Would the household die unwittingly by the hand of Southern troops instead?

George, on his mother's lap, was the first to fall asleep. The others dozed from time to time, but nobody slept soundly that night.

Mary woke sometime in the dark of night to see a candle burning in the front sitting room. She sat up quietly, trying not to disturb others, and looked around. Only one other guard was awake. Was this her chance to ask for freedom? The nearest one caught her eye, leaned forward, and glared at her. The other, who had been reading from a small book, must have noticed his movement. He looked up from this book to see the whites of her affrighted eyes. Mary slunk back down, but noticed a gentle smile from the second soldier. Seeing all was quiet, he went back to reading from his book. How curious the difference between soldiers. It told her that she must wait to find out which ones, if any, she or Nancy could trust.

After some time, she fell into a fretful sleep of awful dreams.

Gran paused for another drink. Her voice had gotten raspy.

"Should we stop for a while?" Part of me hated to ask, but she needed a break. An exciting part was coming up and I wasn't good at being patient.

"Yes, though I hate to leave it right before the battle scene." She coughed.

"Me too. I know what happens, so it's not a total cliff-hanger. It's okay. Rest your voice."

I rose from my chair, and Gran put out a hand to stop me. "You know," she said, "this battle might be a good story for your history class project. Much more interesting than your textbook, I'm sure."

"Wh—? How do you know about my history project?"

"Do you think I sit here all day watching TV when you and Mark are at school? Your mother and I do a lot of talking. I ask her to tell me every little thing about you two. Plus, you mentioned it in my presence once before when your mother asked about your homework."

"Oh." It was a little alarming to think about what things my mother might have told her. I didn't have any big secrets from them and they both loved me anyway. Gran touched on my next alarming thought before I could say anything else.

"You're probably wondering if doing a slave's story might get you into trouble at school. You want to know what I think?"

"Sure."

"I think students these days need to know how it was for slaves. They might have read something about it, but it goes in one ear and out the other. They don't really know or feel anything about it. It's only history. You could bring Mary's story alive for them." She firmly dipped her chin. "Um-hm. I've been waiting for you to have this much passion about this story. Now that you do, and with your talent to present it, you can give this generation something they need to know."

I blinked and then stared at her. Wow. She had a lot of faith in me, and maybe some expectations too. "I uh… How can I do that without anybody finding out Mary is my relative? It might get me kicked out of school."

"I admit it's a risk. Find a clever way of presenting it like the assignment it is. Maybe share it like journal entries or something. Use both Sue and Mary."

The right side of my mouth curled, probably enough to show the dimple I attributed to Dad. She had zeroed in on my earlier thoughts, except I hadn't believed I should do it. Now she was telling me I had the passion and the responsibility to share Mary's story. I bit at my lip.

"You think about it some. Maybe we could continue tomorrow after church."

"Sure. That would be great. Thanks, Gran." She waved the thanks away.

I left to jot down the first half of the story in my notebook for the next hour or so while it was fresh. I lay on my bed and pondered the value of students knowing about personal lives versus traditional historical facts. I knew which I would rather learn. Suddenly I remembered I'd need to study the driving laws of South Carolina, but I had a hankering to go outside for a bike ride. My head was getting too full. If I didn't make plans with Patty for next weekend I just might go crazy.

CHAPTER EIGHT

AFTER HEARING A SERMON IN the chapel, I sat down with the girls for the teen Sunday school class—all eight of them. Brad, the cute guy who had picked up my history book when I stumbled, my brother Mark, and five other boys took the other half of the semi-circle of chairs. The smile Brad gave me when our eyes met sent a jolt through me. Everything I knew about him so far was good. He went back to talking with the guys.

"Hi Charlotte," a petite girl said, but went back to chatting with the girl next to her. They were among those whites that went to Pennfields High.

I was beginning to know them and vice versa from our midweek youth group meetings, yet connecting with them seemed hard. Church had been my safe haven in Maryland. I wasn't feeling it here yet. Saying hello twice a week didn't cut it.

Our teacher, Brother Mike, reminded me of my dad. He had a dimple in his cheek like Dad when he smiled, and the same wavy, brown hair. He asked for a volunteer to read a scripture passage. Nobody responded. I didn't want to be seen as a teacher's pet so I stayed mute as well. The teacher called on Mark to read the part from Matthew 25 about when we do something good to the least of these, we do it unto Christ.

"Today we'll talk about The Good Samaritan," the teacher said. He reviewed the story from Luke 10, making sure we understood that what made the story more amazing was that the people from Samaria were looked down on by their Jewish neighbors.

"Like how some white people look down on coloreds?" a curly-headed boy named Billy asked. His tone indicated it was a sore spot with him. "Or like how Oakmont looks down on Pennfields?"

I tilted my head questioningly at him, not having realized this situation existed. I was pretty sure he went to Pennfields High. I'd never heard anyone at school mention the other high school. But then I'd only gone to school for one week.

"Very few at Oakmont are like that," Brad said.

"How about you?" Billy asked him pointedly.

The strawberry blonde girl cut in, "Sorry, Brother Mike. We've had a crazy week at our school after King's speech about having a dream for the future. Half the school is mad the district still has an all-white school."

What had happened at Pennfields? Was my school turning a blind eye to the real problems around us? It made me more certain that my history class needed to hear Mary's story. I still wasn't sure how to safely do that.

"That's too bad," the teacher said. "Jesus wants all of us to do unto others as we would have them do unto us."

"Then why do the coloreds go to their church and white people come to this one?" Mark asked. "Or that other church for whites in town."

Brother Mike swiped a hand through his hair. "It's been that way for ages, but I'm hoping things will change. There's a time and a season to everything. Usually we're simply happy to see people in church. However, this movement with King might be paving the way for greater things to come. I surely hope so. Now, let's get back to our Good Samaritan."

Billy held up his pointer finger and turned to Brad. "Speaking of being a Good Samaritan, would kids from Oakmont go out of their way to help a wounded colored on the side of the road?"

I raised a brow at Billy. The boy wouldn't let it go. He probably didn't mean to, but I felt like his venting picked on Brad and Oakmont too. I couldn't merely sit here. I stared right at him. "You want to know what Brad would do?" Hearing my voice rise, I took a calming breath. "He would rescue that person because that's what he did for me when someone tripped me and I spilled stuff all over."

"You're new," Billy replied flatly. "And white."

How rude of him to imply that Brad helped me in particular because I was new. I might be ignorant of local politics, but I wanted a final word. "We can't control anyone but ourselves. What matters is what each of us would do."

Brad's eyes widened, and he stared at his knees. Rats! I'd embarrassed him to death. Nice way to pay him back. His expression softened as he gazed my way, and it looked like a smile lived underneath those nearly straight lips.

Flushing, I stared at my knees. I could swear I'd swoon if he did smile at me. His smooth, dark hair swept up from his forehead into a longish flat-top. His eyes—blue as the sky on an emerald pond—held the kindness he had shown.

The teacher took over again. "Well-said, Charlotte. The point here is being a Good Samaritan no matter what situation you're in. Think of a time when you helped someone out and how it made you feel."

We had a pretty good discussion from that point on. By the time Sunday school was over, I had gotten over my silly crush moment. Brad was a good guy and I would love to simply be his friend. I needed more of those at school anyway.

"Hey," I casually said to Brad as we spilled into the church hallway. "Sorry about embarrassing you. It kind of slipped out."

"That's okay. Glad I could help."

"And I'm glad to have someone at school I can rely on as a Good Samaritan." I gave a light punch to his bicep so he could know not to take that too seriously if he didn't want to. "All I know about you is that we have history together and you take debate. Any other secrets you want to spill?"

He cracked a smile and I breathed an inward sigh of relief. "I'm on the tennis team. Pennfields doesn't have a tennis team."

"Huh," I grunted approvingly. "I'm here for drama. With you in debate, we're both trying to convince an audience. Except you have more research."

He laughed and the sound of it turned my insides gooey again. So much for just wanting a friend.

"I guess you're right," he said.

I should say more while the talking was good, but what? I went back to what we had in common. "Mrs. Burkhart's pretty cool."

He nodded. "I have her for debate too."

"Neat. Do you know what you want to do for your history project?" I thought it worth finding out Brad's opinion and if he might connect my project idea as a family story. If he did, I would change that idea. No harm done.

"Hardly, but I don't have to think about it before October. We're getting ready for a debate tournament between six schools. Why, do you?"

Maybe he would think of me as a drip. "Yeah. Sort of. My grandmother has been telling me an interesting story from the Civil War that would make a great project."

"I want to do the Civil War too. Our state was first to secede from the Union and I've visited Fort Sumter. Have you been there yet, to Charleston?"

"No, we've only lived here a couple weeks, and we're taking care of my grandma who broke her leg. Charleston and Myrtle Beach are on the list."

"Fab. I'm up to my neck in debate research, so I was hoping for a partner on the history project. Maybe we could work on it together and split the load?"

Eagerness bubbled inside me. I envisioned spending more time with him. Plus, he hadn't jumped straight to asking if it was an ancestor story. "That would be great!" My thrill deflated as quickly as it rose. "But I'm kind of set on doing a dramatic reading. Is that okay?"

He shrugged. "It's not like I can't speak to a class full of students." He smiled that gorgeous smile that puddled my insides. "Then it's set," he said with a smile. "Meet me at my lunch table tomorrow and we'll figure more of it out?"

Was he kidding me? That might be the best thing to happen on the quiet birthday I expected tomorrow. Lunch with a dreamboat and talking about my favorite story. "Sure."

Patty and I took our lunch trays and scanned the cafeteria, looking for Brad. I had told her the plan to meet him, but I hadn't told anyone that it was my birthday. Nobody needed to know because I wasn't having a party. The friends I would potentially invite could be counted on one hand.

The two best gifts I could ask for were already happening anyway. Nobody had considered me unfit to belong at Oakmont and I expected to get my driver's license in the next few days.

I spotted Brad first, and then I groaned.

Patty stopped and stood next to me, holding onto our trays. "What?"

"To your right. Three o'clock. Melanie."

Patty's glance followed mine.

I studied the group for a moment while Patty echoed my groan. Melanie and two other girls were talking to Jake and Brad. I wasn't about to have lunch with Miss Queen Bee. My birthday would go from unnoticed to undesirable. "We should pretend to forget about—" Brad had spotted us and waved us over. There was no backing out now. I watched Melanie's expression fall as she caught on to who Brad had motioned to. She said something that we couldn't hear. I'm certain it wasn't flattering.

"Hey, you remembered," Brad said. "Have a seat. Hi, Patty."

"Hi," we both said. We slid onto the bench with me beside Brad and the other girls across from us.

"Charlotte, right?" Jake said, looking pleased that we had joined them.

"Yeah." I gave him a smile, delighted he remembered my name from the first day, then quickly squelched it. Melanie was giving me the stink-eye.

"Have a good weekend?" Melanie asked me directly with a slight sneer in her tone.

"I did." I looked right at her with confidence. She didn't need to know the details.

Jake pointed between the female pairs. "So you know Melanie and her friends?"

I silently thanked him for moving past the previous topic. "Melanie's in two of my classes and Ellen in one." I kept my voice light.

They introduced me to the bleached blonde, Gina. I nodded at her and took a bite of the mashed potatoes and gravy, finding it edible.

Brad finished chewing his bite of chicken-fried mystery meat and asked me, "So you got this Civil War story from your grandma?"

Gosh, I didn't want everyone knowing that. Be cool. "Yes. She's kind of a history buff." Totally true—about this story anyway. "When is a good time for you?" I suddenly wondered if I was assuming too much. "You want to hear it, right?" I glanced at him, mostly to avoid the watchful eye of Melanie.

"Of course. I have to know what I'm getting into." I heard the smile in his voice but I didn't dare look at him too often.

Jake leaned in. "Brad told me you might be doing your history project together. Y'all have a great war story?"

Melanie narrowed her eyes when Jake's attention drifted my way.

"My grandmother knows details about one of the Civil War families in Virginia. They were taken under house arrest and endured a battle in their front yard. It will be fun to tell for history."

"That sounds cool," Jake agreed. Brad nodded.

Melanie looked at me like I had cooties. "You've already picked a project? Sheesh."

"Charlotte and I are doing a dramatic reading," Brad said. "Why? You want to join us?" He glanced at me. "How many characters do we need?"

Was that an offer? No, Brad! What are you thinking? I cannot work with this girl! He looked at me for confirmation. I quickly blinked away my widening stare and let out the breath I'd held. I could use another female character for Sue's voice, but this? No. Not happening. I gave him a tight smile.

Melanie huffed. "I'll get my own project, thanks."

She probably saw the relief on my face because she shot me another glare.

"Okay." Brad shrugged and turned back to me. "I'm thinking we could meet early at the church for youth group tomorrow. You can tell me the story and I'll help you write it out."

"I've been writing it as I go, so I can remember what Gran said. Then I'll need to condense it. How are you at typing? Do you want to do that part? Of course, you'll also be in on presenting it in front of the class."

"Okay. I'm not great at typing but it sounds like you're giving me the easiest part." He lifted one side of his mouth. "And I'll try not to sound like a feeb."

Jake pushed Brad's shoulder. "Ha! That could take a lot of practice for you. Charlotte's probably a natural." He winked at me. I didn't think Melanie saw it, thank goodness.

"I'd be willing to listen and give you some pointers," Gina added. A rosy shade came to Brad's cheeks.

I gulped and hoped Brad didn't like her too. Did Jake's wink mean anything more than a simple compliment? This was getting complicated. I wished we'd been able to do this in a private conversation.

Knowingly or not, Patty came to my rescue. "I'm sure Charlotte can handle the acting cues. She's into drama classes."

All the eyes but Brad's were on me. He looked nervous, his smile gone and his eyes darting around.

"It's not that big of a deal to do a dramatic reading," I said. "We sit on stools the whole time. Maybe a hand gesture once in a while, but no stage movement. It's our voices that matter, and we have plenty of time to practice. This cool cat's got it!" I jerked my thumb at Brad. He pursed his lips, shrugged, and then turned to me, looking more relaxed.

"If Charlotte thinks I can do it…"

"Of course you can."

It didn't bother me that Melanie took up a new conversation to draw Jake back to her. What bothered me was that too many people knew the story had come from my grandmother. I was stupid to test it out on Brad. Now they expected I'd go through with it. Hopefully it would turn out okay. I just needed a plan on how to present the story. I didn't want to turn it into Sue's story, but I would be okay with it coming from both.

At least Brad and I had solidified a positive connection. We finalized plans to meet Wednesday night at six instead of seven. Brad knew that the church building would be open for kids who wanted to play basketball before youth group. I was thrilled that he chose to hear my story over playing basketball. A good omen, and as good a birthday present as mom making my favorite dinner and a cake tonight. I couldn't wait to share Mary and Sue with him.

CHAPTER NINE

MOM PULLED UP TO THE church right at six. I admired the tall, white steeple for a second and said, "You don't want to keep shuttling us around. Promise you'll take me to the DMV on Friday?"

'Promise." Mom crossed her heart with her finger.

Mark and I went inside. He didn't mind an hour of basketball before the youth meeting, so my plea to go early worked without a hitch. Or should anyway. Brad was nowhere in sight.

I walked down the hall, peeked in the classroom where we held Sunday school, checked at the outdoor court, and went back inside to sit on the pew closest to the door. After five minutes I saw him get dropped off in the parking lot.

"Sorry I'm late," he said as he pushed one side of the pointed arched door open.

"That's okay. Do you want to sit right here?"

"Yeah." We both plopped down with space between us. "So where do we start?"

"Our focus is the lesser publicized battle of Chancellorsville in Virginia. I doubt anybody else would pick it, so it'll be unique and with the personal effect I want. Let me give you an overview of the situation and the characters in the story first."

He nodded repeatedly like the heads of the little major league baseball figures my uncle collected. "Okay."

"You probably remember that several Southern states rebelled and the war was initially more about bringing them back into unity than the abolition of slavery. Are you familiar with the names of the Northern generals as well as the Southern?"

"I know that Lincoln was president and the Confederacy elected Jefferson Davis." He grinned sheepishly. "Few history details have stuck with me."

I smiled. "Don't sweat it. We haven't got to the Civil War yet in class. I only remember because of my grandma's stories." I proceeded to give him a quick background on General Joseph Hooker of the North or Union after Lincoln fired General Burnsides.

"They're the ones who wore blue uniforms and had more soldiers, right?"

"Right. Burnsides failed at Fredericksburg. It turned out that Hooker wasn't much better—more talk than action—but Lincoln didn't know that yet."

"That sounds familiar," he said. "The Southern Generals were Robert E. Lee and Stonewall Jackson, right?"

I nodded, pleased with his interest. I unfolded a small map from my skirt pocket and circled a spot with my finger. "This is the area of Chancellorsville, practically in the center between Davis' capital at Richmond and Lincoln's headquarters in Washington. Chancellorsville wasn't a town but an inn at a major crossroads that led to Fredericksburg. Here is Fredericksburg to the east, where the armies fought right before Chancellorsville."

"We took a vacation to Washington D.C. a few years ago. I think we passed through Fredericksburg." He shrugged one shoulder. "I liked the monuments and the White House in Washington, but I don't remember Fredericksburg being anything special."

"Yeah, you probably wouldn't with just passing through. I've been to Washington a few times. It's not so far from where we lived in Maryland." I folded up the map. "It's pretty cool."

"Now let me tell you a little about the Chancellor family," I said. I named the daughters and the slaves who would be important in the story.

"Wait." Brad gave me a dubious look. "Your story is full of women? You don't want me to talk like a girl, do you?" He folded his arms. "Can't I be one of the generals or something?"

"The generals don't get speaking parts." I cracked a smile. "Talking like a girl would only make it silly. The audience will know which character you are without speaking like a girl. You'll use your normal voice inflections to make it interesting."

"So you're saying I will be a girl character during the reading? Or maybe a slave?" A look of panic filled his eyes.

"Um." I hadn't expect this to be a problem. In drama class we took on all sorts of roles. I'd had a minor part in a play as a grumpy old man once. I was used to that kind of thing, but Brad wasn't into drama. "I'm writing the script from the point of view of Mary the slave and Sue Chancellor the Southern girl—like opposites, though they were companions. How about I work in a bigger narrator part for you, and I'll handle the girl parts." The girls in the class already had a group or didn't want to do a reader's theater, as far as I knew.

His voice wavered. "Could you please? I don't want to look like a weirdo."

He still might change his mind. I had to sway him. "Look, nobody else has a story like this one. I really think you'll like the story once you hear it. I promise you won't have to speak in a girl's voice. It would be easier if we have one more girl, but I'll figure it out. It's going to be outta sight. Trust me." He didn't know me that well yet, so that might be asking a lot.

He paused. "I guess I won't know until I hear it. Lay it on me."

I exhaled. "Okay. I'm starting where the Union soldiers have made the Chancellor's mansion their headquarters and the entire household is under house arrest because they are Southerners. This scene features the point of view of Mary, the slave."

Mary, May 1, 1863, Virginia

With daylight came the month of May, and a rude awakening to strange noises. Instead of hearing the sisters laugh or tease one another, men's voices called out between the rooms. Mary sat on her blanket, listening intently, her neck muscles tight with distress. What should she do with herself? She couldn't heat water for Sue's bath or make breakfast or any of her usual activities. All she could do was sit here and wonder if her future would ever change.

One guard poked his head in, seeing that nearly all of them had stirred. He was met with stony or fearful faces. When he turned away, Hester clasped her mama's hand tightly.

"It'll be alright, child," her mother whispered, but Mary wondered if Sally was convincing herself.

She glanced at Nancy to read her opinions, since she hadn't voiced them like usual. Nancy patted her skirt pockets for the valuable securities Mr. Forbes had left with her for the care of his fragile daughter, Miss Kate. Nancy gave a sigh of relief, and it somehow comforted Mary as well. The soldiers might use or take other things in the house but they hadn't bothered the women in the night.

Miss Kate rubbed her eyes and stretched. Only when she opened her eyes did she remember their predicament. Fear shone in those eyes. The poor girl's chin trembled and her caregiver became stern.

"Now, now. Don't y'all let those floodgates open," Nancy said, shaking a finger at Kate. "We're safe in here. Aunt Nancy's going to take good care of you. See? They're bringing us something to eat right now, and if'n they didn't, I'd make 'em."

Miss Kate's voice sounded especially high. "Can you make 'em go away so I can use the privy?"

Aunt Nancy grinned. Mary got up, anxious to do more than sit and wait. She knew the coloreds would be the last to receive any food. "I'll help with the curtain."

Sue was first in line, receiving half an apple, a slice of stale bread, and piece of cheese. Apparently, someone had been down to the cellar and found the apples. When Abbie stepped up to the doorway to receive her ration, she batted her eyelashes at the soldier. "May I go to my room for a fresh dress and another chamber pot? Pleeease. I'll be back in a jiffy."

"Sorry, miss. I have my orders."

"Then at least send someone with another chamber pot. It's not right having to share with… so many. This one needs emptying. Can't you tell?" Abbie swung her shoulder away from the soldier who rolled his eyes at her. "Maybe the general should come take a whiff in our little jail cell." Mary thought it smelled much better where Abbie exchanged words with a soldier than the corner of the room where she blocked the privy.

Not surprisingly, the general was too busy for them, it appeared. Couriers came and went up and down the staircase with hardly a glance at them in the crowded back room. The morning passed with boredom and irritability.

Before they could be given anything for dinner at midday, Mrs. Chancellor cocked her head. "Hush!" The room quieted. Faint musketry could be heard to the east—sounds that threatened Mary's chance for freedom if the Rebels won back their ground.

Sue protectively put her arms around her pet lamb. "Will it get closer?" she asked.

"Pray that it won't," her mother answered. A troubled expression remained on her face.

Aunt Nancy closed her eyes and whispered The Lord's Prayer. Hester clasped her hands together and followed suit. Mary joined in too but it didn't make her feel any better.

Fannie made her way to the two guards at the door. "What's happening?"

"Sounds to me like General Hooker was right about the enemy retreating and we're pushing Lee's army back toward Fredericksburg." A satisfied smirk developed across his lips.

Mary didn't know what to think; nothing was certain. She hoped he was right but these weren't the familiar soldiers of General Lee's army. She didn't know if he spoke the truth or was wishfully boasting. Mary sent Nancy an earnest glance until she caught it. The woman gave a little shake of her head. There was nothing they could plan yet.

Mary sighed, a little jealous that Sue had a comforting pet, and simply watched the Chancellor daughters taking turns at entertaining George and Kate, the two youngest of the group. The slaves were neither needed nor invited. Hester clung to her mother and Mary was left to cling to her own worries. Worry alternated with boredom. Finally someone came to change out the chamber pot. The hours passed while the thunder of cannon fire remained in the distance.

After a meager supper of boiled potatoes with a little salt, the same two guards as the night before switched places with the ones who had sat at the doorway all afternoon. Would the kindly one have changed his mood? When he took out his book a little later, she mustered some courage and stepped closer to him, peering over his shoulder. Anything for a change, she supposed, and a breath of fresher air.

When he swiveled around on his stool and stared at her, she stiffened and noisily inhaled enough air to look like a soldier with his chest puffed out, saluting a general. Heat flashed up her neck but she quickly recovered and took a step backward. She felt someone beside her, and recognized the feel of Hester's hand taking hers. Mary glanced from Hester to the book to the soldier.

The soldier's mouth twitched. "Can you read?" he asked.

Mary's eyes opened wider. "No, sir," she lied. She didn't want trouble and yet she was proud that she and others of her people had managed to learn in spite of the laws.

Hester shut her gaping mouth when Mary elbowed her.

"You like reading the Bible?" he asked Mary.

"Yessir. I mean no, sir. I like hearing from the Bible."

His lips twitched again. "I see."

That was enough excitement for both girls and they retreated deeper into the back room. The soldier watched them go and went back to his open page. Mary sat down and listened to what had turned into a quieter night, wishing she could be busy doing chores instead of sitting still like moss growing on a log. Or better yet, dreaming of being set free and earning money for her hard work. Another long day of house arrest rolled over into another long night.

"I'll have to whittle the story down, of course," I told Brad. "Otherwise it'll be too long, but I wanted you to get the full feel of it."

Brad nodded. "It's interesting." He sounded willing to hear more, though I could tell he wasn't sure about his participation.

"The next section of the story I'll tell from the Southern girl's viewpoint, Sue's. See if you think it's a good way to contrast between them." I didn't want it all from Mary's viewpoint or someone would get suspicious of how I knew so much about one slave.

"Yeah, we need to hear the white girl's view. It's cool so far. Like real people from another time. I can visualize what's happening."

I nodded and didn't waste another second.

Sue, May 2, 1863, Virginia

Sue woke to the sound of a bugle at dawn. Her heart skipped as she realized how close and loud it was. Whatever soldiers that had slept in the nearby camp were being called to action. She instantly looked for Lamar and found him curled up at her feet. How she longed to let him outside to nibble the tender grass. The scanty apple cores he'd munched throughout the day was hardly a meal for a growing lamb. Yet she dared not set him loose to run out the door when it opened because the guards wouldn't allow her to retrieve him. Somebody's stomach rumbled beside her and Sue glanced around, aware that all but little George had awakened from the call of the bugle.

Before long, lieutenant colonel Dickinson popped his head in to assess that they were well enough off. He tipped his hat to them without a word and rushed out the front door. Within minutes the drummers tapped out a pattern that Sue imagined called them into formation. Those drummers were likely boys about her own age. Would they live through the day? Would *she*?

"Wow," Brad said. "I'll bet I'd be wondering the same thing. Who was going to live and who would die? I hope I never have to go to war."

I nodded. "Pretty sobering, huh?" The serious mood lightened as I realized he was relating the story to himself. Fabulous! Maybe my whole class would feel that.

Brad glanced at his watch. "Tell me about the battle."

I wasn't sure if Brad related more to Sue than Mary or not, but I decided to keep this next part in Sue's perspective.

Sue, May 2, 1863, Virginia

Stand, sit, a few steps for movement. It all became wearisome. Even Aunt Nancy wasn't up to her storytelling. Sue would gladly choose the monotony of an hour ago if the booming of cannons would only quit. The cannons definitely sounded nearer than yesterday and the spatter of gunfire more intense. This was the first time she could think of where she didn't feel safe in her own home, bringing on another wave of apprehension.

Gazing over the shoulders of the guards, Sue could see a wounded soldier carried in by two men through the front door. A quick glance startled Sue away from her self-absorption. Was his foot missing or simply blocked from view? She quickly turned away, tears springing to her eyes as she recognized charring and blood around his torn flesh. They must have laid him down on the rug around the corner for he gave a loud yelp. She looked again. Another soldier followed on foot, a bag in one hand. *Oh please let it be the doctor!*

The roar of multiple cannons interrupted her silent prayer for the wounded man. George began to cry.

"Lord have mercy!" Aunt Nancy exclaimed. "We all's gonna die!"

Mrs. Chancellor shook a finger at the large woman. "I'll have no talk like that, you hear?"

"Oh let her complain, mother," Bettie said. "It's what we're all thinking anyway, and it's better than listening to moaning men inside and furious fighting outside."

Sue hadn't known her sister to be so bold. Their irritability must be increasing.

"Ooh," a soldier moaned as he was brought through the front door. Despite Bettie's outburst, they remained silent as more wounded men trickled in.

"I can't stand this, mother," Fannie whispered. "Let's make a break for it."

"Hush now. Don't be ridiculous. We aren't the ones with rifles, and where would we go that's safer than in here?"

Were they really safer here? Sue hoped her mother was right. She tried to think of where else they could go but the image of that soldier's missing foot kept returning when she had no better answer to her mother's words. How she wished this was all a drill like when she and Mary watched the soldiers practicing their formations. War hadn't seemed so cruel back then.

Now that the war had shifted to include abolishing slavery, it could take slaves away from people. It could take Mary away from her, and she wouldn't like that, despite having more work to do. War could destroy body parts and take lives. How many of those lives would be people she knew? Her chin quivered, and she fought off crying.

Resigned for now, the household barely moved as sounds of war thundered on and the smoky smell of gunpowder wafted on the air. Booming cannons and the crack of gunfire came from multiple directions. Sue prayed to be kept safe, but everything she heard and saw told her that the chance of peril was real—and not only for her own household. She hoped their other neighbors fared well, and the iron workers had abandoned their work at Catherine Furnace and all gone home.

More wounded were taken to the mansion, filling up the rooms of their house. They would never get all the blood stains out of the wooden plank flooring. She glanced at Hester and Mary, who would work their hardest to clean the floors, and felt a little sorry for them. Perhaps they wouldn't mind so much. They would be glad to have things return to normal and they were used to hard work. Sue watched the slave girls sitting next to one another, squeezing each other's hands and shaking like the warm day couldn't penetrate the thick walls. They had one another, but she had her lamb. She nuzzled her face into his soft fleece.

Aunt Nancy began singing, probably to soothe everyone, but her choice of songs had to do with meeting Jesus after this life. Sue didn't know if that was for their sake or that of the dying soldiers, but she preferred it to complaining or feeling sorry for herself.

Nancy's alto voice was frequently drowned by screams from patients before the ether or chloroform could take effect, Sue guessed. She tried not to look out directly, not wanting another revolting image filling her mind, but constant movement passed through her peripheral vision, and she knew what it meant. She couldn't take enough comfort from Lamar to counter-balance the horrendous happenings surrounding her.

Before a third song could be finished, the guards unblocked the cased opening to let an officer enter, stepping over wounded men to reach the back room. Nancy's melodic voice trailed off as the captain spoke. "I'm sorry. We need every available space to tend to the wounded. I must take you to the cellar."

Moved from the house to the cellar? Bettie huffed and Sue herself cried out her incredulity with a squawk. "Aagh!" How could she handle any more of this?

"What? For...for how long?" Mrs. Chancellor sputtered. "There...there are sixteen of us and the cellar is not fit to inhabit."

"I am truly sorry, Madame, but we have men who will die if we cannot take them in. On your feet, please. All of you."

Abbie mumbled under her breath, "So we get to die in the cellar instead?"

Sue scrambled to her feet, scooped up Lamar, rushed to her mother's side, and filed out of the room without giving in to her threatening tears. She saw Fannie grab a pair of silver candlesticks on her way. Sue's eyes widened at this place that was nothing like her home. Bodies lay strewn on every inch of floor space in the sitting room and into the hall that led to the kitchen, desecrating her good memories of this place. Could she ever walk these floors again and not envision wounded soldiers? Men moaned, some lay still from the effects of anesthesia or simply sleeping. She assumed they would be elsewhere if dead. She recognized some of the bandages as former bed linens.

Abbie shrieked up ahead. Sue stopped to stare at their grand piano, lid shut flat and used as an operating table. A man lay on top of it on a blanket, his uniform blood-red and torn on one sleeve. The doctor had placed a paper cone over the man's nose, but stopped further work while the civilians filed past. Sue caught site of a blood-stained saw on the piano and her stomach convulsed. She quickly averted her eyes and forced her feet to keep moving, stroking Lamar as if she were the one comforting him.

"Aunt Nancy," one of her sisters called back. "Cover Kate's eyes!"

Aunt Nancy took off her apron and threw it over the child's head. "Take her hand, Mary."

Aunt Nancy darted toward the kitchen. What on earth was she doing? A moment later Sue saw her at the end of the group and heard a tinkling jangle with every step Nancy took.

Soon enough they were outside, breathing air that was thick with smoke and hearing the popping sounds of gun volley with sharper clarity. Some shots had already torn into the front lawn and a few soldiers lay lifeless on the ground. She didn't have time to scan any further; they could be seen as targets at any moment.

"Keep your heads down!" she heard the officer yell.

Sue coughed as she ran and heard young Kate go into one of her fits. Aunt Nancy picked her up and hurried toward the corner. That woman was asking to draw fire with the jangling noise she made along the way. Sue couldn't help but look back, worried for them all. Nancy passed Mary, who wretched what little contents remained in her stomach on the grass next to the porch steps.

Before they could round the corner to the cellar on the side of the house, they passed an open window with a pile of bloody arms and feet at its base that no one had found time to bury. Sue's stomach lurched but Lamar's bleating gave her new focus. There was nothing in her stomach to dispense anyway. The soldiers had been too busy today to think about feeding them. It was just as well; she couldn't eat anything now if she were offered her last meal. Had it come to that?

A soldier had unhooked the latch and thrown open the doors to the cellar. They hurried in, stepping into cold water that reached the tops of their shoes. A quick count showed the head guard that they had all made it and fit within the rectangular space. Sue didn't care that things were worse in the house-turned-hospital. Fear bubbled inside her as she breathed in the dank air. She stomped her feet into the water that could become part of her tomb, wanting to stomp away this nightmare. It got her petticoat wet and didn't transport her to somewhere safe, but she took a deep breath and settled. She hugged Lamar tightly and set him down, where he eagerly drank from the musty pool.

The officer let them get their bearings enough to find higher ground on the uneven floor or arrange crates to sit on. Softened potatoes, onions, and apples, dried corn kernels in jars, and a few canned goods sat on the shelves, which were mostly empty this time of year.

George cried as the soldiers shut the doors and hooked the latch. It was dark but Sue found her eyes adjusting to light through small cracks.

Aunt Nancy began to hum as she lifted her skirts and wrestled something with a metallic clang from her large pockets.

"What have you got there?" Mrs. Chancellor asked, suspicion in her voice.

"Your silver tea service, Ma'am."

They could all hear the lady of the house take in a sharp breath.

"I knows how much you care for it." Nancy added.

Nancy was suddenly Sue's mother's best friend. "You angel! That was a gift from the Rappahannock Canal engineers. I would hate to have it fall into the hands of soldiers!"

The sound of Nancy fumbling to set the teapot, sugar bowl, and several spoons on one of the shelves faded into the background as Sue's sister, Bettie, spoke. "I snatched some family photographs, mama."

"And I took the silver candlesticks," Fannie said.

A delicate sigh glissandoed through the cool air—air that grew warmer by the minute with all of them in there. "You dears. Bless you. Bless you all."

Sue wished she had thought to grab something of value besides Lamar.

Hearing his mother's zeal, little George stopped crying. The grateful mood soon dissipated as cannons erupted again with ferocity. The company, more united than ever, prayed as one, led by Mrs. Chancellor.

A little later, the doctor opened the cellar doors. He hurried down the steps. Sue blinked at the bright light, but there was no mistaking the bottle of whiskey in his hand. He held it out to Mrs. Chancellor. "Each of you must take a dram to calm your nerves." Sue's mother took the bottle and worked at the cork with her fingertips.

Nancy put her hands on her hips. "I'd be careful if'n I was you, Ma'am. It's probably pizened!"

The doctor scoffed. "Poisoned, you say? Ha! I risked my life to offer what I could. I've sworn to give aid and do no harm. This here is medicine for your nerves at such a frightful time," he said, pointing at the bottle which Mrs. Chancellor had ceased opening. "Pass it around, Madame, and be done with it. I have injuries to attend to."

Nancy put her hands up. "Y'all can make up your own minds. I'll have nothing to do with it."

Mrs. Chancellor looked from the retreating doctor to Nancy and back, and then opened the bottle. She took a swallow and passed it to her left, the slaves knowing they'd be last. Bettie looked undecided and then took a swig. Abbie grabbed it next, anxious for a medicinal boost. When the bottle got to Sue she smelled it first and wrinkled her nose. It was medicine alright. Her swallow burned as it went down and made her cough. Everyone partook except for Aunt Nancy, who kept her arms folded and her lips pinched tight.

Sue's inkling of fear passed when no one became ill or poisoned to death. In fact, it seemed that Miss Kate's coughing had subsided. Sue smirked. Pizened. Aunt Nancy had some strange ideas and a stranger accent.

They had another visit later on, where one of the soldiers finally brought them some food. With the cellar door open, it was noticeably quieter outside and Sue thought she smelled cigar smoke. Surely it was a sign that things were going well for the Union, which made her frown. She hoped the soldiers that had allowed her to play cards with them were unharmed. Win or lose, she wanted the war to be over and the Yanks gone from her home. She wanted life how it used to be. Her gaze went to Mary. What would happen if their slaves were given freedom because of this war? As much as she liked Mary, she didn't want to end up doing slave chores like cleaning chamber pots and scrubbing blood from the piano.

She dismissed those thoughts and looked longingly at the scraps of food along with a paring knife left for them on a plate. Mrs. Chancellor cut up the link of cured sausage and loaf of stale bread into sixteen pieces. Sue ate heartily, feeling her hunger fade and glad to get the taste of whiskey off her tongue. The food improved their spirits and conversation helped pass time that was laced with worry.

All at once a man shouted from the yard. "Here they come!" At least that's what Sue thought she heard.

Fannie jumped up from the crate where she sat. "Here who comes?"

Sue hadn't imagined the shout. Everyone stilled to learn the answer. Sue heard quickened steps on the floorboards of the house, indistinct voices, and loud curses. General Hooker yelled commands and a bugle sounded. Mary grabbed her hand, bridging the crevasse between whites and slaves. If Mary was scared, she should be too. Not minding the continual clasp of her hand, Sue picked up Lamar with her free arm, set him in her lap, wet feet and all, and let Mary stroke him.

The shouting diminished and was replaced by the boom of artillery loud enough to keep Sue's heart racing. The cacophony lasted forever, it seemed. She heard whimpers and whispered prayers. Lamar seemed tense and baaed more than usual. No light shone through the cellar cracks by the time the noises outside abated.

Exhaustion caught up with Sue, yet she didn't think she could sleep, as full as her mind was. Her eyelids felt heavy so she closed them and leaned back against a hard, wooden shelf, afraid of what tomorrow would bring.

☆ ☆ ☆

I had Brad's full attention, but I stopped to look at the hands of my watch. Too many kids had walked passed for me not to. "Oh, man! It's 6:58." We both stood. "We'll have to finish another time—if you want to." I bit my bottom lip. It was his call now.

"You're right. It's going to be far out." He smiled at me. "Nobody else will have a story like this, and you're good at telling it." His smile faded. "If I do it, I hope I can perform it like you want. Aunt Nancy is funny, but I'm more comfortable doing the narrator or a character who's white."

I nodded encouragingly, but he had to know the truth. "Nancy probably won't get any lines. I have to condense a lot of the story so we don't take the whole period telling it. It's going to be you as a neutral narrator and me as both Mary and Sue. I'll do two different accents."

He pointed at me. "You give me a cool narrator part and it's a deal." We walked toward Brother Mike's classroom.

"Deal."

CHAPTER TEN

"HI." BRAD AND JAKE PLUNKED their lunch trays down across from me and Patty.

"Uh… hi." I sounded like an idiot needing a script.

"Let me know if you're not going to eat your brownie," Jake announced. "Not that either of you need to watch your weight, but some girls don't eat stuff like that."

"Are you kidding?" Patty said, her hands protectively covering the brownie. "That's the best thing on this tray."

I nodded. I recently enjoyed a large piece of birthday cake with ice cream. Why wouldn't I eat a small brownie?

Jake frowned and snapped his fingers. "What a downer."

"You don't mind if we sit here, do you?" Brad asked in a hushed tone. "It's kind of an experiment to see if Melanie and company will follow us." He put his hands up. "Not that we don't like them or anything. They're okay."

"Anytime," I said, smiling. I could do without Melanie showing up, but come to think of it, she hadn't bothered me, only ignored me in either of our classes together this week. Her stupid stunts could have been much worse. Maybe after getting it out of her system she wasn't so bad. Or had she stopped being such a jerk so Jake and Brad wouldn't think poorly of her? What did I care? Her absence and these guys sitting with us put me in a super good mood. I rubbed my hands together and let one eyebrow become expressive. "Ah. Very secretive. Ze mad scientist is performing an experiment. Ve shall vait and see."

"You're pretty good at that stuff," Jake said. "How's your drama class going?"

"Great. They're going to announce the fall play sometime this week."

Jake leaned closer from across the table. "Any two-bit parts in it for me?"

"There always are. I didn't know you had an interest."

Jake half-smiled. "It's kind of a new interest."

I blushed. He was cute, but he didn't make my insides go gooey like Brad did.

"Experiment over," Patty said. "Incoming."

"There you are," Melanie said in a slightly accusatory voice from behind me. I jumped, half expecting her to call me a name or pull some prank on me in front of everyone in the cafeteria. She came around the table and set her tray down next to Jake's. I breathed a sigh of relief. Gina sat beside Brad, and Ellen next to her.

Melanie spoke to Jake. "We couldn't find you for a moment, and I knew you would want my brownie."

I might have indulged in the eye-roll impulse if my heart weren't still pounding in my ears. Far worse than any prank she could pull would be to expose my one-sixteenth. I couldn't yet get comfortable that that might never happen.

Gina held her dessert out to Brad. "You can have mine."

"Thanks." He scarfed it in two bites, and then spoke to me, oblivious of Gina offering her heart along with the brownie. "I guess I'll do the project with you as long I'm the narrator," he said. "You'll make it cool, right? Sorry if I've been a flake about deciding. It caught me off guard to learn the characters were girls, you know?"

"Yeah, I get it. So when do you want to hear more?"

Melanie tore her gaze away from Jake to sneer at me. "He doesn't want to hear more. See how long it's taking to convince him? I wouldn't get excited about a slave girl story either." She covered her mouth with her hand and fake-yawned.

My fists balled and daggers shot through my eyes. How could anyone find a story like Mary's boring? I couldn't come up with a retort.

"I'm free after school today."

Melanie shook her head like we were both pathetic.

"Charlotte?"

I turned back to Brad. "Huh? Oh, great. Me too." Had he considered the source and ignored Melanie or had her rudeness pushed him into a decision?

Melanie said something to Jake. Gina and Ellen held their own conversation. Brad made plans with me like Melanie had never spoken. I could only pray it was because the story interested him. Or me. It wasn't until I'd finished eating that I noticed how quiet Patty had been. I'd completely left her out.

☆ ☆ ☆

Brad and I met at a conference room in the school library. It would be open for another hour. He took one end of the rectangular table and I took the seat on his right. We shot the breeze for a few minutes until Brad said, "I'm impressed how you can tell this thing from memory."

I beamed before reminding myself what I'd already worked out in my mind. If Brad came to feel anything for me through working together, Jake's interest in me would stop it cold. That's the kind of friend Brad was for Jake. I needed to settle for the friendship they both offered.

"Thanks. Gran tells it to me a couple times a year. I'll tell it to you pretty much how she would instead of condensing it, if you have the time. It's much better that way."

He nodded. "Let's hear it then."

☆ ☆ ☆

Mary, May 3, 1863, Virginia

Mary startled at the loud blast that ended her dozing. Hester and Miss Kate, on either side of her, cried out in alarm. George called for his mama on the other side of the long, narrow cellar. Morning had finally come, and with it the raging battle they had feared would sneak up so close. Whinnying horses, the constant ping of gunshot, and the crash of cannons all told them that each breath might be their last.

Mary rubbed her hand over her stomach, amazed that hunger would capture her attention at a moment like this. She felt a little sick to her stomach again today and reckoned that she may as well get something in it rather than wait to die on an empty one. She gingerly ventured away from the conspicuously slave side of the small room, making her way around the others toward a shelf with food, having to rewet her shoes in the puddles that had chilled overnight. She put a few potatoes and apples into her apron and shared them with Hester, Sally, Kate, and Nancy. Kate became grouped with the slaves since staying in the cellar, as if Nancy were her real mother.

Mary brushed the dirt from her potato with her apron, and gnawed slowly at her food. The Chancellors implemented Mary's idea, getting their own potatoes, and eating became the hope for a pleasant alternative to the sounds of destruction surrounding them. The somber group barely spoke, concentrating on eating though unable to ignore the commotion outside.

Nancy chuckled softly but it lacked anything jovial.

"What?" Mary asked.

"I was thinking how glad I am that all y'all weren't pizened. It'd be mighty frightening to be the only one awake down here listening to that hullabaloo."

Mary smiled, but Bettie said, "Maybe it would have been more humane than what's coming."

"Bettie!" Mrs. Chancellor reproved but offered no encouraging replacement.

Mary refused to be converted to Bettie's way of thinking. Nothing inhumane would come her way again that she wouldn't fight her way out of or die trying.

The group fell silent again and waited out their fate. Mary sat, thinking of her cold toes and the acrid black powder smoke seeping in that turned her stomach. The smoky air affected Kate's breathing too, and she began a fit of coughing.

After some time, the fire of cannons grew louder, if that were possible.

"Keep your head up, girl," Mary whispered to Hester. "We'll git through this."

"Why must they fight on the Lord's Day?" Sally, asked. "Nancy, please say another prayer for us?" The "us", Mary knew by how quietly Sally spoke, meant their little group of slaves and Miss Kate, who stuck together for support. Not even the terrible conditions the group in the cellar shared could unify them for long. Habits were too strong. Mary wished with all her heart that it would be better in the North.

"A course," Nancy replied. She closed her eyes and opened her mouth when a horrendous crash sounded and shook the ground underfoot. Lighter thumping followed, like bricks falling onto the porch.

"Something has hit the house!" Mrs. Chancellor cried. She covered her mouth with both hands and moaned.

Hester hugged her mother, and Aunt Nancy lifted Kate's delicate body onto her lap. Mary had no one to cling to. She looked for Sue, but Sue sat with her lamb next to her mother, deep on the other side. They locked glances and Sue sent her a sad smile, almost as if she felt sorry for Mary. Mary looked away and found she had grabbed hold of Nancy's skirt, scrunching it tightly in her fingers. She let go and began her own prayer in a rush with few breaths, doing her best to ignore the whimpers echoing through the cellar. "Our Father who art in Heaven, Hallowed be Thy name—"

Mary opened her eyes and smelled a woodsier kind of smoke. Had the countless dead leaves in the woods caught fire? Her eyes widened. Or was it the house? She scrambled to a stand. "We gots to git outa here!" The words flew from her mouth. She pushed toward the cellar door but others ahead of her caught her meaning and reached the steps first.

Several of the Chancellor daughters climbed the steps and pushed upward on the door. A half inch of light breathed in and out as the seam of the two doors repeatedly separated and closed with each push. "It's no use," one of them said. "Find a stick or something to knock the latch off."

While everyone looked around in the mostly dark cellar, the two doors swung open. A man's voice said, "This way, ladies. Hurry."

When Mary reached the top of the steps and her eyes had adjusted to the light, she could see that lieutenant colonel Dickinson and a couple of soldiers had come to their rescue. "Praise the Lord!" One of the soldiers smiled at her words. It was that fellow who took to reading his Bible at night.

"Is everyone out?" the officer asked.

Mary looked around, but not in response to his question. She could see thick smoke billowing from the front of the house. Too stunned to gasp, tears spilled onto her cheeks without her notice until they tickled under her chin. She wiped at them only to have more blur her vision of the wounded and dead bodies scattered throughout the clearing. Another horrible image she would never forget.

They passed an officer in the front yard who stared at them and said to Dickinson, "You left your post of duty to rescue a bunch of Southern women with slaves? There's war going on, if you hadn't noticed. Leave them be and come back!"

"This way," Dickinson called, ignoring taunts from the officer and prompting the residents into action after their sobering daze. He led the way and the other two soldiers kept the middle and rear moving. They passed more carnage along the out buildings and garden plot until at last there was nothing to see but the landscape of countless sentinels with their budding leaves.

Up ahead, Sue abruptly stopped and stared behind them. Mary turned to see the black plume and licking flames in the distance. "Lamar!" Sue cried. "I have to go back for my lamb!"

"Sorry, Miss," Dickinson said. "We can't. We must retreat further into Federal territory."

Sue sobbed and Mary's heart twisted. There was nothing either of them could do. Abbie took her sister's hand and gave it a tug. "They left the doors open. He'll climb out," she soothed. "Come on." It took another tug plus a nod from the nearest soldier to get her moving again, but the sniffling didn't stop.

"Federal territory," Nancy whispered. The slaves looked at one another. Would this be their chance for freedom? Did Mary dare hope? So far they had been treated as prisoners, though somewhat kindly, but maybe it would be different if they could be separated from the Chancellors. Where was Dickinson leading them?

Miss Kate couldn't take one mile of walking and collapsed. Aunt Nancy lifted her into her arms and carried her another mile or so where Joseph Dickinson led them to La Roque, a home where a New Jersey chaplain would take care of them while Dickinson made further arrangements with soldiers there.

They sat on the columned porch, catching their breath and sipping water. One of the soldiers bragged to another within their hearing distance.

"Did you hear we got Jackson last night? North Carolinians did it for us. The fool was in the wrong place at the wrong time." He chuckled. "Shot in the arm and out of commission."

Abbie shot him a hateful glare. The soldier next to him tossed the root of grass he'd been chewing on at his companion, hitting him on the cheek. "Hush."

Mary glanced over and saw an old black woman, laid out on a patch of grass, stiff as a board. She came down the steps for a closer look and pointed. "Is she…?"

"Yep," a nearby soldier answered. "We found her that way this morning. Chaplain says the war scared her to death." He seemed to be serious.

Mary shuddered. They could be in the wrong place at the wrong time too. She didn't feel any safer here than down in that cellar. War was not for the faint of heart nor the ill. She hoped Miss Kate would recover well. Before she could return to the porch, the book-reading soldier approached. Mary stiffened. He wouldn't do anything bad to her in front of a big group like this, would he? She glanced at the porch to see the watchful eyes of Hester and Sally on her before raising her eyes to the soldier.

"You can read, can't you?" It didn't sound like a question.

Would this skill get her closer to freedom? She suddenly wanted to trust him. "Maybe. So what if I can?"

A smile stretched over one side of his mouth, creating a dimple in his cheek. He pulled out the worn book tucked into his waistband. "I've had this feeling that I should give this to you. The other night and again now." He smoothed one hand over the cover as if he were reluctant to part with it, then thrust it toward her. "You may have it if you'll read it."

Mary's jaw dropped. A white stranger giving her a gift? Her curiosity grew and she took the offering. The title pressed into the hard cover read "The New Testament."

Brad leaned back and laced his hands behind his head. "That's cool. What a hard thing to give up, but I suppose he could access another one. If a slave can read, it would be the best thing she could own."

"Right." It had to be her greatest treasure. Until her children came along. Too bad the book had been destroyed. How would it be to see it and hold it in my hands? Would she have marked favorite passages or dog-eared certain pages? Would the cover have been frayed and worn before she died? I would never know. Yet I could testify how the teachings within had improved life for the generations that followed. I just couldn't tell Brad.

He pursed his lips to one side. "There's something about studying the Bible on your own that's different than going to church and hearing a sermon. You can soak up as much as you want and get your own inspiration from it."

I nodded. "I prefer quiet moments of pondering too." He didn't need to know that I sometimes read the scriptures aloud, using different accents or vocalizations. He would think that was weird. As for sermons, Pastor Jensen seemed biased toward the Good Lord loving white folk more than coloreds. That's the feeling I got anyway.

I stared at him, admiring his faith and love of the Bible. There's something attractive about a guy who followed his beliefs. "I'm sure Mary felt reverence for that book. It was the first thing she owned that made her feel as free as that soldier—a possession she kept in her apron pocket, feeling its constant weight. It represented freedom to her, both as a reminder of the day she left enslavement behind and the new freedom of living the messages within its pages. She studied it every chance she got."

"So we know Mary's going to get her freedom but give me a hint how her life will turn out." Brad's eyes looked hopeful.

I smiled; he was hooked. "She still had a hard life, but she made the best of it."

The school librarian approached the glass wall of the conference room, raised her hand, and spread the fingers of her hand. We had five minutes to clear out before a reservation took the room.

I collected my backpack. "Sadly, her husband grew jealous of that precious book, believing Mary cared for it more than him, which may have been true. I think she loved her children more than him too, but she was happy enough. His mind would sometimes go askew, altered by the war. He did one awful thing that took Mary a while to forgive him for, but he took care of them most of the time. I'll tell you about that later. My grandmother knew the family personally. Luckily her children had become believers and continued going to church after their mama passed."

"Cool. I suppose her descendants today would go to one of those revival type churches," Brad said, rising from his seat. "I want to hear more, but we better go. What about Friday after school?"

I shook my head and grinned. "I'm taking my driver's test that day."

"Is Friday your birthday? No fair. Mine's in a couple weeks."

"Poor baby. But no, it was Monday. I've always been one of the oldest in my class."

He slugged my shoulder without much force. Like a brother would to a sister.

He put on his backpack and fished out a dime from his pocket. "Too bad we can't drive ourselves home. I need to call my brother or mom for a ride. Can we give you a lift?"

"No, thanks. It's only a few blocks for me." I could make it home before his ride showed up. The extra minutes with him I'd be giving up wouldn't change our relationship, and I didn't want to seem overly anxious to hang with him.

"Let's do this again next week. See you at lunch tomorrow?"

I brightened that this could become a regular thing. "You bet."

As I walked home, my elation dwindled as I reviewed our time together. The whole conversation felt friendly but businesslike. Punching my shoulder was brotherly. I had spent an hour comfortably talking with a kind babe-magnet who had faith in God—a real catch!—but his main interest in me concerned a history assignment. I needed to get over him, but I didn't see how when he was so perfect.

CHAPTER ELEVEN

MOM AND I CAME OUT of the DMV with big grins on our faces. I held out my palm for the keys to the Dart and she dropped them into my hand. The two questions I'd missed on the written exam had felt like trick questions, but I'd already let it go, floating on cloud nine.

"Can I pick up Patty and go get ice cream or something after supper? I need to celebrate." I clasped my hands under my chin in a pleading gesture.

"Sure," Mom said. "Just be careful. We need to meet your friend soon."

"I know." All my friends were new and needed at some point to pass what I called parent approval. "Thanks!"

I called Patty with the good news and said I'd pick her up at 7:30. We drove to The Shake It Up diner, singing to the Four Season's *Big Girls Don't Cry* at the top of our lungs when it came on the radio.

First, we checked the place out for who we might know. Patty waved at a foursome of girls in one booth and pulled me toward them. I recognized two of them from school.

"Hi, y'all. Have you met Charlotte?" She told me the names of the girls. "Anything shaking tonight?"

The brunette frowned. "Just food and music so far. We're hoping a couple of hunks will show."

I glanced around. The boys in another booth were about fourteen. Families occupied other spots. The long counter held three singles with empty stools between them.

Patty crossed her fingers in response. "Here's hoping we brought luck in with us. See you later."

It threw me that Patty didn't try to join them. "We're here to celebrate you tonight," she said. I was glad for a private conversation with her. We slipped into a booth and ordered tall chocolate shakes in chilled glasses from a chubby woman with Sarah on her nametag.

Patty popped a quarter into the juke box, selected three songs, and sat back down. "I'm sure lucky having a friend who can drive."

"And I'm lucky to have gotten the car. Hunky guys showing up might be pushing my luck. Just watch. Melanie will show up instead." I grabbed my neck and pretended to choke, earning a smile.

"Hunky guys like Jake? I think he likes you."

So, she'd noticed. "I do too." My voice wasn't as animated as hers. "Not sure what to think about that. He's nice." Maybe I was still holding out for Brad to like me. John from drama was a contender too.

"Yeah. I'm surprised Melanie hasn't been meaner. She has to know Jake is more into you than her."

"I know. What is she up to?"

"Beats me." Patty abandoned her straw and gulped down a big spoonful. She closed her eyes and held her head for a second. "Ooo."

I fished for more of her insights. "It's no secret who Gina likes. Who do you think Brad likes? He's such a mystery."

Patty's enthusiasm dipped. "He's warming up to Gina. They might become a couple by Homecoming."

My heart skipped a beat. What had she seen that I hadn't? "Really? I thought he ignored her."

Patty shrugged. "It's a hunch. I've seen them talking in the halls a couple times. She's probably more talkative when Melanie isn't around."

I stared into my half-full glass, sipping slowly. I needed a minute to untwist my heart.

"So who do you have your eye on?" Patty asked with more lilt in her voice.

I scrambled for an answer that didn't include Brad. "Jake is interesting. I'll see what develops. There's another interesting guy, one in my drama class. John Hagley. He's been friendly, but I don't know. It feels like we flirt because it's safe or harmless. You know? I doubt anything will come of it."

"Oh good. I was afraid you would say Brad. I like how nice he is."

"You like Brad?" My eyes couldn't go any wider.

"Yeah, a little. But I'm not getting my hopes up."

Wow. She had a crush. No wonder she'd been quiet at lunch, wondering if I was monopolizing Brad for reasons beyond my project. I swirled the straw around and around in my shake. Now I had another reason to give up on Brad. Patty had spoken first dibs, if either of us were given a chance. "Well, he is nice."

"And a hunk." Patty giggled.

Three colored boys a little older than us walked into the diner and sat on stools at the counter. Three colored boys. In the diner for whites. Everyone stared. "Hey!" a man at the counter objected. Another man threw some bills on the table and shuffled his family out. My heart pounded.

When Sarah at the cash register finally closed her mouth, she opened it again to speak. "We don't serve coloreds." She pointed at the sign on the door.

"I had a *dream* that you do," the skinny one said, using the same intonation we'd heard from Dr. King on the TV news report of the march. "I'd like a cup of coffee please."

She shook her head. "Sorry. Y'all got to go."

The other two snorted. One added, "You going to deny us a cup a Joe? We ain't hurting nothing. Can't you dream big, as big as Dr. King?"

The cook came out from the back, waving a metal spatula overhead. "Get on out. We don't want any trouble." His brow pinched and his mouth worked like he wanted to say more.

I held a breath. The cook might very well explode. I could see this ending ugly like the sit-ins I'd heard about. For a few seconds, I considered whether or not we'd be safe if we didn't leave, but I couldn't tear my eyes away.

"We don't either," the third said. "We just want a cup a Joe. Got money too."

The cook narrowed his eyes and set a fist on his hip. "Get out or I'll call the cops."

I pictured Mary sitting at that counter. The freedom she craved hit me with a force like never before. There were Marys and Hesters and Aunt Nancys all over this town, desiring an equal chance. A sense of unfairness shot through me, and my fear spiked into anger. Anger that things hadn't changed much over one hundred years. Before I knew it, I was on my feet, leaning forward with my hands resting on the table. "Aw, give 'em a cup, Sarah."

Patty sat up straight, finding that brave voice of hers. "Yeah. Give them a cup. They're paying customers."

"Cup of Joe. Cup of Joe," the foursome of girls chanted. We joined in and so did the boys, and then the coloreds.

A man at the counter stormed out. A child from one of the families took up the chant and her parents hushed her.

"Cup of Joe!" We continued for a full minute until the girl in the booth stood and held up her hands.

"What do you say, Sarah?" she said.

Everyone looked at Sarah, who looked ready to burst into tears, not knowing what to do.

"It's the right thing, Sarah," I called out my encouragement.

Sarah looked to the cook for confirmation. I took the scrunching up of his face as indecision and softening. Whether he had given in for lack of support or hoped it would get them out of his diner faster, I didn't know, but he shrugged. Sarah set a cup and saucer in front of the young man and the diner erupted in cheers.

The family who had shushed their child marched out.

The cook looked more stern than upset, but he wagged a finger at the boy. "You're losing me customers over a cup of coffee."

"Not one but three cups. We'll have a basket of fish and fries too, please," he said. "I'll gain you a whole lot more customers if you take that sign down." He pointed at the door.

Patty and I grinned at each other, the thrill of witnessing history must be shining on my face like it did hers.

The cook pursed his lips. A trade-off the cook needed to ponder. He would lose a certain amount of customers by gaining others. I wondered if the victory would last beyond this moment. It still felt like a victory. I sipped at my shake again, peering at them over the glass.

Patty kept her voice low. "That was so cool! Look at you—getting your license and saving the world all on the same day."

"Pfft. You backed me up. I'll bet they purposely chose a night when more teens could be in the diner for the power of unity."

"Pretty smart. *They* started the chant." She jerked her head in the quartet's direction.

"*They* gave us a reason." I jerked mine at the men at the counter.

"And they—"Patty yanked her thumb toward Sarah and the cook—"made the right choice." We laughed.

I dug a dime out of my coin purse, searching over the selections on the juke box. I searched for a good two minutes, finally finding one I deemed appropriate. More a favorite of my mother than me, I dropped in the coin and pressed the button. A 45 shifted over and the needle came down. Nat King Cole's smooth voice came over the speaker.

The skinny fellow at the counter gave me a nod with his half-smile. I returned it.

CHAPTER TWELVE

ON MONDAY MORNING, I SAW Melanie leaning against the wall as I approached room 209. Her arms were folded and she wore a scowl. When she saw me, her arms dropped to her sides and she took a step toward me. I recognized trouble but went for acting casual. "Hi, Melanie."

She sneered at me. "Don't 'hi' me. The only reason I've tolerated you this long was as a favor to Jake, but he likes you too much. Now I'm telling you to stay away from him."

I crossed my arms. "Why? You have no control over either one of us."

"So you admit you like him? You've been plotting to take him from me since day one."

Like he was ever hers. I squinted at her. "Plotting? What are you talking about?"

Melanie set a hand on her hip. "Finding the best guy to help on your first day, hoping he would show you around. Becoming buddies with his best friend. Taking over the lunch table conversation with your stupid slave story and using your drama skills to act charming. Sound familiar?"

My eyes narrowed further. "You're overreacting. None of that was on purpose."

"I'll bet." She glanced up, and we both saw Brad heading our way. "Just find another lunch table."

I stared her down. "Or you'll what? Put twigs in my locker? You'll lock Jake away so he can never speak to a girl ever again? Sheesh." I stomped away to find my seat.

Brad entered and sat by me. I slipped on a happy-to-see-you face but apparently too late. "What's wrong?" he asked.

Part of me wanted to cry on his shoulder so he could comfort me. "Oh, it's nothing. I'm getting into a character mood."

He smirked. "Drama's not until third hour. You have to get through history and math first."

"But it worked, right? It was a good face—believable?"

"Good if you mean angry." He gazed at me again and I softened. Dang those greenish blue eyes. "You sure you're all right?"

"Yeah. Thanks." I brightened at his concern.

Brad tucked his backpack under his seat. "How was your weekend?"

He'd seen me on Sunday and I'd told him I got my license, but I hadn't mentioned what happened at the diner. "Patty and I went to The Shake It Up Friday night. You'll never guess what happened."

Mrs. Burkhart got up from her desk and moved to its front edge. I didn't have time for the whole story. "Three colored guys walked in to order food, and the waitress ended up serving them!" I cringed, not liking how dull that summary sounded.

"You're kidding!" He looked shocked and alarmed, probably imagining a mini riot with police involvement.

"Don't worry. Nobody got hurt."

The bell rang and the teacher started talking.

I didn't have time to tell it properly. Maybe I could do that later. At lunch? I glanced at Melanie sitting with Ellen on the other side of the room. I figured it was more important to stand up for myself, like those three at the diner, than avoid confrontation. I shouldn't be mean to Melanie, yet I believed Jesus didn't want me getting pushed around either. Maybe Patty would have some good advice.

I glanced at Brad, who faced the teacher. He cared at least a little. Doing this project with me should keep developing that, hopefully into something romantic—if it didn't work out between him and Patty, that is. I guess I was plotting after all.

I waited for Patty by her locker after math. I'd spent that hour thinking about what to do, and I'd come up with a plan.

"What's up?" she asked when she saw me.

"Melanie told me that Jake has a crush on me."

She slapped me on the back. "Right on!"

"No, it isn't, not when she has one on him. She doesn't want me anywhere near him. She ordered me not to sit at the same lunch table anymore."

"Oh." This affected her too, and it showed on her face. She'd probably had visions of me and Jake doubling with her and Brad. She swallowed. "Well, I'll stick with you. We'll sit somewhere else if that's what you want."

"Aw, shucks." I smiled at her. A true friend. "But I have another idea."

Patty dialed her combo, switched books, and shut her locker. "Good, because we shouldn't give her that control. Lay it on me."

"We act like nothing is different and sit with them, only we start talking about how John from my drama class likes me, which he does as a friend anyway, and how he might ask me to the homecoming dance."

"That's a keen idea! We don't give in to Melanie, but she knows you're steering Jake away from you. She'll go with it rather than make a scene."

"Yeah. It's perfect."

Patty's expression fell. "But won't that hurt Jake's feelings?"

"Hm. Perhaps. He'll find someone else. Homecoming is still three weeks away."

"Okay," she said uneasily. "If we can't come up with anything else by lunch, that'll be the plan. We gotta split."

"Thanks, Patty. You're the best."

I booked it to drama class, making it before the warning bell. I slipped into the seat John had saved next to him, my mind whirling. His slicked back, jet black hair revealed a strong forehead and dreamy eyes. Should I start encouraging him more? I hadn't wanted to because of Brad. Now everything was changing.

John would make a far out first date. We were pretty comfortable together in class, enjoying a lot of the same things, but I wondered if dating would mess that up. It happened to my friend in Maryland. Besides, I wondered if John was dating someone. If I couldn't go with him or Brad to Homecoming, I hoped Brad would ask Patty instead of Gina. Brad was perfect. Too bad he didn't feel the same about me. Apparently Jake was interested in me. That alone gave me hope that I might get asked to the dance.

John didn't say hello like usual but greeted me with the chorus of a Beatles hit, singing softly. His hand gestured to me.

I took my turn, swaying in my seat like he did and singing the line that repeated his.

We crooned the last part together, and then laughed. He was fun. Brad's perfection was temporarily overrated. I had to quit thinking of either of them that way. Jake's a good guy too.

The ring of the bell put a huge damper on that fun. We couldn't help sniggering for a bit.

Mr. Dodd gave us a sharp look through his black-frame glasses. "I have some good news that all of you will want to hear." He paused dramatically. "Are you ready to find out the title of the school play?"

I gasped, and I wasn't the only one. I bit my bottom lip. Please let it have a great female lead and supporting roles.

"It's a recent musical but no longer on Broadway."

It sounded like Mr. Dodd chose the latest plays possible, but my lip still drooped. I could sing, but not like a film star. This might take me from the lead role, but there still had to be some great parts I could do. Tell us already!

"It won a Tony for Best Musical and four others. They made it into a film last year and it won an Academy Award for best musical score."

"Oh! Oh!" a girl said, raising her arm high. "It's *The Music Man!*"

"It is!" Mr. Dodd said.

John and I glanced at each other, eyes shining, grins popping out. A rumble of excitement rippled around us. I had seen the movie last year and loved it. As I recall, there was one female lead and a couple minor ones, mostly dancers and townspeople, and a heavily male cast.

"Preference will be given to seniors," Mr. Dodd said in his deep voice. "We'll find a role for everyone that wants to participate. We'll need sets and lighting specialists too. The art and music departments will help. Extra credit will be given for parental help. The school requires chaperones at the practices and some costumes will need to be sewn. I'll post the signup list on Friday with auditions beginning after school next week. You will need to prepare 32 bars of any song to either sing or dance."

I turned toward John and whispered, "Do you think we could get away with 32 bars of the Beatles?"

He chuckled. "Going for a lead?"

I had no idea what the talent pool looked like in the advanced drama class for juniors and seniors, but competition had to be tough. "Do I have a shot?"

"It wouldn't hurt to try. With preference to seniors, I could only hope for a salesman-on-the-train part."

"I'd like to at least end up in the pick-a-little ladies group." I shrugged. "We'll have fun no matter what."

"That's the spirit."

Mr. Dodd formed us into groups and let us practice reading a scene from the script.

I didn't think about Melanie again until the lunch bell after English. Patty waited at my locker. "Any new ideas?" she asked.

I shook my head. "Plan A it is."

We went through the lunch line with our trays, purposely making sure that Melanie and Jake were already at the table before approaching. Melanie sat next to him, facing the lunch line. Melanie's face creased into an angry scowl, burning a hole right through me with her eyes as we neared. I refused to look at her after that one glance. Brad, Gina, and Ellen had their backs to us, and Ellen turned to see who Melanie scowled at. We set our trays down without greeting anyone, Patty and I deep into our conversation.

"John sang to you in drama today? How dreamy." Patty sighed heavily and fluttered her eyes. Her acting was a little exaggerated but effective.

I stepped over the bench as I told her, "I know. It wouldn't be a stretch for him to ask me to the homecoming dance next." Well, it wouldn't be a stretch if John hadn't mentioned another girl last week. I looked up and acknowledged the group. "Hi guys."

Melanie watched us with guarded suspicion while a forced smile came to her lips. I would have to remember that look for drama class sometime.

Gina piped up. "Who's asking you to Homecoming?"

"Oh," I waved away the significance with my hand. "We were just talking about a boy who might ask me to the dance."

Melanie's expression relaxed. I guessed she understood my plan.

"But he hasn't yet?" Jake asked with concern.

"Uh…no." I inwardly cringed, seeing where this headed. Melanie stiffened.

"But he's going to," Patty put in.

"But you'd rather go with me, right?" Jake said with hopeful confidence. "It'll be fun. So how about it?"

"She's taken," Melanie quickly said. "Didn't you hear her? She wants to go with someone else."

"I'm asking first," Jake replied, his eyes still on me.

"I… I wasn't trying to get you to ask me. Don't you want to think about this? Isn't there someone else you should take instead?" I looked pointedly at Melanie and back, hoping he'd either take my hint or Melanie would appreciate my attempt.

Patty hopped onto the convince-Jake-otherwise track. "You don't want to ask her at a lunch table. You should rethink this."

"Too late," Jake said. "I've been thinking about it for days and I'm caught up in the opportunity. I can still be gallant, if that's what y'all want." He remained seated while executing a grand bow extending both arms. "Will you go with me to Homecoming, my lady?" He smiled, not quite masking a look in his eyes that exposed his risk.

It wasn't excitement I felt at getting asked. I wanted to duck my head. To hide from Melanie. To hide from an audience in an awkward situation. To shrug off the urge to say yes out of compassion. But I did like Jake well enough to enjoy an evening with him. He was nice to me that first day of school without knowing anything about me. Now he bared his vulnerability, and that took guts. He might not be perfect like Brad or comfortable like John, but he offered whatever it was he had inside him, and it was good enough.

"I would love to, kind sir." I bowed my head as if I had curtsied.

Jake looked relieved, and I felt good about my choice, even if my plan totally backfired. I might catch Melanie's hateful looks or pranks for the rest of the year, but I was going to Homecoming!

I gave him a smile. "But how about we go as a group?" I swept my hand in a small arc. "Get some of your friends together so all of us can have fun that night? What do you say?"

Jake smiled back. "That's kind of what I had in mind. I'll see what I can do." He lightly nudged Brad.

"That's a great idea," Gina said, smiling at Brad.

Brad looked uncomfortable as he twirled a fork into his spaghetti. Melanie looked like she fought off tears. Ellen seemed to share her distress; she made a good groupie.

Brad looked up and caught Patty's eye. "Would you be my date for Homecoming?"

Patty's slack jaw slipped into a huge grin. "Yes. I'd love to."

I was happy for Patty. Sort of. I'd rather Brad go with her than Gina. Gina's brows pressed together and her lips quivered like she wanted to protest. Or cry.

Melanie stood and picked up her tray. "Don't bother finding dates for us. We've got it covered. Come on, girls." She stalked away with her two followers, leaving the four of us feeling more relieved than anything.

Just walk away for good. No, I wouldn't be that lucky. Melanie had more reason for revenge than ever. I needed to watch my back.

CHAPTER THIRTEEN

MELANIE KEPT OUT OF MY way and I kept out of hers for the next few days. Not an easy thing to do with two classes together, but not impossible. She could be biding her time to spring something terrible on me at a big moment or she could go on acting like I wasn't worth her time. Either way, I had to go on with my life.

Brad and I arranged to meet again in the school library conference room on Thursday for our project. Now that he had me alone, something else appeared to be on his mind.

"Patty's glad I asked her to Homecoming, isn't she?"

I smirked. If he only knew. Patty's interest in Brad had soared significantly since Monday. To a lesser degree, the same thing happened to me about Jake. I thought about him a little more. Mostly I was excited for my first date. My secret hope of winning Brad over if she grew tired of him needed to shuffle to the back of my mind like the winter coat at the back of my closet in the summertime, but with Brad's questioning blue eyes who was I kidding? Why did I always fall for the ones who liked someone else? Get over him! Jake was pretty great too.

I swatted Brad's arm. "Of course she is. She knows a good guy when she sees it."

He blushed. "Thanks. I just…it was sudden, you know. I didn't want her feeling like I simply jumped on the band wagon. She deserves better than that."

I swallowed. The coat didn't belong in my closet at all. "Yeah, she's pretty great. Don't worry about it. She's happy." Discussion over. "So, are you ready for more of our Civil War story?"

It took him a second before he nodded. "That's what we're here for."

"Remember, we left off where the soldier gives Mary his New Testament."

$$\star \; \star \; \star \; \star$$

Mary, May 3, 1863, Virginia

Mary stared down at the small book in her hands and smoothed her fingers over the cover like the soldier had, already feeling a reverence for the book. "Thank you," she said quietly. He nodded and backed up, offering her some space. She'd never held a Bible or any part of it in her hands, only heard readings from it, and now this copy was all hers. She glanced at the soldier and gave him a grateful smile.

She let the book flop open to a page near the middle and read:

Then Peter opened his mouth, and said, Of a truth I perceive that God is no respecter of persons: But in every nation he that feareth him, and worketh righteousness, is accepted of him.

Mary silently stumbled at the hardest words—perceive and righteousness. A warm feeling blossomed from deep inside her. The passage held some strange but exciting words. She wandered away from the cabin to read the passage again privately, staying within view of the guards so they wouldn't worry.

It thrilled her more the second time, like Jesus sent a message straight to her heart. God didn't care if she was black or white, bond or free. She could still be accepted of Him and rewarded in the next life, if not this one. Holding the book to her chest for a moment, Mary tucked the book into her apron pocket and returned to the porch.

"What did he give you?" Hester asked when she neared. "Lemme see."

Mary showed her the book, pleased that Hester appreciated it.

"A Bible? How wonderful!" she said. "Looks like it's been through a war." She chuckled at her own joke, then added, "But I can tell it meant something to him. Why do you s'pose he done give it to you? Is he rich?"

Mary shrugged. "It's the part of the Bible when Jesus lived. It's got some nice words in it. Maybe he knowed them all by now and figured he pass it along."

It was hard to put it back into her pocket without reading more, but she didn't want to do that with so many eyes upon her. Would she ever be free and have time to herself to read and study as she wished? She gazed at Sue, supposing she would take an interest in Mary's gift as well, but the poor girl looked too tired to care.

"Wait," Brad said. "You're not putting scripture verses in the script, are you?"

"No." I squinted at him. "The important part is that she gets her own scriptures to read. It gives her a taste of freedom and it guides her for the rest of her life. I'll have to condense it to something like that, if I mention it at all."

"Okay. God can accept slaves if He wants to, but I don't think we should tell a bunch of white students what they should believe."

"Got it. No preaching during class time," I teased.

"It's not that." He swatted the table. "Oh, never mind. I already know this is way too long and you're making a bunch of changes. I'll read it later and then make my suggestions."

My jaw slacked open. "You're going to make suggestions for my script?"

"Only if the characters' opinions come across too strongly."

I huffed. "The characters become flat if they didn't have opinions."

Brad set his index finger against his lip, appearing thoughtful. "For example," he said, wagging the finger before setting his hand down. "I don't think it's historically correct that Mary would be a playmate for Sue. A Southern parent wouldn't have allowed it. Maybe your grandma added some things or watered it down like a bedtime story. The truth may have been much harsher."

Lips pressed tight, I bristled that he would question my grandmother's integrity. This was no bedtime story.

I let out a breath, believing his sabotage wasn't intentional. Maybe he had a point. Gran hadn't told me about Mary being raped until recently, now that I was older. Could there be other things omitted from or softened in the story? Doubtful. Gran's consistency seemed the important factor.

No, I was sticking with the version I knew and loved. A rare, childhood friendship between a slave and owner could definitely happen, especially when neighbors were sparse. It felt real to me.

I kept calm. "Gran always tells it the same. Don't you like the story?"

"Sure." He leaned forward. "There's no doubt it's better than a book report. I wish you had some documentation. How did your grandma get this story anyway?"

I wasn't willing to risk giving him the whole truth. "It was told to her directly by Mary's daughter. You can't get any better word of mouth than that. Plus, it's known that Sue left a diary, which validates the story—right down to a pet lamb named after a soldier, but I don't know where to find it. It's probably with her descendants."

Brad nodded. "Okay. I can't argue with that."

"That's why I've been writing it down, so there *will* be a record." *For posterity as well as history.* If he figured it out, I trusted he would keep my secret.

He looked satisfied. "Okay. Let's keep going."

☆ ☆ ☆ ☆

Mary, May 3, 1863, Virginia

Lieutenant Colonel Dickinson returned to the guards with whom he had left Mary and the refugees. A picket of soldiers accompanied him, including a drummer boy that Mary thought was mighty young to be in the army. Once again they all marched through the woods until they reached the pontoon bridge at U. S. Ford. Mary wondered how many stops they would have until freedom.

The Chaplain got a horse from the soldiers there and helped Miss Kate cross. She didn't look well. Mary didn't feel so well either.

From the edge of the river, Mary nervously watched the pontoon bridge that looked like boards slapped on top of canoes. The bridge rocked a little under the weight of the horse, though it appeared stable enough. Kate fainted during the crossing, poor girl. Mary fanned her face with her hand, feeling a little faint herself. However there was no other choice but to plunge ahead.

Men pulled Miss Kate from the horse when it reached land, and the whole company stopped to rest while Dickinson sent for an ambulance carriage. "See if you can get some ice and lemons," he told the drummer boy. The boy looked about Hester's age and shot off back over the bridge like he was used to crossing it.

"Don't you worry none," one of the guards told the group. "The lieutenant colonel will make sure you have the best we can offer."

Mary believed him. Dickinson had done so thus far. A glance at two of the Chancellor daughters made her pause. Abbie folded her arms and turned her back on him and Fannie lifted her chin and ignored him. It must be hard for a Southern girl used to her usual comforts to be marched away from her home by enemies of the soldiers they'd hosted so often, but that didn't mean Mary felt sorry for them. She counted on getting her freedom and the chance to have some of those comforts belong to her. If she could stay above Northern lines, that is.

The drummer boy returned with a small sack of lemons and a small block of ice for Miss Kate. He took a pocket knife and cut the lemons in half, offering them as a refreshment. The girls sat on the grass and sucked lemons. The sour soon became tolerable and perked Mary up. Abbie's attitude improved. Sue, however, looked pale and lay with her head on her mother's lap.

Dickinson returned in a one-horse-drawn carriage. He exited and helped the chaplain load the weaker ones. Miss Kate, Sue, Mrs. Chancellor, and her young son rode on ahead. The guards urged the others to follow on foot. They walked to a log cabin at the Eagle Gold Mine, where they were once again under house arrest.

Mary hoped that the Federals had retreated and Lee's army hadn't pursued. In any case, the sounds of war had ceased for now, and she felt safer here than at Chancellorsville. Having cooperated thus far, the soldiers didn't expect any trouble from these women. They were free to move about within the cabin as desired. After a couple days of encouraging words and adequate food, the Chancellor girls warmed toward the good care of the soldiers, playing cards and singing for them.

One afternoon, Aunt Nancy gave Mary and Hester a pointed look, alerting them to pay attention. Nancy and Sally walked up to one of the guards. "Y'all don't mind if we see what's in the cupboards and fix us all a little something to eat, do you?"

He perked up. "Nope. Might be better than what the cook would come up with. Help yourselves."

Once alone in the kitchen, Nancy motioned us closer. "When we gets released," Nancy said, "how we going to stick together and follow the army instead a the Chancellors, so's they don't think we abandoned them?"

Mary spoke up. "I don't mind hurting their feelings if it means I gets to be free. We got to do what we got to do."

Sally nodded vigorously. "We're their slaves, not their family."

Mary would like to have Sue claim her as family if she would, but she would not let this one and only chance at freedom pass.

"You're right, but—" Nancy glanced up at the increasing sound of boots on the wooden floor.

Lieutenant Colonel Dickinson entered the small room. He gave a friendly smirk. "If I didn't know any better, I'd say you ladies were plotting something."

Mary tucked her hand under her collar. Had her heart stopped? As if in answer, her chest now thumped with a vengeance. What did he suspect them of?

Nancy's hands fidgeted for a moment, then boldly asked, "Can you gets us to freedom?"

Dickinson's eyes widened. "Don't you know? You're already free, ever since we confiscated the Chancellor House. We simply had to get you to safety."

Mary and Nancy looked at one another, confusion creasing their brows. Weren't they under house arrest too?

Dickinson explained. "According to the Second Act of Confiscation, the Union has seized you as contraband of war. When we release the Chancellors, you may go your own way."

Nancy clasped her hands together and looked as if she might kiss the officer. Mary was not so easily taken in. "We don't wants to be confiscated property of the army. We wants to be free human beings. Don't we need papers or something?"

"Not if you stay in the North. President Lincoln has signed an Emancipation Proclamation and technically you have been free since then. Southerners are fighting it so even those with papers can't prove to a Southerner's satisfaction that their papers are legitimate. Stay within Union lines until the war is over and you shouldn't have a problem."

"Really?" Mary rose up on her toes as she asked. Could it be that easy? She knew of a plantation that sent overseers to track down their runaway slaves and bring them back. Mrs. Chancellor didn't have an overseer, but other problems could arise.

Dickinson smiled. "Truly. I'm taking you ladies to the Union camp as soon as we are certain that the Rebels have called off the current campaign. That's when I will release your party."

Tears swam in Mary's eyes. She couldn't speak to thank him.

Nancy shook her clasped hands under her chin. "Thank you, sir. God bless you." She paused. "Can I asks one more little favor? When we gets released with the Chancellors, can you make it your idea that we's parting ways from them?"

The lieutenant colonel grinned, and then gave them a nod. "I'll manage something."

CHAPTER FOURTEEN

SATURDAY FINALLY ARRIVED. I'D FELT on edge all week not knowing if Melanie would pull some trick on me. That seemed trivial, however, compared to my bigger fear as Gran felt better day by day. What would happen when she wanted to go places? Somebody would put two and two together and act on it.

Only at Oakmont could I fulfill my drama goals, and I belonged there as much as anybody. It wasn't my fault this Southern town and its schools wouldn't budge an inch away from archaic customs. Patty wouldn't mind meeting Gran when she came over today, but she'd probably be surprised. I watched for her right after lunch, and opened the door when her mom dropped her off. "Hi." I waved her in.

Patty breathed deeply as she glanced around. "Hmm. It smells like cookies."

My living room was about as typical as middle class got. Comfy furniture, pictures on the walls, nothing special but cozy enough. "Uh-huh. Mom's way of welcoming you." I lowered my voice. "My parents want to meet you."

She rolled her eyes. "I know. My mom would have parked and come in if she didn't have an appointment. Parents. Sheesh."

Mom came in from the kitchen, wiping her hands on her apron. "I didn't hear the doorbell, but I heard voices. You must be Patty." She offered her hand and Patty shook it.

"Nice to meet you Mrs. Rogers."

"You too." Mom called to Dad. "Dale?"

Dad came out from his den. "So this is Patty." He grinned, making his dimple appear, and shook her hand. "We've heard a lot about you. Welcome to our home."

"Thank you."

"Tell us a little about you, Patty," Mom said.

I raced through a list before Patty could speak. "She's the youngest of four girls, we have lunch and PE together, she plays the flute in the school orchestra, and does her homework." I sent her a pleading can-we-go-now look.

Mom's mouth turned down for the briefest second. "Alright. You girls go enjoy yourselves and I'll let you know when these cookies are done."

Snatching the opportunity, I grabbed Patty by the elbow and steered her away, but we didn't go to my room. "I want you to meet someone," I said. Patty hadn't shown any signs of bias against the three men who wanted service at the diner, so I trusted her. I needed to know if she would connect Gran as being related to me rather than a visitor like her.

Patty followed me past the kitchen to the small family room where Gran sat in a wheelchair, her casted leg propped on the foot rest in front of a noisy picture tube. "Hi there," I said, distracting her from a show.

"Hello, dear. Who's your friend? Snap that thing off for me, would you?"

I turned off the TV, keeping a close watch on Patty. "This is my friend, Patty, from school."

"Pleased to meet you," Patty said. Her expression changed to one of recognition. "Oh, is this your gran?" She smiled and stepped forward to shake Gran's hand. "Nice to meet you."

"Why thank you, child. So nice to meet you." Gran looked at me. "She's cute as a button." It made Patty laugh.

I reckoned it would be obvious to Patty who Gran was because I'd talked about her and her broken leg before, but the connection still hadn't been instant. That was a good sign. The people I worried about might not make the connection at all.

I turned back to Gran. "Sorry to interrupt your show. I can turn it back on."

Gran waved a hand. "No, I'm tired of it anyway. About all I can do is watch TV or read. I can't wait to get moving again."

The oven timer buzzed and we moved over to watch Mom take cookies from the oven. She set a couple each on three napkins. "Take one to Gran," she said, pushing them toward us.

"Thanks, Mrs. Rogers." Patty looked as delighted as she sounded.

I picked up a napkin for both me and Gran. The cookies warmed my hands. "We'll take ours to my room. I want to show it to Patty."

"Okay."

When we entered the bedroom, I closed the door and went straight over to sit on my twin bed. I expected Patty to come sit beside me and begin eating, but she scanned the pale turquoise walls, my white coverlet with tiny blue flowers and a large, fuzzy turquoise pillow. She examined a Beach Boys poster, fingered my collection of necklaces and bracelets in an open jewelry box on my desk, and picked up a photo of me and my friend from Maryland.

"I need to ask you something." My serious tone brought her gaze to mine before she could gush over the Beach Boys, try on a necklace, or ask about the girl in the photo.

She sat beside me and took a bite. "Sure."

"What do you think of my grandma? I mean really. Tell the truth."

"I like her. It was more comfortable meeting her than your parents." She made a sorry-but-true face. "These cookies are terrific!"

"You're not avoiding the real issue here, are you?"

She tilted her head and frowned. "What—that she's colored? You know I wouldn't care."

I nodded, popping chocolatey goodness into my mouth.

"But it explains you needing the hair relaxer. Why didn't you tell me?"

"I knew you wouldn't care by the way you acted at The Shake It Up. *You* are not the problem."

"What are you getting at?" She sounded a little annoyed.

"Gran's talking about going to church with us soon, and I'm worried about those who would find it a problem. Mom says it will be good for Gran to get out of the house and worship, but I don't think my parents are considering what might happen with me at the school. Gran's feeling better and not content with sitting home on Sunday reading her Bible. That means she'll be sitting with us in a pew and people learning that this white girl—" I pointed to myself, "—has a not-so-white grandmother."

"You shouldn't—" Patty looked glum. "Oh."

"Right. That info gets to some snobbish school official and I'm out of Oakmont."

"That's horrible. Can't you take her to her own church?"

"She's not from Palmetto Peaks. Her church is an hour away and Dad likes to sleep in on Sundays. Gran would rather stick with the family than go to a new colored congregation by herself. Dad's comfortable with the one we've been attending, though there's something about the pastor that rubs me the wrong way. I like the youth teacher though." I was rambling now. I'd never voiced my concern over this out loud.

I didn't want Gran to feel like I was ashamed of her. I wasn't. Having Gran in my life was like starring roles and Christmas and summer vacation all rolled together. I only wanted to keep her away from those who wouldn't understand. It felt a bit selfish, but I also knew that Gran wanted for me the things I wanted for myself—a good education with opportunities for developing my talents and friends who made me happy. I couldn't keep Gran from worshipping.

Patty set her elbows on her knees and rested her chin in her hands. "What will you do?"

I let a deep breath out slow and easy. "I might have to take what comes, though I'm putting that off for as long as possible. That's why I haven't told anyone." Until now. I paused, biting my lip until Patty looked at me, staring me down with her baby blues. "I love my granny. I can't ask her to stay hidden. It gives me an awful feeling—worse than attending school without you and not having plays to be in."

Patty nodded her agreement, looking optimistic. "We'll do something… like make picket signs and rally support."

I shook my head. "That was my first idea. Remember that huge riot at Ole Miss last year, and the Governor of Alabama blocking three coloreds from entering their University, even after a federal judge ordered their admittance? Whites don't want coloreds in their schools and I doubt our little protest would change that. Only thirty-one percent, less than a third, of Southerners approve of mixing with white students in the same school. It would take a lot of time and effort to get a majority."

"Maybe they'd let you be the exception. You're more white than anything."

A pang of regret stabbed my heart that she could be right and wrong at the same time. I looked white and lived white, but people didn't like exceptions. I didn't want to totally lose my African heritage. Was that why I felt so driven to write Mary's story?

Patty broke into my reflections. "Folks won't care about one high school student here."

I pursed my lips. "I can see Melanie putting up a stink until they do."

She frowned. "The federal government already mandates desegregation. We need to stir things up and make them do it."

I ran a hand through my hair. "That's why Pennfields High became a compliant school, so folks would leave Oakmont and their fancy arts programs alone. Like a settlement, because the local government doesn't want to desegregate. It would take the national guard to make a dent." My best chance, for now, was to put off anyone finding out for as long as possible. I had to at least get through being in the fall play. "You can't tell anyone."

"I won't. We'll think of something," Patty soothed.

I put my arm around her shoulder and squeezed. "Thanks."

CHAPTER FIFTEEN

JOHN'S NAME WAS ON THE list for his audition two ahead of mine, but that didn't mean I could watch him or glimpse any of the advanced class talent. The parent volunteers kept us in the drama room until our name was called. I waited off-stage on one side as John came out the other. All I could do was overhear the girl ahead of me from the wing, running dialogue with another boy, and I was impressed. She enunciated well and I could feel emotion in the random lines she read. Her singing was pleasant too, a ballad with melodic lines. She held the last note smoothly and eased into the vibrato. No wonder Oakmont was known for its fine arts. This would be tough.

My palms were sweating, and I wiped them on my skirt. I heard someone thank the girl and call my name.

Heart pounding, I stepped out onto center stage. Only a music stand offered any companionship. Platinum blonde hair stuck up above an upright piano below the stage. Resisting the urge to shade my eyes from the bright lights, my vision adjusted until I saw three figures sitting in the first row. I recognized Mr. Dodd and the choir teacher, but the third woman's face was unfamiliar. The dance teacher or assistant director perhaps? The old joke of picturing them in their underwear flashed into my mind, and I inwardly cringed at the resulting image. "Hello," I said, banishing the image. There was something to be said for it calming my nerves, however.

"Ah, Charlotte Rogers," Mr. Dodd said with a smile. "A promising new student," he told his companions, who looked at my résumé. A boy with a paper in his hand walked over to me from the other side of the stage. Mr. Dodd introduced him as James. "Charlotte, please read with James from the script on the music stand until I stop you, like we did in class last week."

I picked up the first page, quickly scanning it to get the general context. James jumped right in with the male part, giving me two seconds to focus. It wasn't what the previous girl had read.

"Please, Mrs. Burningham. I beg you to let me have Thursday off."

My character was called "Lady." "You simply don't understand that *I* am in charge here," I read, quickly getting into the mood of a snooty, stern woman. I gave her a slight English accent. "I need you, and you shall stay."

His submissive tone deepened and I got more insistent in reply. "Give me a reason so compelling that I shall hate myself if I force you. You can't. Am I not right?" I twirled my hand in air of self-importance and my fingers lightly rested at the base of my neck.

The conflict went on to the end of the page, where Mr. Dodd stopped us. I understood the scene better now, wondered if I had overdone it, and that feeling of wanting a do-over engulfed me. Did they know how passionate I was about acting, how hard I would work, and that this was exactly what I had come to Oakmont to do? I curled my lips into a smile and hoped with all my heart I was what they were looking for.

"Thank you. Please put that page on the bottom of the pile," he instructed, and jotted down a couple of notes.

The choir teacher glanced again at my résumé. "You've had some impressive roles. I see you have taken Freshman Choir and Beginning Dance at your former school. Do you prefer to sing or dance, and would you like an accompanist for what you have prepared?"

"I prefer to sing, but would be happy dancing for whatever part." I walked to the edge of the stage, leaned over, and handed my music to the pianist. Now for the hardest part.

"Whenever you are ready," she said.

As I returned to center front, movement caught my eye. John stood in the sidelines, giving me a thumbs up. I pictured singing the Beatles with him and instantly relaxed. I nodded to the pianist. The first measure sounded better than I'd expected, giving me a boost of confidence. By the last phrase, I felt the music down to my fingertips, swaying slightly and using my hands expressively without excess. I was on stage, doing what I was born to do—perform.

Nobody clapped but they did smile and thank me. "One more thing," the choir teacher said. "Your skin is rather tanned, do you have any allergies to stage make up or talcum powder?"

I blushed. Was she merely thinking of the fair women of the early 1900s who walked around with parasols? "No, ma'am."

She nodded, excused me, and I exited stage right, hoping my skin color wouldn't hinder getting a speaking part. My lips pressed together. How ironic it would be if I'd come to one of the best drama schools in the state only to find that my coloring was too light or too dark for the casting committee's kind of perfect. Maybe she wouldn't have asked if she wasn't considering me for a significant part.

Would they think I was good enough, regardless of the shade of my skin? I'd have to wait until Friday's posted list to find out.

The week crawled by like a caterpillar inching around a flower pot. I spent extra time to understand the math concepts so I wouldn't fall behind when after-school rehearsal started up. I gave up TV and bike rides for the week and worked on condensing Mary's story into a reader's theater script.

It pained me to cut it to the bare bones, but the more I worked on it, the more passionate I became that others could be as inspired by her story as I had been. Mary rose from the dregs of a time when slaves held little value beyond the hard work that was squeezed from them day after day, and yet she kept her dignity and hope for freedom. She may not have led 250,000 in a march on Washington, but she shaped who her children, my grandmother, mother, and I would turn out to be. Mary read her New Testament over and over to her children, teaching them to believe in Christ, who loved everyone and would save them. She taught them to make the best of any situation and be the best they could. By never forgetting the past, sharing Mary's story was my way to honor her.

Friday finally came, but Mark didn't want to leave early for school so I walked by myself. Mr. Dodd had said the list would be posted in the commons area when the building opened up at 7:30. A small crowd waited for the janitor to unlock the front doors, and when he did, I rushed inside with them. We quickly spotted two sheets of paper taped to the wall.

Squeals of delight and moans of disappointment erupted from the press of bodies ahead of me. "Hank Samuelson has the lead!" someone said. "Hank is Professor Harold Hill!" It didn't appear that Hank knew of his good fortune yet. I guessed that he rode the bus.

"I got it! The lead! I'm Marian Paroo!" A girl I didn't know came out from the hive, grinning for all she was worth and bouncing on her toes.

I'd already guessed the leads would be seniors. What would I end up as? Please let me get up there before they ruined all the surprises.

"Who's Charlotte Rogers?" a girl asked, sounding suspicious and disappointed.

What? My name must be on the upper half of the list. "That's me. Let me see!" I pushed my way to where I could see. My heart in my throat, it took a moment to spot it.

Mrs. Paroo – Charlotte Rogers

A main character! I grinned and raised my arms into a victory stance. "Yes!"

Mrs. Paroo was the mother of Marian the Librarian and Winthrop, the boy with a lisp. She sang a song in the movie and had a fair amount of lines, but nothing like the leads. The character was a sweet, kind Irish woman with red hair. I'd need a wig if they were going with that. I inhaled and held it for a second, my eyes opening wider. I would get to use an Irish dialect. Fun!

More students arrived and pressed behind me to see. I got out of the way, but not before a quick glance to find John's name. Constable Locke, a secondary character but with a few lines. Good for him! The other names didn't mean much to me without a face, and I didn't know the advanced drama students anyway.

I walked into my history class elated. "Guess what?" I said to Brad as I sat at the desk next to him.

His eyes widened like he instantly remembered. "Oh, yeah! What part did you get?" We'd spent lunchtime talking about it yesterday, and he knew how anxious and excited I was.

I couldn't contain my eagerness. "Mrs. Paroo. A primary part."

"That's boss!"

I knew he hadn't seen the movie and didn't fully understand the significance, but I appreciated his enthusiasm. A few others congratulated me too.

Melanie had been listening since she saw me walk in. "Congrats," she said, looking at her fingernails. "It'll take a lot of makeup. Mrs. Burkhart looks more Irish than you do."

She wasn't telling me anything new but she hit a nerve anyway. It bugged me that I cared what Melanie thought. Time to ignore her.

"Congratulations, Charlotte," Mrs. Burkhart said. "You'll look great as a redhead." She fluffed her own curls.

I smiled again.

In drama class, several eyes met mine as soon as I walked in. Some faces looked happy for me, some not. John quickly came over and gave me a lingering congratulatory hug. It felt nice, and I secretly wished I could dance in his arms at Homecoming next weekend.

"Congrats, Charlotte," a couple of kids told me.

One girl's voice couldn't mask her jealousy as it dripped with indifference. "Wow, a sophomore got a main part."

It deflated my elation since I knew how she felt. I'd had my share of settling for lesser parts, but she didn't have to be so obvious about it.

A range of emotions wafted through the room. Everybody talked about who was perfect or not for certain parts or what they themselves got to do. Mr. Dodd let the excitement go on for a few minutes before reigning it in. We heard three loud claps to get our attention.

"Congratulations to all of you. Just remember that bigger parts come with more rehearsal time and every part is needed to put on a production like this. We'll make it great!" He went on to explain what we should do for the rest of the period.

At lunch, Brad and Jake sat facing one another, like they did the last couple days. The arrangement invited me and Patty to sit beside our future dates. When I sat down, Jake put an arm around me, pulling me a little closer. "Hey, Mrs. Paroo. Congrats on the big part!" He stayed like that until I thanked him. He slipped his arm off my shoulder, swiped his hand over my back, and then gave it a pat before dropping his arm. It felt as good as John's hug.

I didn't scoot away, though our elbows might hit as we ate. Jake's appeal was growing on me. I'd always thought him cute and nice, but there hadn't been much spark until when—today?

Maybe Patty noticed the coziness. She got a twinkly look in her eye. "Anybody have plans for tonight? We could hang out at The Shake It Up."

Jake swallowed his food. "Maybe after the game, but it'll be packed."

"That's right." Patty laughed. "I forgot it was a home game."

From the dull look in his eyes, Brad didn't seem too excited about getting together. Was he feeling well? "I heard they're letting coloreds order at The Shake It Up," he said, "with two booths for them."

The way he emphasized 'them' made me wince. Was he prejudiced? I couldn't believe it. He was a good, church-going guy. Mr. Perfect. I shrugged it off. I shouldn't judge him by one word that could have come out wrong.

Patty glanced at me, her eyes wide. "I guess serving those guys at the diner wasn't a one-time thing after all. We witnessed history in the making."

"I know." I couldn't keep my enthusiasm from my voice. I explained that night to the boys.

"Wow," Jake said. "You did witness history."

Brad said nothing so I asked, "Has it affected the diner's business? We should support them."

Brad shrugged and clammed up again. I wasn't sure what to make of it.

"That's progress, I guess, but now it'll take longer to get a booth," Patty said.

Brad nodded. "I don't want to wait. We should go somewhere else."

I stared at Brad. It was like seeing him for the first time, only he wasn't so attractive. Maybe I was being sensitive. Nobody else seemed to think anything of it. He'd said it calmly enough. I watched him as I asked, "So you want to go to the game but eat somewhere else after?"

"Sure." He didn't seem especially ruffled. "The other diner has good food too and will be less crowded."

Jake brightened. "Yeah, let's do it! You girls like football?"

"I like Oakmont football," Patty said, making the decision unanimous. "We're in. Let's meet at the bleachers in section F." She looked at me. "Can you pick me up?"

"Probably. I might have to bring my brother Mark, though. I'll call you when I get home."

And just like that, we'd made a date for a non-date.

CHAPTER SIXTEEN

PATTY AND I SCANNED THE bleachers of section F without seeing the boys. Mark waited behind us, hugging a huge box of popcorn to his chest as people bumped past. For him, it was either tag along with us or stay home with Gran. Mom and Dad had gone on a date, and I could only borrow Gran's car if I replaced the gas and gave Mark the option to come. Mark might put a cramp in my style more than the 30 cents a gallon would, but he loved football and I was content to see him happy.

"It seems we got here first," Patty said. She pointed to an empty section of bench that would hold two more. "Let's go there."

We climbed to the bench. I tossed out a folded blanket for our cushion. If the air chilled as the sun set, we could use it for warmth. As planned, we sat on either side of Mark, leaving space for Jake and Brad like book ends. Or we could scoot to the end of the blanket and they could sit together. I was curious to see what they would choose.

We watched the crowd, nibbling from Mark's popcorn box. He couldn't complain about our snitching out of his box because I was the one who paid for it.

I recognized several faces and waved at two friends. This place was starting to feel like home.

Patty waved to a friend, then stood and waved her arm overhead. "Here they come."

There wasn't any discussion between them as Jake plopped down next to me and Brad shuffled past our knees to sit by Patty. They'd already decided where they would sit, and my insides came to life like a flashing strobe light.

"Hi." Jake gave me a grin. "This is your brother?"

"Yeah. This is Mark. Mark, meet Jake." They lifted their chins to one another.

Mark offered the box like they were old friends. "Popcorn?"

"Thanks."

I could smell Jake's cologne as he leaned across me. He smelled better than the popcorn. I'm glad Patty suggested we get together. This would pave the way for a more comfortable date next week.

Melanie walked by below us with Gina and Ellen. She threw a glare our way and kept going, her chin held high.

"She's going to Homecoming with Don Burton," Jake said. "I heard she asked him."

"Really?" It was either gutsy or desperate. Maybe both. "Good for her." If she had fun she might get over Jake for good. Keeping him to myself sounded better all the time, especially when Patty looked so happy next to Brad.

We chatted for a few minutes, watching the crowd and snatching handfuls of popcorn, until the announcer came over the loud speaker. We jumped to our feet as our team ran onto the field. I cupped my hands around my mouth. "Go Vikings!" They'd won a game and lost one, so I really had no idea how good they were.

We kicked off first, and before long, it became obvious that the Rebels had better offense than our Vikings had defense. Three minutes into the game they had a touchdown and extra point scored on us. "Maybe our boys need to warm up," I suggested.

The Vikings marched down the field but couldn't quite get into field goal territory. The Rebels scored a field goal this time and Mark propped his elbows on his knees and set his chin in his hands. I didn't remind him he could be watching TV with Gran instead. He perked up again after our guys made it to another set of downs.

A player caught a long pass and everybody went ape when he ran it for a touchdown. We jumped up, screaming. Pom poms flew into the air. Jake pulled me into a hug. It quickly evolved from celebratory to cozy, and then awkward. He released me, but we both knew that we'd passed a milestone. We settled back onto the bench and his arm slid across my back over to my shoulder. Tiny bubbles of happiness fizzed like soda inside me.

I gave him an approving smile that had nothing to do with scoring the extra point.

In the end, we lost the game 21-10, but I felt like a winner all night. Jake put his arm around me in the booth as we sipped malted shakes. Mark kept the guys talking about the game, but I didn't mind. I'd learned we could spend more than lunchtime together and find it comfortable. When it was time to part, Jake winked at me and said, "See you Monday."

I dropped off Mark first so Patty and I could talk in the car without him. I parked in front of her house, unable to keep the smile off my face.

Patty pushed my arm. "You guys started cookin'. You think it'll sizzle at the dance?"

My cheeks grew warm. "Maybe. Not too fast, I hope. What about you?"

"What about me? All we did was talk. It was comfortable thought." Patty sighed. "Do you think he likes me?"

"He sat by you, didn't he?"

"Golly, our shoulders even touched!" She giggled. "I'm ready for more, you know?"

How much more was Patty talking about? We'd never had a reason to discuss specific values. Patty was a nice girl, and I couldn't see her being easy, but I didn't really know what she believed. She only went to church on Easter and Christmas. Come to think of it, I didn't know what Jake believed either.

"Want me to ask Brad how much he likes you at church on Sunday? It's a good time to talk to him without Jake or you around."

She looked horrified. "No! Don't come right out and say it like that." She paused and shrugged. "But maybe you could dig a little if it comes out naturally."

"I dig."

She rolled her eyes at me.

☆ ☆ ☆ ☆

As much as I'd mentally prepared myself for this, the one pancake I managed to eat felt like a brick in my stomach as we drove to church. I gave my cause one last effort, "Wouldn't you be more comfortable attending the colored's church, Gran? I'd be happy to sit with you." It crossed my mind that they probably cared far less that a white girl was among them than Granny being welcomed in my church.

"Thanks, honey, but you don't have to change your routine for me." Gran chuckled. "I'm a big girl. My pappy brought me up as white as him, no matter what other folks thought. I've had funny looks and slap-in-the-face words flung at me before. I'm right happy to be out worshipping on this fine day instead of stuck in the house. At least I brought my own seat so no one will fault me for contaminating their pew."

She smiled like it was a joke, but it wasn't funny. Not one bit. I'd been so worried about my own backlash that I hadn't considered the possibility of Gran being shunned. Did people make their objections known in churches too?

Gran saw my frown and added, "That's the beauty and the curse of my skin color. I can fit in with either group or I fit in with neither. Sometimes it's my attitude that makes all the difference. Mostly it's only one or two who care, and other times... If you got to face a whole group, I'll take my chances with a church-going congregation. Besides, your Momma said Pastor Jensen gives a splendid sermon."

I was still reeling from what might happen to Gran. I'd been thinking too much about repercussions for me. There was no turning around at this point. If Gran could do this, I guessed I could too.

I smirked at myself, hiding my shame. "Splendid if you don't fall asleep." Pastor Jensen had a voice that lulled. Maybe that's what people liked about him, but I liked my Sunday school teacher best. Brother Mike never preached fire and brimstone and always had an interesting story to go with his lesson.

I might have had more faith in the congregation, but it only took one person to get me kicked out of school. I silently prayed that they would have compassion, or better yet, ignore us. That was impossible. Who wouldn't notice a woman in a wheelchair with darker skin?

Dad parked the car in the lot and helped Gran into her wheelchair. We'd come early for plenty of time to maneuver.

Gran's eyes lit up when she looked up at the steeple. She closed her eyes and breathed deeply. I felt guilty for wishing she had stayed home.

We bypassed the three porch steps where the pastor greeted his congregation inside the doorway, and wheeled her around to the back with only a threshold to lift the wheels over. Dad parked her on the left edge of a pew on the second row.

I swallowed. "Shouldn't we sit in the back so the wheelchair doesn't block anyone's view?"

"She's not in the way on the side, and nobody will have to go around her to take a seat." Dad had made up his mind.

I sat on the far end next to Mark, with my parents nearest Gran. My mouth felt dry. Mark elbowed me when I fidgeted next to him and started chewing on a fingernail. I told myself to get a grip. Gran was here to worship. My reasons shouldn't get in her way. That's what I kept telling myself.

With only three churches for white folk in our town, it was likely we had a school board member among our congregation. Patty had suggested the board wouldn't care about one person, but I swallowed hard. Closing my eyes and clasping my hands together, I prayed that the time would be later rather than sooner. *Just let me do the play—please.* That's not all I wanted, but asking for more felt selfish.

The gray-haired pastor stood and smiled from the microphone as he looked over his congregation and welcomed them. His gaze jerked back to Gran in an obvious double take; his smile faded. During the slight pause before he composed himself, I turned around to catch several who followed that gaze. Most only glimpsed a graying-haired woman in a wheelchair because of her long-sleeved blouse. Perhaps being near the front was better after all. I relaxed enough to join in singing the last verse of the opening hymn.

Pastor Jensen began his message boldly. "We have sung unto the Lord as David did in Psalm 101. It is from that psalm that I will make some initial remarks before I begin with the sermon which I have prepared." He glanced at our pew, then faced forward, took in a big breath, and let it out. "A few here are not pure before us. They are deceivers." He pounded a fist on the podium—a first that I'd ever seen—and it made me jump. "Beware, for David tells us that the wicked will be cut off from the city of the Lord. He will cast off the impure, as will I."

Something about his intensity strengthened his Southern accent. He had me sitting up straight. I swallowed hard, fearing that the kind of purity he was talking about was white supremacy.

Right then he shot a sharp glare at my mother as he quoted, "He that worketh deceit shall not dwell within my house; he that telleth lies shall not tarry in my sight." I didn't know he had that powerful of a voice. Then he lifted his chin away and turned toward the other side of the room, ignoring our pew as he delved into his planned topic. He'd washed his hands of us.

I closed my sagging jaw. One woman in a wheelchair had done that to him? The image of all clergy that I'd grown up with since before I could remember had cracked. My respect for Pastor Jensen shattered, falling as slivers in slow motion, pricking and stabbing at my insides. I flinched twice and Mark looked at me like I had cooties. He slumped forward, setting his elbows on his knees. Did he not feel wrongly called to repentance as I did?

I looked beyond him to my parents. Dad's shoulders sagged, his hands clasped over his middle. I couldn't tell if he felt scolded or bored. Maybe he hadn't seen the pastor's glance at us. Mom crossed one leg over the other as she folded her arms, her mouth tight, with eyes focused on the pastor. She looked annoyed but not shaken. Gran caught my gaze and sent me a wink from her twinkling eyes. She might have enjoyed that she could be the cause of riling the pastor.

I worked it over in my mind again and again, always coming to the same conclusion. This man believed that we had come into his little white flock, gained acceptance, and then one day sprang Gran on him to reveal our true natures as deceivers. He would no longer cast his sight upon us, the liars that we were. Didn't the rest of my family see that he meant the psalm to refer to us? The back of my neck prickled. Well, his interpretation was wrong! Plain and simple.

"What's with you?" Mark whispered.

I became aware of my fidgeting hands and the tension in my pressed lips. I clasped my hands in my lap. "Nothing." Nothing I could talk about here and now, anyway.

I had expected a man of God to rise above the prejudice all around us, expected him to be better than the majority of Southerners. But this one wasn't. My mind burned with betrayal that any from my family could be considered deceitful liars by someone who wasn't any better than the rest of us. Judgment is the Lord's. We were good Christians. And God knew it. He would accept us like He would accept Mary for her righteous works. The hairs on the back of my neck laid down, a measure of peace returning.

Even Gran's mother had come to be accepted in her husband's white neighborhood, through the respect he held and his insistence. Her kindness and goodness had made that transition easier. Though some had bristled around her, others had looked upon her heart more than her skin. It probably helped that they lived in a Northern state. Mary's descendants had blended into the white culture ever since. I didn't want Pastor Jensen's kind of white living. My African heritage had enriched our understanding and tolerance. That sounded better to me than being a hundred percent white any ol' day.

I huffed. Maybe I should quit hiding who I am. Maybe I should stand up right here in this church and introduce my granny to everyone, school board members included.

I took a few deep breaths. Gran would soon be back in her own home, going to her own congregation after her cast came off. She didn't need to own this temporary problem. I studied my mother, whose expression looked peaceful. Had she learned from Gran to shrug it off or was she glad that the reprimand was over and done with? It had seemed severe to me, but maybe nothing more would come of it.

The choir stood to sing a closing hymn. The music soothed me. That's what it must be. I'd hate to think I lost my nerve already.

On my way to Sunday school class I remembered to gather info about Brad's feelings for Patty. Suddenly Brad was there, standing right next to me in the hallway.

"Who was that in the wheelchair?" His tone sounded snappish.

"Oh, that's my grandmother. Did I tell you she came to live with us when she broke—"

He quit walking and someone behind bumped into him. "Your grandmother is colored," he whispered.

People walked around us. I pulled him by the shirt sleeve into a cloak room alcove. "I know. She's one-fourth colored."

"That makes you…" His lips thinned.

Annoyance blossomed, and I set a fist on my hip. "One-sixteenth colored and fifteen-sixteenths white. You got a problem with that?"

He snorted. "That slave girl, Mary. She's one of your relatives. That's how you know the story so well."

"That's right. She's my great-great-grandmother."

He looked like he would be sick, which made me angrier. I hadn't expected this from a friend. A school board member, perhaps, but not Brad. I struggled to keep my voice low. "Put that in your pipe and smoke it."

I stared him down, daring him to upset me further. Perfect Brad was prejudiced like the pastor. My eyes stung, but I fought the tears. I'd been so blind. Patty could have him! I squeezed my fists. He could go do whatever he darn well pleased with that piece of information. I didn't care…for the next two seconds. Would Brad do what I'd feared Melanie would?

I breathed in deeply, needing to calm down. "You said you liked Mary's story."

"I did. I do." He threw up his hands. "She was one slave girl. It was only history. You hadn't made it personal before."

"Yeah? Well, it's mighty personal to me."

He nodded but his jaw was still tight.

"You want to tell the school board on me?"

His jaw relaxed, shifting from smugness to sadness. "I don't know what I want." He turned and walked away.

CHAPTER SEVENTEEN

I WOULD HAVE SAT IN the car through Sunday school if it had been unlocked. Instead, I fidgeted and picked at my nails through the youth lesson, wondering where Brad was, what he was thinking, and scared to death of what he might do. Brad knew the whole truth and held the power to ruin everything for me at Oakmont. What would he do with that power? He never did come in.

Only one person said anything about Gran—the boy in Sunday school, Billy, who had made an issue of bigotry during our Sermon on the Mount lesson several weeks ago. Near the end of class, he leaned close and said, "I have a grandma like yours."

I whipped my head toward him. "What?"

He nodded and gave me a knowing look. As for the rest, they hadn't noticed or didn't care.

With two other churches for whites to choose from, why the loyalty to Pastor Jensen? Were habits so hard to break? Did the pastor have us all fooled until now? He had been crafty enough not to outright declare his bias while chastising us. I supposed Billy would have switched churches long ago if it had been obvious to him. Would he change now? Or was he trying to make converts?

Mom or Dad never came to get me and Mark out of class, so they must have tolerated Pastor Jensen through the adult Sunday school class. Would they ask him about that part of the sermon? Maybe he would deny having meant us because he didn't want to lose his newest generous donor. The pastor probably figured Gran was visiting and wouldn't be back. I could see him shaking Dad's hand in the future but none of the rest of our family. Bile crept upward into my throat.

Once we were all in the car, Gran summed things up. "I'm not sorry I came and you shouldn't be either. Don't any of y'all let that pastor try to pin a little old scripture on you that don't fit. That was nothing."

Nothing compared to what she grew up dealing with. Nothing if the pastor could get over it enough to shake my hand next time. Nothing as long as it stayed here and didn't get to the school board.

"It was something, but nothing that we're going to let get to us. Right, family?" That was all my mom said.

"Right." Dad had answered for everyone while I was still trying to figure them out. "The good Lord knows the intent of our hearts."

Mark piped up. "Hey, what are we having for dinner?"

It appeared the former subject had been covered. They didn't know about my worry or the power that Brad held over me. I guessed I could tough it out until there was a reason not to.

At home, nobody really talked about what happened. I certainly wasn't in the mood to start an argument—not when Gran and Mom wore thick skins. I tried to be tough, but moped around most of the day and tossed in my bed that night. When morning came, I still dreaded facing Brad, but with play practice starting right after school, I couldn't fake an illness. I planned on slipping into class right before the bell to avoid a confrontation, but there he was, leaning against the wall next to the door, waiting for me.

"It's about time," he grumbled. "We need to talk."

I walked into class without a word. He might want to talk but I had nothing to say. Whatever happened was up to him. He could ruin my life or simply hold his knowledge over me like a time bomb ready to go off if he needed some big favor. I could be out of Oakmont on the first week of play practice, never having the chance to build a decent drama résumé for college scholarships.

"I talked with Pastor Jensen after church," he whispered as he followed me in.

I stiffened, then took my seat. I swallowed hard and looked at him.

"What he said in church…it was about your family, like I thought."

The bell rang and I startled—the only thing that kept me from slumping low in my seat.

"He said that some people's outward appearances, like being church goers, are merely a cover. He warned me to stay away from you."

My stomach lurched. How many times had Gran gone through stuff like this?

Mrs. Burkhart began speaking as she leaned against her desk. I couldn't listen. Dozens of consequences from Brad's few words pushed their way in front of me—none of them good. Tears burned behind my eyes, and I struggled not to let them fall. Moments later, Brad shoved a note at me, breaking the awful spell. I discretely opened it and read:

Please forgive me. I was raised differently than you. This will take some getting used to. Until yesterday, I believed Pastor Jensen's and my father's opinions were right because, well, he's the pastor and my father is my father. I've trusted them for years and I've only known you a month. I can tell you're a good person. We still need to talk, but for now I'll keep your secret.

Relief rushed at me, making the tears pool into my eyes. I blinked them back and dared a glance at him. No smile, but he gave me a nod. He would keep my secret. I closed my eyes and exhaled. Someone snatched the paper from my hand. Not Mrs. Burkhart, like I first imagined, but Melanie.

I whirled in my seat to find her diagonally behind me, reading the note. I tried to grab it.

"Charlotte," Mrs. Burkhart warned.

I opened my textbook to the pages Mrs. Burkhart assigned and pretended to read. I went over the note in my mind as I turned around, hoping it was gibberish to Melanie. Within a minute, a note appeared on my desk. I opened it. *I'll find out your secret.*

As I walked toward the stage for play practice at the end of school, I couldn't quite shake Melanie's pestering from the locker room. Her incessant questions still swirled inside my head: *How come the pastor doesn't think you're a good person? What's your secret? Does it have anything to do with Jake? What's your secret?* Ending with: *Don't worry, I'll squeeze it out of Brad.*

Patty didn't know anything about the note, but she probably guessed the gist of what happened at church. She played along and got Melanie off my back, thank goodness. "No big secret," she'd said with a shrug. "The pastor found out how provocative her Homecoming formal was, that's all. Wait until Jake sees her in it." For emphasis, she added a whistle. It shut Melanie up for a while, though she probably wasn't buying it.

Melanie slammed her PE locker shut and departed with, "This isn't over. I'll find out your secret."

It might be an empty threat, but I doubted it. Melanie had probably left me alone this long because she couldn't find any ammo to use on me that wouldn't be seen by others as juvenile. Until now. She might do anything to learn my secret—even talk to the pastor. Then she would complain to the school board. They would kick me out of Oakmont and she would have Jake all to herself. Stupid girl. Didn't she know that Jake wouldn't go for someone that devious? But it would put me away from both of them. Not so stupid girl.

I rubbed my temples, took a deep breath, and opened the door to the auditorium. The room buzzed with excited chatter, which I wasn't quite ready for. Where were one of those relaxing lava lamps when you needed one?

John saw me approach, and a look of concern filled his face. "Hey, what's wrong?"

I gave a weak smile. "It's nothing. Melanie gave me a headache."

He gave me a sympathetic look. "What's she on your case for?"

"The usual. She wants to stick her nose into my business." I rolled my shoulders.

"Have a seat. Let's loosen you up." He pointed to an aisle seat and stood behind me. John's fingers magically smoothed out the tension in my neck and shoulders until Mr. Dodd called everyone to attention. About seventy-five students gathered around him for orientation, stage hands and all.

"Welcome, everyone," Mr. Dodd projected without a microphone. "If you haven't already, sign in on the roll and pick up the schedule." I joined several others at the little table below the stage while Mr. Dodd kept speaking. "This is an important commitment. Attendance is mandatory. If you can't be here when it's your scene, I expect a parent or doctor's note upon your return. Is that clear?"

Mumbles of, "Yes, sir," flitted around the stage.

I glanced through the detailed schedule. It mentioned everything from the school's selection of costumes to patterns, from parent assignments to the final cast party. Even the set painters had specific time allotments. Just as professional as I'd hoped. I needed to stay here. Oakmont's reputation would give me an edge on scholarship applications.

"Take out a Hi-Liter or pencil." Mr. Dodd went through each page and had us mark the items pertaining to us. He gave an overview of each scene in *The Music Man*, handed out specific parts, and answered questions. I felt better, the meeting pushing traces of Melanie into the background.

I would report to the choir room during the next two practices to learn the piano lesson song and go over my lines at home. On Thursday I would get personal instruction on speaking with an Irish brogue. Groovy! My main scene would be blocked out on stage next Monday, and I needed to know my lines fairly well by the end of next week. The thrill of it all shivered through me.

CHAPTER EIGHTEEN

SUCH AN EXHAUSTING, STRESSFUL WEEK! I looked at my bedside clock and smiled. I'd slept in ninety minutes extra, which would help me be fresh through my date tonight. With a smile on my lips, I let myself daydream about that for a moment before the press of life slipped back in place.

I'd also made it through the week without being summoned before the school board. I needed to keep it that way. How did I do that when it wasn't up to me? At least I wouldn't worry about Brad. He'd said our friendship was too important to him. Good thing too, or tonight's double date would be awkward.

I no longer felt the stomach-punch of Brad's lack of personal investment like I had when I sat down each evening to condense Mary's story for the midterm assignment. Last night as I wrote out the ending, a burden had lifted. Now I needed to show it to him so he could type it up and we'd start practicing. How I hoped it would mean something to my whole history class and not only Mary's descendants. I envisioned it making a difference to many people.

I smiled again in remembering his words.

"It's hard giving up long-engrained concepts," he'd told me, "but I'm seeing the world with new eyes."

Brad's high opinion of Pastor Jensen had some cracks in it now, and I felt bad that I'd brought that on, but also glad I'd forced him to reevaluate. We'd made a truce. He would continue with the assignment and I had accepted that his lifetime of conditioning wouldn't change in an instant.

If Melanie had gone to Pastor Jensen to check up on me, I'd heard nothing about it. She was in history class Friday morning but not PE at the end of the day. Odd. I didn't want to think about her anymore. The big day had finally arrived.

I quickly got up, pulled some clothes on, and went into the kitchen. Mom was at the sink. I shifted into my Irish brogue, focusing my words at the front of my mouth. "Top o' the marnin' to ya."

"Good morning, Charlotte. You look chipper."

"Ya tink so? Well, yud be right. Everuh-ting is narmol wid me."

Mom laughed. "You call that normal?"

There was one strip of bacon—Mark had hogged more than his share—a slice of toast, and half a banana on a plate on the table. I grabbed some cereal and a bowl to go with it. "Thanks for saving me something, Mom."

"Sorry about the bacon. It was nearly gone when I checked. What time do you get your hair done?"

"Two o'clock at Patty's sister's shop. Can I take the car?"

"I don't need it, but ask your father. Remember, I want to take some Polaroids of you with your date when he comes to pick you up."

"Oh, didn't I tell you? Sorry. I'm dressing at Patty's and they're picking us up there."

Mom frowned. "Then take the camera and have Patty's mom do it."

"Okay." Whew! I'd just avoided having Jake see my granny—a temporary precaution that I intended to remedy once the evening went well. He didn't need all my family details before our first official date. Jake didn't struggle with bigotry like Brad, but I didn't want any chance for confrontation.

Patty and I did our makeup in her parent's bathroom. A large mirror hung over the sink. Patty added eyeliner after I'd applied mascara. I liked the result. We tried out soft shades of pink lipstick, of which she had no less than a dozen. I took the one with a coral shade. "I like this one best."

She liked the light champagne one for herself and set them aside. "We'll reapply it right before the boys come." Patty made two kissing sounds. "There may be magic tonight."

"Not between you and me, I hope."

Patty swatted my arm. "Ha, ha. You know what I mean."

"Your kissing noise reminds me of a story about two men who entered a train. The first man finds a bench facing two beautiful women. He slides over for his friend, but the second man sits right between the women instead. When they enter a tunnel, the jealous first man makes a kissing noise and slaps his friend's cheek in the darkness. The girls each thought he had kissed the other girl and ignored them. Miffed, they both move across to sit by the first man, who gives his friend a smug look.

"A few miles farther, they came to another tunnel. The man who got slapped leans forward and gives both women a kiss, finding one mouth and one cheek in the darkness. He returns to his seat in time to hear two slaps before light brightens the train. The women end up trading back to their original spot beside the man who kissed them."

"Cute. So the moral of the story is what—don't be jealous of your friends? Be wary of trains in tunnels? The good guy gets the girl?"

I shrugged. "The real thing is better than a fake kiss?" We laughed. "I don't know. I only told the story to make kissing sound less daunting. I've never had a real kiss."

Patty cocked an eyebrow. "Trust me. If there's any kissing tonight, you don't want it to be fake."

I nodded, unsure if I was ready to be kissed by Jake but kind of hoping for it.

"You'll get the hang of it pretty fast. Now grab your keys. We're due at my sister's salon in a few."

After an hour of primping at the beauty shop, I stared into the mirror. My eyes popped like Lucy Riccardo's do when Ricky catches her at something, only this didn't mean trouble. My hair was piled higher on my head than I'd seen it and not frizzy at all. I could be a model. I kept grinning at myself, pushing back the tinge of sadness that I would never be able to replicate this. I hadn't imagined that Lauren could make me look as beautiful as Patty.

"What do you think?" Lauren asked.

"I love it!" *Stunning* came to mind first, but I felt too modest to put it that way. I couldn't wait to put the dress on and see the whole package.

Patty agreed. "Jake will drool like a fool." Lauren had already worked her magic on Patty so we were both anxious to dress. Patty gave Lauren a hug and off we went, strutting past the other hairdos in progress.

Back in her mother's dressing room, I zipped Patty's peach taffeta gown. It hugged her slender figure in all the right places. Brad's boutonniere, waiting in the fridge, was a perfect color match. She smoothed the skirt admiringly in front of the full-length mirror. I hooked a string of her mom's pearls around her neck, which perfectly adorned the plain space below the high Audrey Hepburn neckline.

I whistled low and slow. "Classy lassie."

"Not like the dog, I hope." She giggled. "Not bad for a Spiegel catalogue order, eh?"

"Oh, yeah. Brad is going to flip."

She pulled my dress from the hanger. "Your turn. Speaking of Brad,—" she looked at me sideways "—what's up with you two? It's like you hardly had two words to say to each other all week until yesterday, and now you're buddies again? You gotta spill the full story."

I hid a frown. I'd given her pieces I hoped would satisfy. Brad and I had come to an agreement, but the buddy-buddy relationship still felt like an act. We needed time to solidify trust. "Brad knows my secret, but he's going to keep it."

"Well, yeah. I know that." She held the dress open while I stepped in. My dress had a fuller skirt that flared from its satin sash around the empire waist. "You said the pastor wasn't happy with Gran showing up. Was that Brad's reaction too?"

"The pastor indirectly chewed us out for being sneaky in attending his 'white church'. He called us deceitful."

Patty's head slowly rocked side to side and she growled under her breath. "I'd go somewhere else. I don't go that often but my pastor reaches out to the whole community. Now, what's between you and Brad?"

"Brad was surprised by Gran but he's given me his support." She didn't need to know of Brad's struggle to give it or that our truce was still a little shaky.

Patty zipped my dress. "Of course he gave you his support. What did you expect?" She hadn't said it as a question.

I couldn't verify that what she expected of Brad was a given, so I stared into the mirror.

Patty looked into the mirror from behind me, her head tilted and her brows pressed together. "You...had doubts?"

Yeah, I had doubts. I'd found out the guy I once thought was perfect had a glaring flaw—one he could use to dismiss me from the school. It made for some chilly encounters before he came to his senses. I couldn't watch Patty's eyes on me anymore and glanced away from my reflection. "I'm simply saying that we cleared the air and he's on my side. Don't you think that's great?"

"Sure." She folded her arms. "What are you not telling me?"

My whole body got hot and I was afraid I'd make a perspiration stain on my dress in the first five minutes.

"C'mon, Charlotte. What happened?"

I fanned myself with my hand. Both gowns were sleeveless— perfect for a warm October night in the South if you didn't have to deal with extra stress. She shouldn't hear this right before her special date with Brad, but I knew she'd be persistent. I sighed. "Brad grew up trusting Pastor Jensen, so of course he was torn when the pastor said those bad things against us."

"You mean he agreed with the pastor?" Patty had a look of horror on her face.

I had to fix that. "No, not totally. He was confused. He knew I was a good person and imagined my grandma was too. Like a lot of people, he was raised to believe that whites are better. Finding out I wasn't pure white wouldn't immediately change that. It gave him something to think about." I couldn't believe I was defending him. He'd had me scared all week long, wondering where he stood and what he might do about it. Yet I couldn't have Patty upset with Brad and ruin her night.

Patty's horrified expression softened to a frown. "So he's changing his opinions for the better?"

"Yeah, I think so."

Brad's reaction made me question if I'd done the right thing. I needed to confide in someone about my inner struggle. "Brad always considered me as white and accepted me that way, so it shook him up when someone he respected challenged that. I realize now that Brad typically judges things as strictly black or white. No pun intended." I formed a smile that made Patty smile too.

"I've only ever thought of myself as white. It makes sense to me, with such a small percentage of Negro blood and the way I was raised. We all have red blood running through our veins, right? But is that a cop out? Have I lied?"

I searched Patty's eyes, pleading for understanding. "I'm afraid my hopes and dreams have influenced me. I took Dad with me to register instead of Mom on purpose, never realizing how serious and picky the board would be. I swore to a notary public that I am white because that's the closest fit I have. What does a person do with those slivers of gray areas? I'm not 'colored' or 'white'—I'm 'other'. I don't fit anywhere. Not since coming here." I hung my head.

Patty's voice was kind. "Yes you do. Nobody's one hundred percent everything in all situations. I fit in a category full of blondes, but look at all my highlights. You'll find reds and browns in there too. You were asked to choose from only two categories: white or not white." She set a fist on her hip. "I'll bet they didn't give you any guidelines before having you swear, did they."

I lifted my head and shook it.

"Well then, you've lumped yourself where you belong the most, and that's the best you can do. You weren't being deceptive. You made your best judgement with your heart in the right place. If someone else doesn't think you fit, then that's their problem."

"Yeah. Thanks." I hugged her. Patty had validated my choices. I felt my spirits lift.

Too bad Brad had seen it as me lying, but he seemed to be over that now, or adjusting anyway. I wished he'd had more good experiences with coloreds so he could trust them.

The significance of Brad making this adjustment was starting to hit me, and I wanted Patty to understand it too. "Everything Brad had believed about coloreds was shaken up last Sunday. It all hit him at once, you know?" I revisited the look of sadness he'd given me when we parted that day.

Blinking back tears, I felt a little sorry for Brad being so sheltered and then hit with a whammy. "He struggled with that for a few days, saying he prayed until he gathered the courage to make a stand for something new. For me." I whispered the last two words and wiped at a tear.

Patty handed me a tissue and took one for herself. "You're going to have us both ruining our makeup if you don't shut up."

I blubbered a laugh. "He's not perfect, but he's a good guy."

She nodded. "That's good enough for me." Her smile looked genuine.

Patty's mom knocked on the door. "You girls need any help in there?"

"No. We're almost ready."

"Okay. I'll be back in five minutes for pictures."

We touched up our makeup and I wiped my moist palms on a towel before donning our long, white gloves. When Patty's mom raved about how gorgeous we were, I truly felt like a princess. We twirled and made exaggerated poses as she snapped some Polaroids on hers and Mom's camera too. We laughed at ourselves. We'd have to be more dignified when the boys came. Mom and Gran would love seeing them all. Dad would roll his eyes at some of them, but he'd love seeing me all dressed up.

The doorbell rang and we quickly ran for the master bedroom. It was all about the grand entrance. We had Patty's mother open the door. We heard her welcome the boys and gave it another minute before we stepped into the living room. Their appreciative smiles were priceless.

"Wow," Jake breathed out barely above a whisper. His lopsided grin grew into a full one.

My heart squeezed with emotion. I not only cherished his appreciation for all our effort, but he looked as handsome as anything in his sharp, charcoal suit. It was all I could do not to rush over and hug him. Jake was my date! How did I get so lucky? I closed the distance but stopped short of reaching for his hands. "Hi. You look good yourself."

"You look more than good. You're beautiful."

My face warmed and I grinned.

"I'll go get the boutonnieres from the fridge." Patty's mother hurried into the kitchen.

We were aware once more of others in the room. Brad looked good too in his subtle pin-striped suite with wide lapels and a flared leg. He and Patty seemed to have good vibes going. I set my hand on Brad's shoulder. "I'm glad we could double."

He lifted one eyebrow at me, and I hoped he could tell I wasn't acting. Two steps and I was back in front of Jake. "This will be so fun!"

Patty's mother returned with two small boxes and handed one to me and one to Patty. "Y'all can do the flowers and then we'll take a few pictures, okay?"

I could smell Jake's cologne as he leaned in to pin a rosebud and carnation corsage on my dress. His hands trembled ever so slightly. We all got the job done and stood together for some pictures. Then we switched places so that I was between Jake and Brad, and I put one arm across each of their backs. Brad gave me a sideways glance before doing the same and smiling at the camera. I couldn't help it. Reconciliation felt too good.

The boys escorted us to Brad's father's car, a white '59 Chevy Impala with that cool fin-like flare at the back and a chrome stripe down the sides. It gleamed like Brad had polished it. "Wow," I said. "You get to drive this thing much?"

"Psh. Are you kidding? My first time since getting my license was last night when he had me practice night driving with him. He debated being our chauffeur instead. You should have heard his list of rules."

We shared driving stories until we got to the restaurant.

"I hope you like steak," Jake said to all of us as Brad pulled into the rather full parking lot of a local steakhouse.

A line formed out the door, including other couples in formal attire. "Good thing we made reservations," Brad said.

Within five minutes, a waitress seated us in a semi-circular booth. I felt both elegant and comfortable, with conversation flowing between the four of us like it did at school.

A waiter set down my beef tips and gravy over rice. It smelled heavenly. A side of collard greens and biscuits rounded out my plate. Jake had chosen a steak, Brad the barbeque ribs, and Patty had the shrimp and grits.

"Is there anything else I can get you?" the waiter asked.

"Ketchup please," Jake said.

I held back a smile. He always had some on his lunch tray.

I picked up my fork and knife, and cut a tender morsel to taste. The beef was tender and the gravy flavorful with a touch of wine. "Mm." It was my first time eating with gloves on, giving me a constant reminder for best behavior and not to touch my food. We all dug in with more manners than we used at the cafeteria lunch table.

Jake swallowed a bite. "I'm glad you fine ladies didn't simply order a silly salad. Girls on diets don't belong at a restaurant like this."

"This place is fab," Patty said. She looked around. "Oh, there's Gina and Ellen with their dates. Don Burton too, but I don't see Melanie."

I looked in the direction of Patty's gaze. "Maybe she's powdering her nose." I buttered a biscuit and took a bite. If I didn't see Melanie until the end of the night it would be fine with me. It would be nice to see her dress, though, and find out if she and Don were enjoying one another enough to leave me and Jake alone.

Several minutes passed before I glanced at the other table. "That's odd."

"What?" Jake asked.

"Melanie hasn't returned."

"Who cares?" Patty said.

I shrugged. "It's just weird, that's all. I wanted to see her dress."

I checked again a little later and still no Melanie. Was she sick or something? She hadn't been at PE yesterday. All her whining about not going with Jake and she ends up sick? I felt a little sorry for her.

"Anybody want dessert?" Brad asked.

I shook my head. "I'm too full."

"Me too," Patty agreed.

Jake set his cloth napkin next to his plate. "They'll have punch and cookies at the dance. Shall we go?"

Everyone nodded. A shiver of excitement filled me as I anticipated more of the evening. Dancing with Jake sounded heavenly.

The waiter brought the check and Brad took it up to the register. We all followed, finding Don Burton's group there ahead of us. He laughed at something Gina said, not seeming at all distressed about being the fifth wheel.

My curiosity got the best of me. "Is Melanie sick?"

Don winced. "She had her appendix out." He shook his head and then smiled at me and Patty. "Save a dance for the poor sap who has to go stag, would you?"

"Aw. Of course." Patty put a hand on his arm. "Don't worry. You'll have fun."

So that explained it. "Is she still at the hospital?"

"Yep. She'll come home tomorrow or the next day. She's pretty upset at missing tonight, but what can you do?"

"I'll bet." Jake shook his head, offered his arm to me, and led us to the door.

"Poor girl," I said. Even Melanie didn't deserve being stuck at the hospital and missing the dance.

Patty snorted and leaned toward me. "I'm sure you feel reeeally bad for her."

Patty had a point. At least Melanie wouldn't ruin the night for us, but still... Getting one's appendix out wasn't something I wished on anybody. "This is like the worst night of her life. She's lying in a bed eating hospital food while we're all enjoying steak and shrimp. She doesn't get to dance or dress up or see anybody dressed up."

"Right, but there's nothing we can do." Patty spread out her hands.

A small part of me wished it wasn't true. "I suppose you're right."

We were blocking the door so we started moving again.

"Look, we can always show her a Polaroid if she's interested. Let's go to the dance."

CHAPTER NINETEEN

A JAZZY SAXOPHONE SOLO ACCOMPANIED softly brushed cymbals and a light drumbeat as we entered the school gym. Twinkling lights and crepe paper streamers draped from the ceiling, making it hard to believe that this is where we usually got sweaty in ugly uniforms. Everything was beautiful, especially with colorful dresses and handsome guys in dark jackets beneath the strings of lights. I inhaled deeply. My first formal dance.

A sweet smell hung in the air from the punch and cookie table further ahead to our right. A tropical sunset backdrop was set up on our left, where a young-looking photographer snapped photos of happy couples. Next to that was a wrought iron arch flanked by matching bushes pruned into three round balls stacked like a snowman. I guessed that would be the backdrop for the Homecoming king and queen.

The sax dropped out and the band's lead singer took over. He crooned the last verse with a silky voice, catching my attention as we made our way into the transformed gym. The band stood on a large, foot high wooden platform. The lead singer was white but the band behind him consisted of five colored people who looked about college age: a bass player, drummer, guitar player, the saxophonist, and a young woman with a tambourine. Seeing them at a white school took me by surprise. They sounded good, not like a garage band.

Did the school board know they were here? Would they care? I supposed the band was hired help, like the school's janitor. The board's rules were about the students who attended. This was my first big event at the school and I didn't know what normal looked like. Still, a teacher rep had approved the committee's choice, and I should learn who that was for future support.

Couples broke apart as the slow dance ended, and we filled in the space around them. "Don't you look fab! Very elegant," a girl from my math class appraised, looking at me from hairdo to heels.

"Thanks. You too!" I was right about girls caring how we all looked. She obviously found it part of the fun like I did. I glanced around. Half the girls had short or long gloves on, a third of the dresses were knee-length. I spotted John and waved at him. He looked so handsome and his date was a knockout. When I turned back to Jake, his eyes were on me. Only me. He didn't care what the other girls looked like or which friends were here. I no longer needed to scout out the rest of the dresses.

The band started a new set with a faster beat, and the girl was singing this time. Jake bobbed his head to the beat as he watched me. I swayed to the music and he took my cue. "Shall we?"

He held out his hand and I took it with my gloved fingers. He pulled me into a one-handed swing step and we pushed and pulled to the lively music. He knew the basics, could twirl me in and out, and that was about it. Nothing fancy, but I didn't care. I was dancing with Jake Notley, who only had eyes for me.

We did the twist on the next dance, and I saw Mrs. Burkhart twisting away with a man who must be her husband. She wore a shimmery black cocktail dress with a fitted bodice and fully gathered skirt, which swished back and forth as she twisted. They both laughed at something he said and seemed to be having a good time. Weird seeing her here as a chaperone.

I fanned my face when the third song of the set began. "Time to rest," I told Jake.

"Okay. Want something to drink?" he offered.

I glanced at the sweet red punch and wrinkled my nose. "A sip of water." I pointed to the gym's water fountain and we headed that way. Jake took my hand and I suddenly believed gloves were a terrible fashion idea.

After our drink, Jake tugged me back to the dance floor. The band resumed with a slow song. Neither of us spoke. I looked into his eyes, saw anticipation and tenderness there, and we were drawn together by the music—just like I'd fantasized about. Jake pulled me close to him, with one arm around my waist and his hand taking mine at shoulder level. My chest brushed against his, and our faces were close.

It only took seconds for our sway to feel natural, and moments later I rested my cheek on his shoulder, feeling content. As if in a dream, I closed my eyes. I listened to the lovely blend of voices as the girl harmonized on the chorus with the lead singer, and felt Jake's touch on my back. Safe. Content.

The band rolled into a second slow song, so I laced my fingers behind his neck and gazed into his eyes for a moment before resting my head on his shoulder again. Not quite hugging, but close enough. I didn't want the music to end.

All too soon I heard clapping. Was the song over? Not really wanting to, I took a step back.

A voice spoke over the microphone. "We're taking a short break so they can present your Homecoming royalty." He waited for the cheers to subside. "We'll be back in a flash so all y'all can keep grooving to the music."

We applauded the band and moved along with the crowd closer to the arch and those perfectly rounded bushes where the royalty was bound to have their photographic moment.

Mrs. Burkhart and three other teachers stood beside the arch. She took the microphone from its stand and got everybody to quiet down with her hands. Once she had our attention, she cranked up the noise again by asking, "Are you ready for your royalty, Oakmont?" The crowd went wild. "Then let's get to it!"

The second burst of noise quickly died out. We were anxious for the results.

The copper-haired teacher continued. "As rep for the freshman class, it is my privilege to announce the 1963-64 Freshman Class Prince and Princess." She opened a small envelope in front of the hushed crowd. "The freshmen have voted. May I present Todd Pullman and Abigail Lush."

A squeal pierced through the cheering and the prince and princess took their places under the arch. The professional photographer snapped the happy moment.

The sophomore teacher rep repeated the process, and I was happy that the princess, Dolores, was a nice girl in my PE class that I had voted for. I'd seen the prince but didn't know him.

"I voted for Roger," I told Jake.

"Chris is a good guy. I'm good with him as our sophomore prince."

"How come you didn't run?"

Jake puffed air out of the side of his mouth. "Right. Because I'm so big on having the spotlight."

Next, the junior names were announced, and finally the rep for the seniors made the big announcement for king and queen. I didn't know the royal couple but I loved her dress. We all watched as the photographer clicked away at the king and queen and then the entire royalty.

"You should be a candidate for prom princess," Jake said into my ear. "You've got my vote."

My ear tickled and my heart thumped. "That's sweet." I could see the two of us posing for pictures underneath a similar arch, in spite of what he'd said. Would we still be together at the end of our sophomore year? Would I be at Oakmont? I pushed aside the nagging question that wouldn't leave me be.

We helped ourselves to a cookie while the band returned and did a quick tune up. Brad and Patty caught up to us.

"Dolores made it!" Patty gushed, rising on her tiptoes.

I shared her enthusiasm. "I know! That's so cool."

Patty's heels landed. "Melanie won't like it. She'll make trouble for Dolores during PE."

"Melanie didn't get enough votes to be on the final ballot," Jake said. "What does she have to gripe to Dolores about?"

"Consider the source," I said with a shrug. "I don't think we'll have to worry. Melanie will get a medical pass out of PE for a few weeks. Maybe they'll send her to study hall instead."

"So what do you think of our king and queen?" Brad asked.

I shrugged. "They're seniors. I don't know either of them."

The dateless Don Burton walked up, pointed at me, and asked, "Charlotte, next dance?"

I glanced at Jake. He'd heard Don mention it at the restaurant, so I assumed it wouldn't be a problem, but wanted to check. He winked at me, keeping his happy expression on me as he said, "How about you borrow her for the first fast dance after the royalty dance. I get her for this one."

"Got it," Don said. Then he winked at Patty. "You're after Charlotte." Patty nodded, looking satisfied with that arrangement.

The guitarist strummed a chord to announce that they were ready. The lead singer leaned toward the microphone and said, "Let's have our royal couples dance a few bars before y'all join in."

The music started when the king and queen, who were already an actual dating couple, stepped to the middle of the floor. The princes took their royal counterparts out to dance, leaving three single girls standing by and watching their dates perform the tradition without them. Don should take advantage of that. I elbowed him, "Go on. Ask one of them. You won't have as good an opportunity as this again."

"Thanks." He quickly took off before someone else asked the ladies-in-waiting.

As couples joined on the dance floor, Jake and I did too, savoring the slow song. I couldn't help but feel that it had been way too long since I was in his arms, that this was where I should be. Before long I felt light pressure above my ear. A kiss? His warm breath confirmed it, though I heard no sound of it over the music. He'd kissed me! Sort of.

After the song ended, I sent Jake an adoring look that conveyed my happy feelings. When I finally tore my eyes from him, I saw Don waiting with his partner until her date returned, and then he headed toward me. He must be expecting a fast song. Suddenly he veered off in another direction. I watched as he approached the female singer at the drinking fountain. She refilled a container. They talked for a minute and the music started without her. I guessed they didn't need her to sing or play tambourine for this song. She took a big drink, dumped the rest from her cup, and the two of them started dancing to the moderate-paced music.

Jake must have been following where I focused because he said, "Would you look at that."

I watched her doing the Mashed Potato with the Jerk thrown in. "Yeah. She could be a regular on Bandstand. Don's not bad either." Grinning like a Cheshire cat, Don looked like he was having the time of his life dancing with a college-aged girl.

They started capturing more attention, and some of those nearby stopped to watch, clapping to the beat or trying to copy her steps. Three bright flashes in a row popped. She'd caught the attention of the photographer as well. Curious, we moved closer.

A teacher whom I didn't know raced up to him. "Those photos will *not* be submitted to the yearbook committee with your other ones. Do you understand me?" Half the gym must have heard her.

"Yes, ma'am." He backed away, not looking scolded at all.

The teacher spoke to Don next. "Mr. Burton, this is a member of the band, and you need to be associating with your fellow students." Don's cool-cat demeanor deflated.

By now the two had stopped dancing but the music continued. I felt bad for the band member, for them both. She looked like she was having fun showing off her moves, and Don no longer had his fifteen seconds of fame.

The lead singer finished out his verse and signaled the electric guitarist to go into his solo while he motioned her to get back on stage, keeping a watchful eye on the situation.

"Let 'em dance," somebody called out.

"Yeah, let 'em dance!"

More and more students clapped along to the lively guitar solo so the girl began to dance again, ignoring the teacher, who looked agitated. Mrs. Burkhart came up to her co-worker and said something that only she could hear. Her expression smoothed and the two retreated to the wall. My respect for Mrs. B went up a notch.

If I recalled the song correctly, the band skipped one of the verses to end it early, and moved on to something safe. A lot of the students applauded the dancer, but I noticed a select few who stood with their arms folded or whose backs were turned away from her. She gave a low Jackie Gleason bow, took Don's hand, shook it, said something that made him beam, and stepped onto the platform.

The lead singer held out his hand to her. "The lovely Claudia, ladies and gentlemen." More applause and a few whistles. "Spread out, y'all. Let's do the Madison!" A handful of students cheered. "Claudia will demonstrate the steps. Those who already know it, join right in."

The drummer started a soft tapping against his cymbals and a light beat with his drums. Claudia hopped off the platform. The lead singer interchanged counts to four with calling the steps to the line dance as Claudia demonstrated them. "One, two, three, four. Slide, slide, touch, four. Tap that toe, kick, four. Heel, heel, quarter turn."

Just when I got one part figured out, they moved on to the next. Brad, Jake, and I gave up before long, but Patty and several others knew what they were doing. We stood there watching Claudia and the dancers with awe.

"Having fun?" I asked Brad.

"Yes, but I'll stick to the Swing and the Twist."

We watched a couple sequences. "How is it that coloreds are so good at music and dancing?"

I looked at him sideways, thinking it was a racist question, but by his expression he simply wanted to know. "Nobody has the corner on dancing and music because of skin color. If that were true, I'd be better at dancing than Patty." I smiled to show I wasn't offended, but he blushed anyway.

He looked at the floor. "Sometimes I'm an idiot."

"Sometimes?" I laughed and he lifted his eyes to me. "I've seen some real progress from you. And real courage." I lightly punched his shoulder. "You're alright, Brad."

He gave me a shy look. "You're alright too."

"Aw," Jake said from behind us. "Does this mean we're one big, happy family again?"

Brad rolled his eyes but heat spots were back on his cheeks. "I'm going to find Patty."

Jake took both my hands in his and glanced after Brad. "I've got to hand it to him. He's trying hard, you know. For you. Because you showed him your true colors—ones that go beyond patience with Brad. You felt compassion toward a certain girl in the hospital who might tell the school board your biggest secret."

I took in a sharp breath. "You know my secret?"

"Yeah. I hope you don't mind. Brad needed to confide in someone."

He tucked a strand of hair behind my ear, looking at me tenderly. "You're probably the kindest person I know."

His eyes searched mine, and I could feel my unease melting. His gaze went to my mouth. I don't know what I did next to show my yearning for that first kiss. My lips may have parted slightly, or I leaned into him, or returned the same gaze. Maybe all of those things. We could have been anywhere. On a hilltop, by the ocean, under the moonlight. Maybe all of those places, but certainly not surrounded by a crowd. As his lips touched mine, it was hard to distinguish the source of my happiness. Brad respected me, Jake didn't care one cent about skin color, and I was experiencing my first real kiss that tingled all the way to my toes.

For one blissful moment, all was well in the world

That is, until one of the teachers tapped us on the shoulder and wagged a finger at us. Heat filled my cheeks and was gone just as fast. Nothing could ruin this night. Nothing.

CHAPTER TWENTY

MOM SHOOK ME AWAKE WITH a cheery sing-song voice. "Time to get ready for church."

I bolted upright. "No! We can't go." I'd been so focused on other things that I'd forgotten to let my family know I had a problem with Pastor Jensen, and they should too.

"Of course we can. You know getting in late doesn't change that." She ruffled my hair. "Sounds like you had fun. Do you have anything for me—you know, photos, juicy stories…?"

"No. I mean yes. I have photos. But we can't go to church. Or at least we can't put Gran through that again. We're not welcome there." I took a breath. My head spun and I plopped back onto my pillow.

"Gran took sick last night. She's staying home, but the rest of us are going."

"But—"

"Don't worry. We're attending another church." She propped her chin in her hand. "That's right, you weren't there when we talked about this. It was yesterday when you were getting ready for the dance with Patty."

I sighed with relief. "Good. I don't think I could stand listening to that hypocrite."

"Charlotte! That's not nice. Pastor Jensen spends a lot of time looking after widows and keeping kids off drugs."

I folded my arms. "He makes us believe he is a friend to all but only helps a certain group." Brad popped into mind. At least he was humble enough to admit he needed to change. I doubted the pastor would change anything.

Mom blew out a breath. "Having biases is not the same as being a hypocrite. The pastor doesn't pretend to love all men. He simply focuses on helping whites. It's hard for people to get over generations and generations of engrained beliefs."

"He's the deceiver, hiding his biases. Look how long it took us to find out about him."

"Well, let's keep an open mind about this other pastor. Now get up. You need to hurry."

"I heard Gran coughing when I came home last night. How bad is she?"

"Some congestion. She'll be alright. Hurry now, won't you?"

Mom waited for me to get out of bed before closing the door behind her. I looked at myself in the bathroom mirror. My hair still looked pretty good from last night so I smoothed it. I had a quick shower and threw on a Sunday dress. My stomach rumbled as I brushed on my mascara.

Mark poured the last of the milk bottle onto his cereal when I reached the kitchen. "Save some for me!"

"There's another quart in the fridge—" he said, taking a spoonful of cereal, "—and the milkman comes Tuesday." He swallowed. "How was your date?" He waggled his eyebrows at me and took another bite.

"Good."

"Is he a good kisser?"

"Ha ha. Wouldn't *you* like to know." I struggled to hide my dreamy reflections. Jake had kissed me three times last night, if I counted the brief one on top of my head. The one on the front porch was a soft, tender one, where he lingered long enough to savor the touch without becoming sloppy. It left me wanting more. My favorite was on the dance floor. It's hard to compare the perfect first kiss that I'll always remember. I almost sighed reliving it, minus the part where the teacher caught us. He had me totally hooked on him. "Jake was a perfect gentleman."

Dad came in. "I'm going to warm up the engine. Don't make me wait too long."

I shoveled down my last three bites, set the bowl in the sink, and joined them in the car.

We pulled into the parking lot next to a quaint church with a tall steeple. It was smaller than the other one, but the two circular stained-glass windows on either side of the front door gave me a cheery welcome. I almost wished Granny could have come so we could gauge a truer reception of us, but I didn't need more of the town sticking their noses into our business. Folks should let one another be.

I heard a car door shut and glanced back to see Mrs. Burkhart and her husband walking hand in hand toward the church. I took it for a good sign that we would like this preacher. If only they had a Sunday school teacher as good as Brother Mike, maybe then I could get Patty to come with me sometime.

I checked on Gran as soon as we got home.

"No chills, no aches. Just a sore nose from blowing it," she said, poking a finger in one ear and wiggling her jaw. "And stuffed up ears too."

"Well, you've got to eat." I handed her the crutches and offered my hand so she could get out of the easy chair. "I want to tell you how church went."

"And I want to hear all about it. We better go wash our hands first."

I did at the kitchen sink, but not finding a towel, I dried my hands on Mom's apron.

"Hey!" She wagged her spatula at me. "Toss that salad and get the dressing, would you please?"

I settled Gran, tossed the salad, and set it on the table. It signaled everyone to gather 'round. Dad said grace like every Sunday, and we started passing bowls of Mom's spicy red beans and rice and pan-fried catfish. I served Gran so she'd get enough before Mark took it all.

"Thanks." Gran looked around the table. "So how did y'all like church?"

"Good," Mark said as he piled food onto his plate. "Dad didn't fall asleep and we didn't get yelled at."

Dad exaggerated a hurt look. "I don't sleep through the sermons. I close my eyes to avoid distractions. It's a peaceful way of listening."

Mom rolled her eyes.

"I see," Gran said with a knowing smile.

"Pastor Hall likes to read scriptures and tell stories," I told Gran. "I like him."

She nodded. "I like it when preachers show the Bible relating to real life. That's good. You keep that passion, child. Them scriptures feed our faith." She took a sip of water. "Does Pastor Hall seem like he wouldn't mind too much if I was in the congregation next Sunday?"

I shook my head. "I don't think he'd mind, but you know you'd still be the only colored there. Don't know if other folks might care."

Mark waved his fork in the air like he'd had a brilliant idea. "Hey, maybe the colored's church has a Saturday or Sunday night session. Then we could get Gran there and she wouldn't feel funny going to ours."

Dad poked his fork toward Mark. "So you'll be there to wheel her around in her wheelchair? Would you feel funny being the only white 'cause that's what Gran puts up with?"

Mark lifted his shoulders.

"I don't mind and I don't want to be no bother." Gran sighed. "I grew up with the colored kids calling my daddy names and the white kids calling my mama names. I'm still waiting for the day when nobody cares who sits next to who."

"Oh, Gran," I said, my thoughts shifting. "I got to sit by a good friend of mine during Sunday school. Remember me telling you about my friend John from drama? He goes to that church."

"How nice. I don't think I'll live long enough to see a church that don't care about skin color."

Her mind was still on the past. I propped my elbows on the table and threaded my fingers together. "Then why not continue to fight for equal rights?"

"I used to do more, but fighting your whole life is tiresome," Gran said with a sigh. "I have to do it now and again, but today we see peace marches turn violent and Freedom Riders risking their lives. I'm too old for that. I've seen progress through the years, and that does my heart good. I had it better than my grandmother, Mary, and you have it better than I did. It may come slow, but there's hope."

Whatever Gran had done in her youth, it had paved a way for me. Could one person really make a difference? My parents switching congregations wouldn't make a difference outside of our family... unless they became an example to follow. Mary had made a difference to her children by taking them to a congregation of coloreds rather than stay at home with her husband, like Henry preferred. "They needs church learning," she'd insisted.

I hadn't done anything to forward the cause of civil rights because I hadn't had much to lose. And I hadn't thought of the next generation. Until now. Now I could lose doing something I loved and be yanked away from my friends. It would affect scholarships and college opportunities. My future. Me, me, me. I set my fork down, suddenly not as interested in the food on my plate.

I hadn't believed I could make a difference. Heck, I hadn't believed I needed to do a darned thing. All I needed to do was get in the school allotted more money to their drama program and life was good. For me. But what about the students who were ineligible to attend Oakmont—didn't they deserve to have choices?

Of course. While true that one person could make a difference, I didn't know what I should do about it.

CHAPTER TWENTY-ONE

JAKE WAITED AT MY LOCKER on Monday morning. My heart skipped into double dutch. "Hi, handsome."

"Hi yourself. How's my girl doing today?"

His girl. My insides fluttered. My resolve to take on the school board, if it came to that, kicked up a notch. No way was I missing out on the play *and* walking the school halls with a hunky boyfriend.

"I'm great now. How are you?"

"Couldn't be better."

I grabbed what I'd need for history and shut the locker. Jake took my hand and we wandered around to find Patty or Brad, possibly both together. It didn't happen by the time the bell rang. "See you at lunch."

He shot me with his finger and made a clicking sound with his mouth. "You got it."

I approached my teacher's desk. "Mrs. Burkhart?"

"Good morning, Charlotte," she said.

"Good morning, ma'am. I saw you at the dance. You can really twist."

"Thanks. Did you have fun?"

"I did."

A couple of students walked in.

"Oh," Mrs. Burkhart said, "I need to speak with you and Brad. Can you stay after class for a minute?"

"Uh..." Complications flooded my mind. She'd learned something from the school board. I couldn't do Mary's story. It was too long or too controversial or too—

She shook her head in tiny movements, probably seeing worry on my face. "No, you're fine. I need a favor from the both of you about your project."

"Yes, ma'am." More students shuffled passed me.

"Great." She noticed I continued to stand next to her desk. "Can I do something for you?"

"Do you go to the school board meetings?"

She smirked. "Not if I can help it. I've been a time or two."

"How often do they meet and what are they like? Do they make a lot of rules? Are they super strict?"

She tossed her reddish curls away from her face. "They have issues that need discussion about twice a month, but they don't make rules for the fun of it. What's this all about?"

"I might need that information for something pretty soon."

"I see. The secretary in the office can get you a list of school board members and their meeting schedule. Let me look the list over and I'll tell you what I know about any of them."

I brightened at having a starting place. "That's a great idea. Thanks!"

"You're welcome. If there's anything in particular that I can do, please let me know."

"I will."

She stood and took her usual perch at the front edge of her desk. The tardy bell rang as I reached my seat. I noticed that Melanie was still gone. I whispered to Brad that Mrs. B wanted to see us at the end of class. He made a questioning grunt that echoed my curiosity. "It's about our project," I whispered. "I've already cut the story down as much as I could and still have it make sense, so it better not be that." I turned and faced forward.

We had a class discussion and a worksheet on the 1800s that averted my concern. Before the bell could ring, Mrs. Burkhart called me and Brad to her desk. "I received a note from Melanie's mother that she'd had surgery and would be out for a few days. She's worried about Melanie being on pain medication and feeling overwhelmed with makeup work. Melanie had planned on writing up her report this week."

On Homecoming weekend? I crossed my arms. "Sounds like she procrastinated."

Mrs. Burkhart's lips twitched. "Perhaps. But no matter. I'll grade her as I see fit."

"Why are you telling us this? I thought she was working on something with Ellen."

Mrs. Burkhart sighed. "It seems Ellen got bored with the civil war book they were reading and quit. Melanie's mother said she won't be able to make sense of her notes and write a good report on it with the pain medication she's on. The point is that I must make an attempt at placing Melanie in a group because of her medication. In looking over the project proposals, I wanted to approach you first. You two have a small group and have chosen the same war."

A shrill bell interrupted us, and students shoved books and papers into their backpacks. Mrs. B spoke above the noise. "Your homework this week is to finish up your midterm presentations. We will work on those tomorrow in class. Dismissed." She turned back to me and Brad. "I'm asking you if she could get in on your reader's theater presentation. Would that work for you? From what I read of your proposal, she might fit well as one of the two female characters. I'm excited to have you share your script, by the way."

She looked sincere, and I didn't think the flattery was meant to sway me. Brad and I looked at one another.

He shrugged. "It's your call, Charlotte, but it might be easier than you doing two parts." He looked at the teacher. "She found the story and wrote it out. I did the typing."

Mrs. Burkhart nodded and looked to me. "Do you want a day to think about it?"

I'd wanted another female reader all along, but everyone had their group or project already and I preferred to read the whole thing myself than invite Melanie. I didn't feel as sorry for her now as I had Saturday night, but she was still in a pickle, and this was Mrs. B asking. "No. Brad is right. The reading will go better with another female to read that character. As long as she's able to run through it a couple times ahead with us." Melanie had better appreciate this favor because she didn't deserve it.

"Thank you, Charlotte. I'll put your presentation farther down on the list and I'll let Melanie know."

Out in the hallway I turned to Brad. "What have I done? Melanie will probably sabotage us."

"Don't worry. She'll do it for the grade, and she'll do a good job because she cares what people think of her."

"Hm. That actually makes sense. I hope you're right."

"And by the way, I respect you for saying yes."

I stared at him.

"Let's go visit her after your play practice and bring her a copy of the script to look over. The sooner she sees what she's in for, the better job she'll do."

"Or the sooner she can change her mind." Having another female voice is really what the script and audience needed. She better not turn into a prima donna.

Brad looked confident. "Nah. Not unless she really did read a whole book and took good notes, I'm betting she'll take the easy route."

As Brad and I approached Melanie's hospital room, a woman's voice sounded through the open door. "How about a crossword puzzle then?"

"Ugh. Puzzles are stupid and there's nothing on TV." Melanie's familiar complaining wafted to our ears. Stuck in the hospital, Melanie was likely to be more crabby than usual. I considered backing out.

Brad knocked, and entered first. "Hey, Melanie."

Melanie gaped at us as we drew near her bed. She wore a silky pink robe over her hospital gown, and quickly smoothed her hair. "What are you guys doing here?"

"We came to visit you, of course." Brad sounded cheery, but I was still leery of the climate in the room.

The woman I assumed was Melanie's mother, smiled. "How nice." She turned toward her daughter. "See, I told you some friends would come."

She ignored her mother's comment and asked us directly, her tone sarcastic, "Why? Missed me in class today?"

"You could say that," Brad said, unruffled. "We're your new history midterm group."

I couldn't let him do all the talking. "We're doing a reading on a Southern family and their slaves who lived through a Civil War battle. You don't have to act, only read with good voice inflection. Would you like to see the script?" I held it out until she took it. "I've highlighted your part. You get to be Sue Chancellor, a fourteen-year-old Southern belle." I added the last part so it would sound more attractive.

She flipped through the pages. "Looks like this Mary person gets to say a lot more."

There was no way I was giving Mary over to Melanie. "She's the slave. I thought you'd rather be the Southern girl."

"A Southern belle, Melanie," her mother cooed, "and a smaller part won't tax you so much."

Melanie shrugged, which I took as her acceptance. "How was the dance?" she asked in a tone that I imagined played down her curiosity.

"Uh, it was good." I kept it vague, not knowing what would upset her. "Great band and decorations."

"Did you hear who made the royal court?" Brad asked. I inwardly cringed and sent him a look.

She nodded, a sour expression coming to her face. "Ellen phoned me. How y'all picked Dolores, I'll never know."

Brad changed the subject. "Want to see a photo? We clean up pretty nicely, if I do say so myself." He pointed to my purse and I dug out one of the Polaroids of all four of us. She held out her hand for it and scrutinized.

A nervous chuckle slipped from my mouth. "Better than our PE uniforms, don't you think?"

"Yeah." A small smile crept onto Melanie's lips. "Much better." She sighed and handed it back. "You should have seen my dress. Emerald green and sparkly."

"Sounds perfect for the Christmas dance," I said encouragingly.

Melanie's mother slapped a hand to her thigh. "That's exactly what *I* told her."

"When do you go home?" Brad asked.

Melanie's grumpy tone returned. "It should have been today, but now they say tomorrow morning."

Her mother explained further. "Her incision was weeping fluid. They wanted to make sure it wasn't infected. She'll be fine. She might be to school on Wednesday."

Melanie sent me a big, fake smile. She must not take after her mother.

I reckoned Melanie wouldn't exactly be charmed by our visit, but I hoped she would appreciate it anyway. With our effort to be nice, I also hoped it would make her forget about Brad's note.

She didn't look too ill for me to ask, "When do you think you could practice the script with us? We can come to your place if that would help, but we need to run through it this week sometime. Presentations start next Monday, but Mrs. B said she'll put us toward the end."

"I'll let you know." Melanie's voice softened after she glanced at her mother. "Thanks for including me in your project."

Maybe this wouldn't turn out to be such a nightmare after all. Or maybe she didn't want to be a total snot in front of her mother. I reminded myself this wasn't her fault, and the timing was terrible. "You're welcome. You'll do a good job on Sue's part."

She nodded soberly. "I'll do my best." There was an awkward pause as she tensed up, licked her lips, and expelled a breath. "Well, if we'll be working together, I guess I should warn you."

"What?" As soon as I asked, I knew what she would say. It didn't matter that I had previously mentally prepared for this possibility. My throat clogged and goosebumps rose on my arms.

"I went to see your pastor last week." She gazed at her lap while I stared at her. "I... I wrote a letter to the district superintendent. It went out in Friday's mail. I'm sorry. I wish now that I hadn't sent it. I'm really sorry."

I couldn't breathe.

CHAPTER TWENTY-TWO

I WALKED TOWARD THE DOOR, rubbing my arms, but my knees kept buckling.

Brad grabbed my elbow. "Are you alright?"

I could hear the worry in his voice but I couldn't talk yet. Or maybe didn't want to. My breath came in short rasps. All my fears were crashing in on me.

Brad kept a hold on me, his steps labored as we moved down the hallway. "I should have realized something like this could happen. I never should have written that note."

My breathing had evened out enough to speak. "It's not your fault."

"It's not yours either," he shot back.

I gave a frustrated sigh. It might have been better to blissfully go about daily life until the last minute when I got a summons of some sort.

I did some quick calculations. Mail sent on Friday within the same town could get to its recipient by tomorrow. Then what? Would the board of directors call a special meeting or wait until the next regularly scheduled one? The schedule I had picked up showed them meeting twice a month. It seemed they would need to discuss it and pass judgement before notifying me. I prayed for governmental red tape. A couple weeks would get me through the midterm history assignment but not the play. My knees buckled once more.

Would they have to prove their allegations? That could buy some time, but I wouldn't put it past them to have me suspended. I silently prayed over and over, pleading that I could still be in the play.

Brad opened the door for me and the outside air did some good. I wasn't so overwhelmed with the immediacy of decisions anymore. I needed to talk to Dad about this.

"Do you need me to drive?" Brad asked as we approached the Dart.

"No." My mind was still tortured but my knees would hold.

After seeing to my condition, Brad started his own rant. "I can't believe she did that." He punched a fist into his hand. "We'll fight it if we have to. We'll get the whole student body to fight it." I never thought I'd hear him defend my civil rights like that.

I touched Brad's arm. "Thanks. Your support means a lot to me."

Dad was sitting in his favorite armchair, reading the evening newspaper when I got home. He lifted his paper toward me. "Have you seen—" He glanced at me. "What's wrong?" Mom came into the family room from the kitchen. Gran asked Mark to shut off the TV.

"There's a girl at school who turned me in to the superintendent for not being one hundred percent white. She did it to spite me." My chin quivered. "I'll have to tell Mr. Dodd he better find another Mrs. Paroo for the play."

"Oh, honey." Mom's voice dripped with empathy. She came over to give me a hug. "Not the play."

"They can't do that!" Mark said. "They already accepted you. You went to the courthouse and everything."

"They'll claim I lied."

"I'm sorry, Charlotte," Gran said. "Truly I am. But what's wrong with going to Pennfields High? Oakmont sounds stuffy to me."

"It has more of those privileges you wanted me to have. Like one of the best drama programs in the state. It's my best shot at a college scholarship." There was the me, me, me again, but I couldn't help feeling sorry for myself.

Dad thrust his index finger out and wagged it at me in that thinking way of his. "So you'll go to school and listen to one or more teachers that could be as prejudiced as Pastor Jensen, but you don't want to sit through any more of his sermons?"

I frowned. "Teachers don't talk about church stuff. They talk about math equations and grammar and who Napoleon conquered."

"And Pastor Jensen talks about the Bible and God's love." Dad's friendly stare made me squirm. He had a point.

The face of the teacher who told Don not to dance with Claudia popped into my mind. I hadn't noticed much of a problem with prejudice at Oakmont but it could be lurking under the surface waiting for something like this to explode. Southern traditions were everywhere. How many of the student body would side with Melanie instead of me? I honestly didn't know because we Oakmont students were in our own little white world.

I raked a hand through my hair and let my frustration out. "I just want to do the play and have everything work out for everybody." I sniffled. "I see what you mean now, Gran. Fighting for what you want your whole life sounds tiresome."

She handed me her tissue box. "That don't mean you shouldn't try. Some things I fought for did see success. Because doing the play means that much to you, you'll never forgive yourself if you don't give it your best shot."

"Right," Dad said. "If the board doesn't accept fifteen-sixteenths as white, we'll insist they get some kind of genealogist expert to prove your heritage, simply to take up a whole lot of time and put them in a court situation they may not want to deal with. I'd hold off telling Mr. Dodd anything yet. We will do everything we can to keep you in the play."

Mom nodded. My eyes brimmed with tears. "Thanks."

Gran said, "I've seen lots of school board cases in my day and they don't win 'em all. This board—are they all hard-headed?" She had a small coughing fit, then reached into her apron pocket for a peppermint lozenge.

I took a folded piece of paper out of my backpack. "I've got a list and I'm going to find out."

Gran nodded. "Good. Do the homework on them ahead of time."

"What do you think of this?" Dad picked up the newspaper from his lap. "There's a picture of a boy from your school dancing with a colored girl from that dance you went to."

I leaned closer. "Let me see that."

At the top of the Social page was a photo of the entire Homecoming royalty, listing their names in the caption. Right below it, I could see Don and Claudia in a two-column square. "Well, I'll be."

The article headline read: *Oakmont Dances around All-White Restrictions.* I quickly read through the article. It gave a description of the school's long-held policy, explained that the girl in the photo was a member of the band, and brought up the question of how much longer Oakmont would defy federal mandates in favor of states' rights. Principal Morgrin was quoted as saying, "It has been a long-standing tradition here at Oakmont to provide the best education and programs available for our students. We strive to uphold the preferences of the parents who send us their students. These dances enrich their social experiences and provide a wholesome recreational outlet as a secondary form of learning." The article overall showed a slight bias toward desegregation, but done in a reporting-the-facts way.

"That sneaky photographer." I smiled for the first time in the last hour. "He promised not to use it in the yearbook but nobody imagined he'd put it in the paper."

"There will be a ripple effect over this," Dad said. "Newspapers sell when folks get riled up."

I inhaled through my teeth. "That's bad timing for me. Either the papers or the school board will want to make an example of me for sure now."

Dad reached for my hand. "I'm sorry. You might be right about that. We can still fight it though."

"How? Maybe we can stall but it's like our opinions don't matter. They won't see the real me." I could feel my emotions rising toward my tear ducts.

"Hm. You may be on to something. Let's make our opinions matter. I'll write a letter to the editor and see if they publish it. There's some people at work I could talk to about doing that too. Our first step is to flood the newspaper with opinions promoting civil rights."

"The power of the press. That's brilliant, Dad!" I slipped behind him and threw my arms around his neck. "I knew you would have an answer for me."

CHAPTER TWENTY-THREE

I WENT TO SCHOOL EARLY Tuesday morning with a mission. If Dad could talk other adults into promoting civil rights through the newspaper, then so would I.

Mrs. Burkhart's door was open but I knocked anyway. The halls were noisy but her room was empty of other students. "Come in, Charlotte," she said. "Did you get everything squared away with Melanie for your midterm project?

I nodded. She continued to watch me expectantly, with her chin propped up by one hand, as if she knew I wasn't here to talk about the weather. "Did you see the newspaper about the dance?" I asked.

"I did."

"Can I ask you what you said to calm that teacher down when Don was dancing with the singer?"

She smiled like she knew a secret. "I told her to give it a minute, that it would all blow over without making a fuss."

"Hm. You were right. How did you know?"

"I didn't. I had a good chance at being right, but it could have backfired."

"Oh." I'd expected her answer to reveal her personal opinion about mixed-race dancing. I'd have to come out and ask. "Did it bother you that they were dancing?"

She lifted one eyebrow. "Is there a reason you're asking?"

A question for a question. Great. This was supposed to be easy. My sigh was more noticeable than I wanted.

"Does this have anything to do with your question yesterday about the school board?"

I returned my focus to her. "Yes. Yes it does."

"Care to tell me about it?"

I only had a few minutes before students would start showing up, but for her to side with me, she would need to know more. "You know that story I wrote about the slave, Mary?" She nodded, so I continued. "She's my great-great-grandmother. The school board will find out and I need to stop them from expelling me."

She kept her expression calm, like she knew all along, and I wondered if I had been that transparent. "I see. Is there something I can do to help?"

"Yes." I drew out the word in a breathy burst of relief. "I hope so. It doesn't bother you to know that, does it?"

She smiled. "Not at all."

"Then can I ask a favor? Could you write a letter to the editor of the newspaper giving your opinion in favor of civil rights? We're trying to flood their office with positive public opinion."

Her forehead wrinkled and her voice held regret. "I'm sorry. I can't."

Of all my teachers, I counted on Mrs. B and Mr. Dodd to help. Strike one punched me hard in the stomach.

"It's not that I don't want to," she said. "I can't. All the teachers got a message in their office inbox this morning saying we were not to make any statements with any reporters whatsoever or discuss civil rights or school policy in a public setting. The principal and the school's lawyer are trained to handle school-related issues, and teachers are to only teach their specialized subjects. If I went against the principal, I could be fired."

"Oh." I didn't want her to get fired. That nixed asking Mr. Dodd too. It sounded like the principal would never take my side, and my hope for school support just went down the toilet. "That's okay. We'll manage." I shuffled to my seat, feeling glum and helpless to change anything.

"I'm truly sorry, Charlotte."

Thinking about the notice and expecting it to come in the mail was making me crazy. I continued on with play practice and school as if

nothing had happened, but my stomach squirmed as my mind ping-ponged various outcomes and ways to handle them. Dad and I checked the opinions column every night. They seemed to give equal attention to both sides of the hot desegregation topic. I stayed busy and swallowed down my sporadic worrying. Jake was the best distraction of all. We walked hand in hand everywhere at school and talked on the phone every evening. I told him some of my ideas and fears.

Melanie came to school on Wednesday, shuffling in with small steps like a little old lady. She gave me a tentative smile as she headed for her desk. I wasn't sure how to respond to that or if I felt like being friendly to her, so I pretended not to notice.

Brad came up to her at the end of class, motioning me over. "We need to get together for a practice. Are you up to that soon?"

I was glad Brad had taken over. He probably knew I was uncomfortable.

"I'm still a little sore. Can you wait until Saturday?"

She looked at me with pain in her eyes, and not from her surgery. I didn't want to see it. I was the one who had been hurt. I watched the students exiting as if they had caught my attention.

Brad hadn't answered so I looked at him. He waited for me to confirm. "Saturday sounds good." I glanced at Melanie and in that moment I saw her expression smooth out. She saw my casual response as compassionate. I needed to work on that more.

I didn't see Melanie in the lunchroom at all the rest of the week. Maybe she was embarrassed or hated me more than ever for having confessed to me. She barely noticed me in class but it wasn't quite like the air of being stuck up. Shyness? More like embarrassment. Whatever it was, things were weird between us, and I hoped it wouldn't affect her doing the project with me.

On Saturday morning, Brad picked me up to drive to Melanie's. She welcomed us, and then we sat on three chairs turned away from her dining table, our noses in the script. I could tell Brad had been practicing. Melanie, on the other hand, sounded formal and stiff. I gave her the benefit of it being her first run through, but on the second time through I had to stop her.

"Sue is worried about her lamb and she can't find him, Melanie. She's scared. Show that in your voice."

She frowned. "I'm trying."

Brad snorted and received a sharp look from her before she ran the line again.

"Lamar! Lamar!" She finished the whole paragraph with more emotion.

"Much better," I said.

The encouragement didn't help for long. After Brad's next paragraph of narration, Melanie's voice was once again stilted. Yep. She would ruin my project. Nobody would feel sympathetic toward the slaves with a performance like that.

I tried a different tactic. "Think of the story, the message, not individual lines. Find Sue's emotion and put that into your voice."

"I just…I messed up, okay?" Her shoulders slumped. "Maybe this is easy for you, but I'm fighting my own emotions, so how can you expect me to feel Sue's? I feel bad that I wrote that letter. Now, every time you try to help me, I feel worse."

"Killed with kindness," Brad muttered under his breath.

I stared at her. "Great honk," I said. Was Melanie trying to apologize?

She felt her nose. "What is 'great honk'?"

I waved it away. "Something from *The Music Man*."

She gave a disgusted huff.

"Look," I said, "what's done is done. We can't take it back."

"But I need to do something to make amends. I don't want you to hate me. I don't want to hate myself." She sniffed.

"I don't hate you." I'd said it automatically but it gave me pause. I still harbored ill feelings toward her. She'd done more than a prank and it would probably cost me dearly. But hate? No. That cankered souls. Jesus taught us to love our enemies. I needed to offer Melanie something tangible.

I softened my voice. "If you want to make it right between us, then put your heart and soul into reading your lines. What I want from you is to quit worrying about what you did to me and do your best job on this."

She threw her hands up. "See, there you go being nice again." She expelled a breath and looked submissive, less annoyed. "Okay. I'll try harder." Her eyes glistened. "Can you really forgive me just like that?" She snapped her fingers.

Is that what I was doing—forgiving her? I pictured Brother Mike with his upturned hands out to his sides, weighing the options like a scale. His voice in my mind said, "The freeing feeling of forgiveness on the one hand or cankering hatred on the other?"

Even if Melanie wrote a second letter to the school board saying it was only a joke, they would still investigate. There wasn't a thing she could do to make amends for her deed. The damage was done. Why keep tormenting ourselves? She probably only sped up the inevitable because several people had seen me with Granny. Why not show mercy and let it reconcile us? I looked her in the eye and nodded. "Mary's story is what I care most about."

"Really?" Her eyes shone.

In my mind, Brother Mike beamed proudly at me. I felt warm inside. "Yeah. Don't beat yourself up too much. If you didn't bring up the issue to the board, somebody else would have. It was only a matter of time." Time that I couldn't afford, but likely true anyway.

Melanie's face brightened. "Let's start at the beginning again. I promise I'll do a better job this time."

CHAPTER TWENTY-FOUR

I AWOKE BEFORE THE ALARM and bounded out of bed. Our turn at the history project had finally come. Melanie had been putting some heart and soul into the part of Sue Chancellor and Brad was so familiar with his narration he barely looked at the script anymore. This was my chance to tell Mary's story to a bunch of sophomores who may or may not care about today's news or anything to do with slavery during the Civil War. Not that I expected a great change to come about, but informing was a start.

Most of the presentations so far had featured reports on battles and soldiers. A few of them were actually pretty good. A handful of parents came to watch their student. That's the kind of support this school earned. Oakmont parents practically demanded the best programs, the best teachers, and they kept track of opportunities like this to check up on things.

Knowing a few parents would be there again today made me feel guilty that I hadn't invited Mom. Inviting Mom meant inviting Gran— who gave me the story, after all. Yet I didn't want her presence as visible evidence against me. People couldn't help but notice her and that might rile up students or teachers, causing the school board to speed up their process. Delays might be my only chance for participating in *The Music Man*.

I'd learned that our local Boxwood County Community College gave a couple part-tuition drama scholarships but only one fulltime award each year. A primary part in one of Oakmont's plays might give me a shot at the part-time scholarships, which would really help because Dad had already said I was on my own for college costs.

I stood before the bathroom mirror, going a little heavier than usual on makeup, almost like I do for plays. I came down for breakfast, watching

Gran hobble over on her new walking cast to wish me luck. Mom echoed the sentiment. They had no idea that they could watch the presentation, and I wasn't telling them. On my way to school, I let go of the guilt and replaced it with a shiver of excitement after Mark wished me luck and we parted ways. My group would present second today, and I pictured success. A long, bright yellow school bus pulled into the front circular drive, signaling that I only had so much time.

Jake caught up to me as I put my backpack in my locker. In my other hand, I clutched the sack holding some costumes I'd rounded up. Melanie said she would get her own, but I had an extra apron just in case.

"Good morning, Miss Mary," he said with a flourishing bow.

I giggled. "You're not supposed to how to the help…unless you're one of them yourself and you're sweet on me."

"Oh, I'm sweet on you all right," he drawled with exaggeration and pecked my cheek. "I can't wait to see what all the fuss my two best friends have made is all about."

"See? You can't cut class to attend mine!"

"Just watch me. How could I miss it? If your teacher won't give me an excused note, I'll play hooky."

I warmed from his support, and then grabbed his hand. "Come on then. I've got to give this old vest and hat to Brad and then find Mr. Dodd."

I'd asked Mr. Dodd if we could borrow three stools during first period today. I found him setting them up at the front of Mrs. B's classroom right before the bell. He didn't leave.

"Don't you have a first period class?" I asked, my breath coming a little fast.

He tilted his head. "What, and miss this? My student teacher can handle it. After John told me one of my little drama stars wrote the script, I had to come."

My heartrate picked up with his enthusiasm. I would have to thank John later.

Mrs. Burkhart was setting up a row of folding chairs along the back wall for parents. She gave me a big smile when she looked up at me. "Ready?"

She didn't need an answer but I nodded anyway. Parents and students began filling the room, and I recognized Melanie's mother. The first performance went well. Four mothers, one for each student in that group, stood and clapped at the end of the presentation. Now it was our turn.

Melanie and I wore typical school dresses, but we quickly donned our bonnets and long, white aprons to create the setting. Someone sniggered but most of the students sat up and took notice. We took our places on the stools, with me in the center. Brad's strong, practiced voice caused everyone to hush.

Narrator: "By Christmas of 1862, the war between the North and the South had been going strong for twenty months—longer than anyone had predicted. When would it end, and could the nation be unified? Would Southern plantations know economic destruction if their slaves for which they had paid good money were allowed freedom? Would this Civil War be the great equalizer for slaves with dreams of freedom, or would hundreds of thousands of deaths be in vain?

"The war had already caused a handful of slaves to run away from the Chancellorsville farm in Virginia. That was only the beginning of its effect on Mrs. Chancellor and her daughters. Let's drop over to the Chancellor mansion and listen in on fourteen-year-old Sue and a fifteen-year-old family slave, Mary. The lives of both Southern belle and slave are about to change."

Melanie spoke next as the character of *Sue:* "Mama, we have visitors! It looks like refugees fleeing Fredericksburg. Come see! Mary, put some tea on, and then set to hanging up their coats."

Narrator: "The Chancellors offered Southern hospitality to these acquaintances, helping them forget the horrors of artillery firing upon their beloved city of Fredericksburg. Two slave girls, Mary and Hester, along with Hester's mother, were stuck with the extra chores of a full household. Other slaves had already run off. Aunt Nancy, a nanny for one of the guest's children, pitched in where she could."

Mary: "Sue and her sisters don't mind cooking and such, but the worst chores are left to us. Come on, Hester, let's get after those chamber pots."

A student squeaked out an "ew". Brad continued without missing a beat.

Narrator: "The guests at the inn started to leave as spring arrived, but not before one of the young men had violated Mary without suffering any consequences. After she recovered, it only made her more determined to be free. When Southern troops came 'round to guard the river access, Mary couldn't help but be leery of the soldiers, even those who acted like gentlemen."

Mary: "I'm keeping a fork in my apron pocket to poke a man in the eye if need be—officer or not! I'd rather have a whipping than be taken advantage of. Mistress Chancellor is as nice a mas'er as any can git, but she ain't above teaching me a lesson. I gots to be careful and avoid them soldiers as much as possible. I'll not be alone with any one a them."

I break character long enough to glance at my audience. I see the enthralled but somber looks on their faces. Exactly as I'd hoped.

Melanie put a hand up to shield her eyes from the imaginary sun. *Sue:* "Mary? Mary? Oh, there you are. It's such a nice day today. Let's go spy on the army camps. Doesn't that sound fun? Then maybe we can play with my lamb."

Mary: "Maybe the mistress will spare me an hour with you, on account of you needing a companion and all, but I gots chores that got to be done before bed. I don't want no whipping."

Narrator: "Chores soon became the least of their worries. Little did they know that a battle would soon arrive with a vengeance at their door. General Hooker and his Army of the Potomac set up headquarters right there at the inn, putting the Southern family under house arrest."

We continued on, describing the horrible sound of guns and cannon fire blasting in the yard and seeing wounded men fill up the floor space and the dead litter the yard. Melanie had mastered that scared look on her face and in her voice.

Sue: "I held my lamb tightly in my arms as the officer led us past moaning men and a pile of surgically removed limbs to the safety of the cellar. I almost vomited, but fear triumphed over nausea."

Mary: "I did throw up, my secret condition aggravated by the sight of blood. I was with child. There was no time to think about it though. We spent the rest a the day praying and huddling in the cellar. Nightfall gave some relief, but the dreadful din struck up at first light. A cannonball hit the front porch, setting the house on fire. We had to git out of there but we was locked in! It scared me to death! If it wasn't for Lieutenant Colonel Dickinson coming to let us out…" I hung my head and shook it.

Narrator: "The officer led the company to safety across the river and away from the battle."

Sue: "'Lamar! Lamar!' I cried as we left, but couldn't find my lamb through all the smoke and the rushing around. We had to get out of there fast. Lamar meant more to me than losing our home, but I could never go back there either. The soldiers ruined our land, our crops, and set our slaves free. Eventually, we were able to reunite with family in Charlottesville and start over. Not one of us was lost to the war, yet it was a terrible time that I will never forget."

Mary: "When I learned we was on Northern land, I couldn't believe I was free! A slave no more! But where would I go? What would I do?

"I took the first job for real money I could git, as a cook in a Union army camp. I had a baby growing inside me to think of, and needed to save up. That baby also needed a father, and I needed a husband. The only men around me were white.

"One a the soldiers took a liking to my cooking and my smile. He say I'm pretty. We spend some time talking and gitting to know one another. He say talking to me helps him forget some a the bad things about war that he see in his mind. Some a the soldiers give him flack but he tell them they jealous 'cause they ain't got no woman. There's no white women for miles.

"Though scorned by some, it wasn't illegal at the time for him to marry me. I needed to git married fast so he can believe and accept my baby as his own. I feel a little bad having to trick him. He say he loves me, so I see it for the best, and ask God for forgiveness. True love don't mean nothing. He treat me like I's worth something, and that be good enough for me. We got married right away in front of the army preacher. I couldn't be happier. I had my freedom, and a white father for my half-white baby.

"After the war, he gave us a good home—a real home with a warm fireplace and food I could eat myself instead a serving to others. Not all the freed slaves had it as good as I did. My firstborn daughter lived like a princess compared to my childhood as a slave. She was a beautiful child with long, black hair and a pretty smile. She charmed her way into the lives of our white neighbors. Not everybody accepted us, a course, but I dids my best to fit in.

"I became deeply religious, determined to give my life to God for blessing me so much. My husband sometimes resented this, and he suffered with those war nightmares a his. Life ain't ever easy. It takes hard work being a wife and a mother, but I still counts my blessings.

"After a few years and a couple more chilluns, my husband said I paid too much attention to the chilluns and that New Testament book given to me by a soldier during the battle at Chancellorsville. He don't understand my gratitude and my desire to give our offspring a better life 'cause he never had the life of a slave. He want more respect but I tell him I respect him plenty. I simply have my hands full. He's missing the attention he once got for being a soldier who fought in the war. He can't let go a some things he saw in battle. They mess with his mind. Other soldiers have moved on, but I guess he couldn't, and it affected our relationship. The casualties of war took many forms."

Narrator: By the time the youngest grew taller than Mary, Mary got consumption. She lived long enough to see her firstborn daughter marry in a church that allowed all the family members of both bride and groom to attend, no matter their skin color. By the end of her life, Mary still kept her hope for the future. Her dream of freedom, for which brother fought against brother and father against son, would carry on." Brad gave a small bow and said, "Thank you."

Applause broke out. I stood, my chest thumping. I hadn't planned this, but my emotions were too strong for this to solely be about the Civil War. I shoved the bonnet off my head to hang by the tie under my chin. I looked into the eyes of my classmates and spoke to them, emotion thick in my throat. "If Mary were here today, would she see progress? Would she believe that her dream of freedom had been achieved? Or would she listen to Dr. King's speech and wonder why people of color must still plead for their dream of freedom?"

The room was silent. Students stared at me. Melanie slipped off her stool and slunk back to her desk, signaling to them that no, this was not part of the script. Mrs. B was grinning at me, and my passion couldn't be deterred, like something inside me had changed.

"I only ask that you ponder Mary's story for meaning in your own life. Thank you."

Mr. Dodd stood and applauded from the back of the room. Jake and Melanie's mother joined him. A handful of other students stood too. One of the parents huffed and a student folded her arms and frowned.

Mrs. Burkhart came out from behind her desk, and Brad and I returned to our seats. "Well done," she said. "Thank you for an enlightening presentation and a unique perspective. War didn't only affect the soldiers, but the communities as well. Our next presentation will be..."

I tuned out, watching Jake give me two thumbs up as he, Mr. Dodd, and Melanie's mother quietly excused themselves. I recalled the student reactions like replaying a reel-to-reel tape. At least one of my goals had been accomplished: I'd given information. Whether I'd started a snowball rolling that would grow in size or fizzle and melt, I'd have to wait and see.

The class had been digging our presentation. I was certain of it. It was my request at the end that made a few feel uncomfortable. That was all right. People who were too comfortable weren't motivated into action. We needed more action. My heart boomed in agreement.

I'd been a little uncomfortable sharing that passion myself. In fact, the biggest impact had likely been on me. I couldn't blend in any longer. Though I didn't plan to parade my ancestry, my desire to promote racial freedom and civil rights had welled into something I could no longer keep locked away.

CHAPTER TWENTY-FIVE

WHEN I WALKED INTO DRAMA class, John immediately asked me how it went. Before I could answer, Mr. Dodd appeared at my side and gushed, "She was fabulous! Such passion! Your friends did well too. Fervent voice inflections and the best student script of its kind I've seen in years. You should perform it at the regional drama festival in January. There are student categories for directing and—" he paused for a big breath, "— script writing!"

John looked at me with a raised brow and whistled softly.

"Indeed," Mr. Dodd continued. "She practically had us waving little flags at the end."

I grinned with pleasure, too overwhelmed to speak.

"We'll talk about it more later," Mr. Dodd said, giving me a firm nod and whisking himself away.

I told John a bit more about it before class got underway. A couple of kids might have been listening in, the way I kept getting glances. Maybe word was spreading about the crazy new girl who made an impromptu political speech in her history class. If so, negative publicity was still promotional. I would continue to show them the positives.

Later, at lunch, Melanie and her girlfriends joined our table as if they belonged there all along. She must have gotten over the earlier strain between us. Oddly, it wasn't awkward at all. Her first question was directed to me. "So, were you satisfied with our presentation?"

I liked the sincerity in her voice. "Yes. Thank you. It was fab, wasn't it?"

We all talked about it for like ten whole minutes. Melanie listened more than talked and didn't monopolize Jake at all. After spending time practicing with her and Brad, it felt like she belonged. So far, she did.

"So Charlotte," Jake said, chomping down on a carrot stick. "You obviously want to support racial freedom. Got any ideas for kids like us to make a difference?"

"Not yet, but Mr. Dodd said we should repeat the readers theater piece at a drama festival. That would get some good exposure."

"Yeah," Brad agreed.

Melanie sat up straighter. "Cool."

A girl came up and squinted at me, a distrustful look on her face. We all stared at her, waiting for her to say something, but she left instead.

"What's her problem?" Ellen asked.

I shrugged but deep in the pit of my stomach my sloppy joe sandwich wouldn't settle properly. Too bad I'd saved the chocolate pudding for last because I'd lost my appetite. Maybe it was nothing to worry about.

Nothing else weird happened until I started dressing for PE. Miss Zindle handed me a note. "No dressing for you, Charlotte. Principal Morgrin wants to see you."

All I could hear as I walked down the empty hall to the principal's office was the soft pad of my pumps and my heart hammering in my ears. I swallowed hard and opened the office door, handing my call slip to the secretary. "Wait there," she said, pointing to a chair.

Just what I wanted—more time to panic. Had gossip about my speech gotten back to the principal? If so, I'd done a faster job at sealing my own fate than Melanie had. Did he want to congratulate me for all my effort? Who knew? I sent up a silent prayer for further help.

Principal Morgrin's door opened and the chubby-bellied man with a crew cut stared at me. "Come in, Miss Rogers." His tone was business-like, neither friendly nor harsh.

I could do this.

"Have a seat."

He went around a large wooden desk to take his own seat. I let him do the talking, since I didn't know what to say yet.

"I got a call from the district office about a letter they received."

I inhaled. It wasn't quite a gasp, but it may as well have been. He watched me carefully, and a slight smile curved his lips.

He poked a fat finger in the air at me and leaned in. "You don't belong here, do you." It sounded like a statement but his piercing gaze demanded an answer.

My throat felt thick and dry, and I couldn't speak. I wasn't prepared for my drama dream to crash down on me yet. This wasn't fair! I didn't see any way out.

He continued. "You are ineligible to attend this school. I have no choice but to put you under suspension until your records can be transferred to the proper school you should attend, when you will be expelled from Oakmont. Do you understand, Miss Rogers?"

My brow furrowed. "W…wait. Please, sir. I didn't admit to being ineligible."

"Did you not lie to the notary republic to get into Oakmont? I've looked up your records, Miss Rogers. Math might be your poorest subject, but I'm sure you are smart enough to know that having colored ancestors doesn't add up to you being white."

Didn't my white ancestors count for anything? "Well…actually…" I bit my lip. It felt weird telling the principal he was wrong. Would he believe me? "I don't believe that I lied, sir. I've been fitting into the white culture all of my life. I have some African ancestry back four generations but I've been raised white and consider myself thus. I am fifteen-sixteenths white, which is definitely the majority of me. Don't I look white to you, sir?" It sounded rather logical to me, but it wouldn't show him that my heart had been in the right place.

His voice edged toward gruffness. "I am not interested in a lesson in fractions. It is more a social phenomenon than a biological one that I speak of, but if you want to get technical, one-drop of Negro blood is all that is required in the South. Oakmont does not consider you white. Your suspension will remain."

I could almost hear the crack of a gavel against his desk.

Make him prove it, Dad seemed to whisper in my ear. I tried to be polite but there might have been a little growl coming into my voice. "Can I see Oakmont's policy statement? Does it mention drops of blood or percentages?" I couldn't help but over-enunciate so he could hear how

---

ridiculous it sounded. "The notary public never asked me anything like that."

His lips pressed together before he spoke. "You'll have to go to the district office for that. I'm through arguing with you, Miss Rogers. You may get your belongings from your locker and go home. Do not return tomorrow." He rose from his chair.

How was I supposed to accept that answer? He'd acted as if his opinion was as good as law. I too stood, challenging him with a look as I kept my voice controlled. "Mr. Morgrin, sir? What if I do return tomorrow?"

"Then I shall be forced to call the police to escort you away."

CHAPTER TWENTY-SIX

THE PRINCIAPAL HAD ME SCARED. Mentioning the police was a low blow. I wasn't a criminal, but he'd made me feel awful just the same. I hid my fear by walking steadily away, but after I'd rounded the nearest corner of the hallway where I couldn't be seen through the office windows, my knees buckled. I slid to the floor with my back against the wall, my elbows on my knees in an unladylike pose. I didn't cry by sheer willpower. It would make me feel beaten. This had gotten serious way too fast. But I wasn't ready to give up.

Play practice. If Principal Morgrin didn't allow me at school, I couldn't go to play practice today. Or tomorrow. Or ever. Tears pooled in my eyes now. I wiped at them furiously, telling myself it didn't mean he'd won. What was I going to do? Dad would know. It took me another minute or two, but I got up, emptied my locker, and walked home.

"What are you doing home already?" Mom asked when I walked in the front door. "Don't you have play practice?" She looked at the clock on the wall. "School isn't out yet. Are you feeling all right?"

I shook my head and dropped the sack of costumes. "Something happened, but can we talk about it when Dad gets home? I'd rather explain only once."

Gran thumped over from her easy chair. "Does it have anything to do with your presentation? I'm sure it was wonderful, wasn't it?"

"It went well." I managed a small smile. "Please, let's wait until supper."

As I headed to my room, she called after me, "Can I call you 'wonderful' as long as I don't call you 'late for supper?'" She'd tried to cheer me but the old joke lost its charm for now.

I laid on my bed and sorted through my feelings, staring at the ceiling, my fists clenching and unclenching. Melanie's letter had done this, not my little history speech. She'd stolen my chance to shine in drama. She'd ruined my life! I knew she hadn't intended all the consequences that would occur, but man! I threw my fuzzy pillow at the wall.

I was angry…but I didn't hate her. I hated the new course my life would take. I'd forgiven Melanie once, when it seemed easy, and if I couldn't forgive her again now that the consequences had come to a head, then I was a hypocrite. That wouldn't sit well with me for long. But I didn't want to think about that any longer. I would let go of my anger when I was good and ready.

I may as well have invited Gran and Mom to come watch my project for all the good keeping them away did. Gran had been my inspiration and I loved her to death. She should have been able to come. I scrunched up my face. She'd missed my performance because of my fear, but it hadn't mattered in the end. She would have loved to see me sharing her favorite story—her grandmother's story. My face smoothed out and my shoulders slumped.

I reviewed in my mind the part of that story that I hadn't been able to put into the scripted version. I'd skipped some hard parts to show a hopeful ending, but Mary had dealt with fear and shame and anger too. And forgiveness. I mustn't forget about the forgiveness.

Mary, February 1877, Maryland

Mary sat reading a passage from her beloved New Testament when she felt a chill. The embers in the fireplace glowed red but the flames had died, so she tucked the blanket on her lap in around her legs. After washing all the bedding, cooking supper, and fussing over the children, God's word was the very thing to soothe her mind at the end of a long day. She only needed a few more minutes of study before going to bed. The children were sound asleep, and perhaps Henry had drifted off as well with how hard he'd worked today.

A floorboard creaked and she looked up. Henry stood there in his nightshirt, a scowl on his face. Why had he been so crotchety lately?

"What's keeping you, woman?" he grumbled. "A man needs his wife beside him on cold nights like this. That book again?"

"I'm sorry, Henry. I just wants to finish this parable. I'll be there before you knows it."

"You'll do no such thing." Henry stomped a bare foot. "That book has come between us for the last time. You come right now."

Mary was out of patience tonight. "I said I'll be there in a minute."

Henry matched her tone. "And I said now. I put up with you leaving me every Sunday for the Lord, but I shouldn't have to wait for my wife during the week too. I am a soldier and the man of this house." He strode over and plucked the book from her fingers.

Mary gasped in surprise and then shrieked in horror as he tossed it into the fireplace. "No!" She rushed to retrieve it when Henry stepped in her path, grabbing her around the waist.

"Let me go!" She pushed his chest with her hands, but he held tight. A quick glance told her that the cover was smoldering, a gentle wisp of smoke rising. She could still save it. "Let me go! You know what it means to me."

He held on tighter. "I'm beginning to. Looks like it means more to you than I do."

The pages ignited, bursting into flame. "No!" A sob hitched in Mary's throat as she watched her first true possession go up in bright flames. Henry relaxed his hold and she slipped to her knees, sobbing into her hands.

I could hear Mark calling me to supper, rousing me from dozing off. Dad should be home. I hopped up and dashed to the dining table. He set aside the newspaper and took his seat.

Mom gave me a sympathetic look as she set a casserole down. "The school called about your suspension. Want to tell us more about it?"

"Yeah."

We said grace and I launched into the details of my day, starting with how awesome my presentation turned out and onto the part about what Principal Morgrin said to me and how I responded.

"You mean Principal Morbid," Mark deadpanned.

Dad ignored Mark and said, "That's my girl! You handled yourself quite well."

I'm glad he approved, but I needed advice. "What am I going to do?"

"You should go to school tomorrow," Mark said. "Stick it to the man!"

Gran chuckled.

I turned to Dad, waiting for his answer. He leaned back, looking thoughtful.

Mom ignored Mark and focused on Dad too. "What about the police? Is that simply a scare tactic?" she asked.

He pursed his lips. "Not necessarily. She is on suspension. He could claim disruption of the peace or trespassing. If the cops were called, they would certainly take the principal's word over a student's. She could be arrested."

Everyone heard my sharp breath and my mother's slap to her chest.

"I don't want you to get arrested," Gran said. Everyone's eyes were on her now. "But that's like Rosa Parks and those fellas eating at the Shake It Up. That's being brave, that is. There's a time and a place for it." She bobbed her head. "Um-hm."

My heart pounded. "Granny, you want me to defy the suspension?" I still wanted Dad's opinion, but Gran's was just as important.

"There's no shame in attending Pennfields instead. You're the one who has to figure out if you can live with being brave enough to fight it. It's not for everyone. You don't go about it stupidly either. Don't go in seeking to disrupt the peace or making a fuss for the cops. You make your point in the most respectful way possible so you can gain respect back. No sticking it to the man." She wagged a finger at Mark, who grinned with his mouth full of food.

What Granny said made sense. "Yeah." I felt like eating, and took a bite of the cheese-topped whipped potatoes.

Dad leaned in again. "That's what you did in the principal's office. You were brave and respectful."

I frowned. "But I didn't really make a point."

Mark waved his fork. "Because he didn't give you a school policy or enough information to make a point. There was no proof to contradict." He took another shovelful of shepherd's pie. Mark could be a pain but sometimes his genius came out.

My enthusiasm surged. "There needs to be a point to my suspension. It's not like a punishment to get a student to change. There's nothing I can change about my ancestry." I looked at Gran and splayed my hands. "Not that I want to."

She chuckled at that.

"It's the policy that needs to be suspended, not me."

Dad nodded.

I took a drink of milk and worked through what point I needed to make. "I'm going to school tomorrow."

"Groovy!" Mark said. "Wish I could be there to see it."

"There won't be much to see, and hopefully the police won't show up. I have an idea. Dad, I need your newspaper, and I need to make a phone call."

CHAPTER TWENTY-SEVEN

THE YOUNG PHOTOGRAPHER THAT WAS at the Homecoming dance met me at the corner where Mark and I split off to go to our separate schools. "Good luck," Mark said as I turned toward the photographer.

"Hi Mr. Wadsworth. I'm Charlotte, the one who called you."

The photographer shook my hand with a good, firm grip. He was kind of cute, with light brown hair and black glasses, and not much taller than me. "Thanks for the opportunity. Call me Scott."

"You're welcome, Scott. Please remember, you're here if there's anything newsworthy that happens. We're not starting a fuss on our own."

"Got it."

I looked him over. He had a boyish grin, perhaps fresh out of college, with hair as long as our school allowed. The camera hanging around his neck would be a dead giveaway that he didn't belong. That made two of us. I noticed he sported a backpack where he could stash his camera and blend in.

We approached the front of the school. Not a cop car in site. So far so good. "I know you said you could spare all day, but I hope I'm not wasting your time. On the other hand, I don't really want to see a cop on the other side of those doors either."

"Be prepared," Scott said. "The motto works for Boy Scouts, reporters, and apprehensive students."

I appreciated his easy manner with a half-smile. I looked for Jake, who was meeting me out front today instead of at my locker. He wasn't here yet. I'd called him last night to get him up to speed. It was sweet, his offering protection and all.

Melanie's groupies, Gina and Ellen, spotted us. "Hey, Charlotte, who's your friend?" Gina asked in a flirty manner.

Ellen fluffed her hair. "You can take my picture."

I waved the idea away. "He's only here for a school project."

Ellen showed me her pouty lip. "Come off it. Your school project was yesterday. I'm in your class, remember?"

"I heard you got in trouble for it," Gina said, wide-eyed. "Got sent to see the principal."

I neither confirmed nor denied. "Who cares about yesterday?"

Jake burst through the front doors toward me, fighting the crowd. "Hi." He gave me my usual peck on the cheek. "I've checked out the foyer and commons area already. I think you're safe from Morgrin." He glanced at Scott. "So this is the guy that's documenting for you?"

"Only if need be. Scott Wadsworth, *Palmetto Peaks Press*." He offered his hand to Jake and I introduced my boyfriend.

We kept an eye out for Principal Morgrin as we joined the crowd entering the school. Apparently he'd expected my obedience because he was nowhere in sight.

I moved to the side of the front doors when we reached them. "Thanks, Scott. I feel bad that you came so early for nothing."

"Are you kidding me? You're a big story, even if not today. I'm the one who will get it, thanks to you. That piece I did from the dance generated extra sales all week long from the opinions page. My boss was as pleased as a palmetto swaying in the breeze. Your story will double that. I guarantee it. I'll go with you to see if your first period teacher lets you attend. Then I'll meet you outside the cafeteria at lunch—if nobody stops me."

"Great."

Jake and Scott walked me to my first class a little early, both wanting to make sure I was okay before leaving me.

"Charlotte!" Mrs. Burkhart said, her head pulling back in shock. "I got a notice that you would not be in school starting today. I'm surprised to see you. What's up?"

"Yes, ma'am. I'm declining Mr. Morgrin's offer of suspension on the basis of prejudice and poor school policy. I'd like to be in class today please, if you don't mind."

"Oh, dear! I hope that doesn't cause any more trouble for you."

"I don't intend it to."

"Poor school policy, huh?" Her mouth twitched. "In that case, I must tell you that if you were to sit among us, it would in no way be construed as me encouraging your presence here. Understand? This could have serious consequences."

I smiled, though her look had turned serious again. "Yes, ma'am. Thank you, ma'am." I waved goodbye to Scott, who watched from outside the doorway.

"I might also be talking to myself right now," she said without looking at me. "I'm remembering lunch in the teacher's lounge yesterday where Mr. Dodd and I discussed the possibility of three student presentations with the quality and educational value worthy of a student assembly."

My eyes bugged. "Really?"

Her beaming faded, and then she sighed. "A certain issue will need to be resolved first. I doubt now if we can get Principal Morgrin's support for one of them."

Melanie entered with Ellen, looking right at me. "Ellen said you have a photographer."

"Photographer?" Mrs. B put a hand on her hip and her other grabbed her chin. "Charlotte, this sounds like trouble. Do you know what you're doing?"

"Yes, ma'am." At least I hoped so.

Second hour didn't go so well. My math teacher wouldn't admit me into class. I respected his position, like I'd decided ahead of time, and left. Besides, he said he would report me if I stayed. I hid outside, sitting down with my back against a wing of the school where the drug addicts didn't hangout, thinking and picking little pieces of grass until I heard the bell. Time to try again.

Third period was drama. I was a little nervous facing Mr. Dodd because of the likelihood of him having to replace me as Mrs. Paroo. I still hoped it would work out.

Mr. Dodd rushed to me as soon as I entered. "Charlotte!" I was afraid he might hug me. "You're here! Does this mean you can still do the play? I was so upset this morning with that note in my box and only three weeks until the play. Did you get reinstated?"

"No, sir. Technically I'm not supposed to be here. I'm trying to work it out. Can the play be considered an outside-of-school activity since practice is after school?"

John came in and stood next to me, his face scrunched in confusion as he watched.

"Oh dear. Hm." Mr. Dodd mumbled something, frowning. It wasn't like him not to enunciate. "Doubtful, but I'll check on it as a general question—without mentioning your name."

"Thank you, sir." I bit my bottom lip. "I really want to do it if I can, but I suppose you should get me an understudy…just in case."

"You're not going to be in the play?" John asked, horror written his face.

Mr. Dodd ignored him. "How can I get someone to master that Irish brogue like you did?" He sighed in exasperation. "Technically, I should report your presence, but I'll do it non-verbally. I'll mark you as absent and not turn it in to the attendance office until the end of the day. You be careful, Charlotte. I recommend you don't return tomorrow. I shall call your home as soon as I get an answer on the question about the play."

"Yes, sir."

John followed me to my seat. "What's going on? You cut play practice yesterday and now you're talking about an understudy?"

I didn't like telling him. "Principal Morgrin put me on suspension."

He snorted. "You? On suspension? You'll have to do better than that." His face fell when I didn't laugh. "Really?"

I nodded. "I'm not supposed to be here. Just crashing the party." He didn't smile. I whispered, "It's a question of whether or not I'm white enough to be a student here."

John put his arm around my shoulder and patted my back. "Oh, Charlotte. I'm sorry." He released me and sad puppy dog eyes stared back. "Sounds like you need a miracle."

"I know." He almost had me crying. Drama class was supposed to be fun. Not today.

I wasn't certain I had the stomach to attend fourth hour but I'd resolved to finish out the day as planned, seeing what responses I got. My English teacher simply dismissed me with his arm extended toward the door. It took him all of three words to make his point known. "Out, Miss Rogers." I wasn't making a point at all this way.

Jake waited at my locker right before lunch, looking relieved to see me. I couldn't muster my usual enthusiasm in return. I felt a little better when we found Scott.

Jake tried to give me an out. "I have a friend who will let us ride with him to McDonald's if you want to avoid Mr. Morgrin."

"Or I could take you," Scott offered.

I shook my head. "No. The whole morning has been slow. I need to make something happen."

Scott perked up. "So you want to make a fuss now?"

Jake looked worried. "Like what?"

"No. I don't know. Let me think about it while we get our lunch trays."

Scott made a face. "Is your school's food as gross as I remember mine being?"

"Yes," I said at the same time Jake said, "No." I gave Scott one of my lunch tickets. "My treat. I hope you don't die."

"It's the chicken-fried special," Jake said. "Your lucky day."

Scott took the ticket. "Do I need a student ID number or anything?"

"Nope," I answered. "Just a ticket. Anyone with a ticket gets food. The lunch ladies won't know I'm on suspension."

Melanie, Ellen, and Gina were already at our table with Brad and Patty. They stared at Scott as we brought our food to the table. Ellen batted her eyes at him. "Hanging around so you can shoot me?"

"High school," he muttered softly. He smiled at the girls and his normal volume resumed. "I would like to shoot something today."

"So he's the photographer?" Melanie asked. "Yearbook stuff?"

Scott looked like his smile was forced. "No. It's school district research for Charlotte."

Ugh. He'd passed further questions back to me.

I'd attended first hour with her so Melanie didn't know I was suspended. Hardly anybody knew. Nothing worth mentioning had happened yet. I needed to make some kind of point out of my being here. It could be a school project of sorts.

I looked around. Not a teacher in sight. Only the lunch ladies. I grabbed my fork and glass and stood on the bench. "Hey everyone! Attention, please." I tapped my fork against the glass cup. People quieted and stared at me. I wasn't disturbing the peace; I was interrupting the noise. "Attention, please. I have an important announcement."

"Groovy. You inviting us all to a Halloween party?" somebody drawled. A few more people looked my way.

Scott moved quickly, whipping his camera out of the bag, setting one knee down on the floor, and aiming his big, silver flash attachment up at me. It went off with a poof like mini-explosion that temporarily blinded me. The bright flash turned the attention toward me more than anything.

One of the lunch ladies yelled for me to get down, so I did. The majority of students were seated so they could see me standing. A few ignored me, and somebody called out, "Who does she think she is?" My mind answered that I'm Mary's great-great-granddaughter. Not everyone had to know that part yet, but they would.

"I'm doing a survey for a school project. How many of y'all would be open to accepting colored students at Oakmont? Come on. Raise your hands. I need a count." I elbowed Jake and he stood to take a tally. Melanie decided to be helpful on her own. A few arms raised.

"What's with the photographer?" somebody yelled.

"Ignore him. He won't take your picture." I shot him a glance and he sat back down on the bench. A few more arms raised, but the amount was clearly in the minority.

"Thank you. Now, how many want to keep Oakmont the way it is?" Jake and Melanie counted again. About double the previous amount.

Another choice came to mind. "Thanks. How many don't know or need time to think about it?" The largest number of hands shot into the air as one of the lunch ladies marched out from behind the metal counter.

"How many don't care?" A boy shouted and then laughed.

There were more questions I'd like to ask, but the kids were getting bored fast and I could see a lunch lady marching toward me. "Sorry, ma'am," I told her as I swung a leg over the bench. "I'll eat my lunch now." I picked up my fork.

A couple of people laughed at me as she glared and said, "We have rules here. I should kick you out!"

"I'll behave. Scouts honor." I held up three fingers like Mark does at Scouts, and took a bite of fruit cocktail using my other hand. I smiled as I chewed.

Her tight mouth relaxed a bit as she shook a finger at me. "No funny business. I'll be watching. The principal will hear about this." She turned on her heal and the normal chatter instantly returned. My eating something had won her over. Barely.

My survey wasn't scientific or private, but at least I'd introduced a certain topic. That might be the best I could do today.

"Good start," Scott said. "Now what?"

Melanie handed me a torn piece of paper with some numbers on it. "Yeah. What are you doing? I thought you were hiding your secret but you're stirring things up."

Curious expressions surrounded me. I hadn't told Patty what happened, though Jake must have told her and Brad the basics. "I'm not supposed to be in school today. I'm on suspension for breaking Oakmont policy. Morgrin doesn't think I'm white."

Gina's eyes bugged out. "No way!"

"Why did you come to school then?" Brad asked.

Gina nodded. "Yeah? I wouldn't."

Ellen crinkled her nose. "Aren't you white? Not that I care," she added when the whole table cocked their heads at her.

Scott jotted down a few notes.

"I'm making the point that this policy is wrong, and I'm seeing where we are with the student body." I looked down at my food tray getting cold.

Jake smoothed his hand over my back and gave it a pat. "You did well. That was brave, and I'm proud of you. We'll get a bigger reaction from adults than the students."

His touch soothed, but really I liked that he used 'we'.

"Maybe we visit the district office next," he added.

Scott tapped his nose and then pointed at Jake. My silent partner had an opinion.

I trusted Scott's assessment that I needed to think bigger. "Yeah, I need to grab a copy of that policy and see when the board meets next. We could go to city hall and find out what is required for a petition or picket signs." I shrugged like it was a question. Was that too much?

"Sure." Patty waved at Scott's notebook. "You take notes while we brainstorm. We need a plan."

'We' again. I loved my friends. Strange how that included Melanie and her counterparts. Nice to have them on my side.

My stomach rumbled. I popped a hush puppy into my mouth. It was okay cold, but I wasn't touching the gross-looking cold meat patty. I chugged the fruit cup and opened the milk carton to go with the cookie. Everyone started spouting ideas from getting an article in the school newspaper to something related to Halloween on Thursday.

Scott held up a finger. "There's one problem. I can't take Charlotte as the only one in my car. I need another volunteer."

"Company policy?" Jake asked.

Scott shook his head. "Her mom's."

Patty chuckled.

Jake turned to me. "Wish I could go but I have a test next period."

"I'll go," Melanie said. "I'll get somebody's notes for health and then it's only study hall for me to miss. I'm not cleared for PE yet so nobody will care."

I looked at her with wonder.

She lifted a shoulder. "Sue and Mary have to stick together."

That did my heart good. "Thanks."

Brad lifted a leg over the bench. "The first bell is about to ring. Anything else you need today, Charlotte?"

"I don't think s—" I ducked my head. "Quick! Hide me from Principal Morgrin. He's coming this way!"

Seven heads turned to look at the same time, like a neon sign showing him where to focus. His red cheeks puffed out and he picked up his pace from across the room. "I see you Miss Rogers. Stay right where you are!"

"C'mon." Scott led the way for me and Melanie to follow him.

Brad, Patty, and Jake made a barrier of sorts with their bodies. Mr. Morgrin still had to navigate around tables and students to get to our table while three of us slipped away toward another exit. I saw movement from Ellen out of the corner of my eye. She approached him, stepping directly in front of his path. I could hear her voice. "Hey, Mr. Morgrin. There's something I need you to tell those lunch ladies for me."

"Out of my way!" his voice boomed. "Where did she go? Ah!" He'd spotted us again.

I heard a lunch tray clatter to the floor and a man's voice bellowing, "Awk! Ow!"

Patty spoke up quickly. "Oops. Sorry, Principal Morgrin! Someone bumped me."

Students were sniggering, but I couldn't look back. The last thing I heard was Brad saying, "We'll help you up, Mr. Morgrin."

Man, I wish I could have seen that!

We hightailed it to Scott's car and Melanie and I collapsed with laughter in the back seat as my newsman screeched out of the parking lot.

CHAPTER TWENTY-EIGHT

"YOU CAN'T GO BACK TO school tomorrow," Melanie said from the back of Scott's car as soon as we got serious. "Morgrin will have a cow."

"I know. He'll call the cops for sure. Probably have them waiting for me."

"Like he wishes he had done this morning." We shared another small giggle fit.

Scott parked at the curb in front of the school district office. "I'll wait here," he told us. Had he tired of our laughter?

"I have to do something though," I said, opening the building door. "I can't let them decide my fate without putting up a fight."

"I know." Melanie's voice sobered. "I'm sorry you have to go through all this. I'm so sorry I sent that letter."

"I know. It's okay. You've been forgiven, remember?" I gave her a warm smile.

I approached the receptionist. She had a little bowl of Halloween candy on the counter right in front of me, but I resisted. I had only one purpose in mind. "Do you have a printed school policy for Oakmont High and a schedule for when the school board meets? I'd like two of those, please."

She looked at me longer than needed, and then went to a file drawer. "Here you go." She handed the papers over. "And here's the form to register. New students must fill it out and verify their race in front of a notary public."

I'd already done that. Back when I wanted to blend in and not rock the boat. If it weren't for the fact that I would no longer have a superb drama program and I'd miss my friends like crazy, a little boat-rocking sounded exactly like what Oakmont needed. "Thanks."

Once outside, I muttered, "Verify their race. Fiddlesticks. There's only one race—the human race."

Melanie stopped right there on the sidewalk and set her hands on top of her head. "That's the perfect slogan!"

"What are you talking about?"

"That slogan would look great on a protest sign, but a *sweeter* approach would get more attention. That Halloween candy in there gave me an idea." She explained it to me as we walked to the car, and I found it to be the perfect next step. I gave Scott the extra copy of the policy and schedule.

"Thanks," he said. "There might be a good quote in there I can use."

I hated asking Scott for more favors, but Melanie had a good plan. "Can you take us to the library next? We need to make some copies, and they'll have a typewriter and mimeo or ditto machine."

He rolled his eyes, then smiled. "Sure, why not. It's a good thing this has potential for a great scoop."

Melanie turned to me. "The five and dime store is across from the library. I'll go there while you make the copies. How much money do you have on you?"

I dug into the zipped compartment of my backpack to find some leftover birthday money. "Eight dollars and eighty-three cents."

"Give me your five. You'll need the rest for copies. I have ten I can put in."

I shook my head. Was she still trying to make amends or simply being a friend? "I can't ask you to—"

Melanie held up a hand. "Don't mention it. This will be fun!"

"What are you girls cooking up?" Scott asked, breaking into our bonding.

I glanced at Melanie, who zipped her lips with her fingers. I liked having it be a secret. "You'll have to come to the school at 7:30 tomorrow morning to find out."

Granny hobbled to the kitchen table to see me and Melanie cutting little slips of paper from the ditto sheets that I quickly typed at the library and ran off on the machine's drum. "One Race: the HUMAN Race. Stop Segregation." She looked at me. "What's all this?" She looked at Melanie. "And who's this?"

"Gran, this is my friend Melanie. She goes to Oakmont." I enthusiastically explained our idea, sniffing the sweet smell of the cookies Mom had put in the oven, which added to my good mood.

Granny peeked into my bag and sat down at the table. "That's a mountain of candy. Looks like y'all could use some help."

I showed her how to wrap the paper slip around the candy bar and tape it on the back. She copied my example and said, "Are you in drama too, Melanie?"

"No, ma'am. We have History and PE together."

Gran reached for a piece of tape. "I know why Charlotte wanted to go to Oakmont, but why did you choose that uppity school?"

I laughed. "She means no offense. She calls it like she sees it."

"None taken." Melanie pursed her lips. "You know? I really don't know. We always assumed I'd go there—my family and me."

"Like most other whites." Gran sighed. "It's not your fault you followed the norm. It's the norm that's twisted. Been that way for centuries." She shook her head. "Separate but equal? My foot. If the city was fixing to incorporate constitutionality by having an integrated high school, why didn't they open up Oakmont instead of Pennfields? I'll tell you why. They still want segregation." She left it hanging in my mind as we both reached for another candy bar. We all sat quiet for a while.

Mom brought over a plate of snickerdoodles and a letter in her other hand. "It got mighty quiet in here. Is your granny behaving herself?"

I quirked a half-smile and took a bite of cookie, the taste of sweetened cinnamon delighting my tongue.

"There's mail for you, Charlotte. From the school board." Mom plopped the envelope down in front of me and looked over my shoulder. I pushed the cookie away.

Melanie groaned and put her head in her hands. "Of all the days for me to be here! It's all my fault."

"You're supposed to quit apologizing once you've been forgiven."
I slid my finger under the seal. Mom and Gran hovered.

"Dear Miss Rogers," I began. "It has come to the attention of the
school board that you are attending Oakmont High under fraudulent
circumstances. Therefore, we hereby revoke your eligibility. Your records
will be transferred to Pennfields High, where you are expected to attend
as soon as this is received. Please report to the school office on or before
Friday, November 1st." I looked up. "Sheesh, that's in three days!"

I continued reading aloud. "They will give you your schedule,
which we have matched appropriately to your current courses so that you
may have an undisrupted educational transition."

"Ha!" I said without humor. "That doesn't mean they can match
the drama program or teachers like Mrs. B."

Mom put a hand on my shoulder. "I know. Honey, I'm sorry."

"Yeah," Melanie said. "And what about your social or emotional
transition? Do they care about that too? And your chance to be in plays
and earn drama awards. I'd like to write a different kind of letter."

I shook my head. "It won't do any good. Their minds are made
up."

Only Granny smiled. "That gives us a few days to figure things out
and complete your initial plans. Good thing you're starting on it already.
Let's get cracking." She grabbed another candy bar.

"What else does it say?" Mom asked.

"Uh…" I scanned the rest. "School address, blah, blah, blah.
Signed by a board member."

"Are you okay?" Melanie asked.

"Yeah. We knew this was coming. They don't know that I'm
fighting their decision. Gran is right. Let's get cracking."

Four hundred mini candy bars and a roll of tape later, dad pulled
into the driveway. "C'mon. Let's meet him before he cuts the engine." We
raced to the carport and he cranked his window down. "Hi Dad. Can I use
your car to take my friend Melanie home?"

He stepped out of the car, leaving the engine running. "Okay, but
come right back. No dawdling." He gave me a hug and shook Melanie's
hand. "Nice to meet you, Melanie."

After supper I stretched the long kitchen phone cord around the corner into the living room and sat on the couch with my feet tucked under me. I spoke with Jake, then Brad, and then dialed Patty to enlist their help the next morning. Melanie had said she would call Ellen and Gina. I knew they would do whatever she asked of them. All seven of us ought to get the job done in good time.

When I talked to Patty, she had an odd, higher-pitched whine in her voice.

"Why are you using Melanie's idea anyway? I'll bet we could come up with a better one on our own."

"She's trying to make amends, and it's a good idea on short notice. Besides, it's already done. We bought the candy, attached the notes and everything."

"So Melanie was at your house wrapping those candy bars clear until supper? Why didn't you call me to come over? I would've helped."

I could hear the pout in her tone. How could my best friend be jealous? I'd only spent one afternoon with Melanie. I appreciated that Melanie wanted to be my friend but we weren't best buddies. Melanie had given up her Jake obsession enough to become nice, and she wanted to help. She was cool with me now.

"I know you would've, but I didn't know if you could get a ride and I couldn't stop to come get you. We were truckin'. Granny too."

Patty was silent. I had to lighten things up. "Besides, I didn't want to torture you with all that tempting chocolate."

"Right. Like you didn't indulge?" Her playful voice returned.

"Mom baked snickerdoodles. I did have to do one chocolate quality control check though." That was before reading the letter.

"I knew it!"

"You can have one tomorrow. I'll bring you some snickerdoodles too. Hey, what happened in the cafeteria after I left?"

"Man, you missed a good show! I bumped into him with my lunch tray and he slipped on the milk I spilled. It was crowded but I didn't exactly need to be pushed, if you know what I mean."

"You didn't! What a friend."

"I did. Food went flying! Brad and Jake offered to help Mr. Morgrin up but he refused to take their hands. He didn't trust anybody. It was hilarious watching him get up off the floor with his cheeks red and puffing. Students everywhere were sniggering and he scowled at everybody. He dusted off the food on his shirt and marched away. Then some kid did a hilarious slip-on-a-banana-peel routine, faked slipping, and scrambled awkwardly to get up like Morgrin did. The whole room roared with laughter. The janitor and three teachers came into the lunch room right before the end-of-lunch bell. Now there's all kinds of rumors going around about why you're in trouble. Melanie too."

I frowned. Too many people had seen us running away. "Like what?"

"Everything from poisoning the food on the lunch tray to lingerie modeling for that photographer."

"You've got to be kidding! There goes my rep. How can people believe stuff like that?" I clamped my jaw and squeezed my eyes shut. "Stupid idiots!"

"I know. I'm sorry." Patty paused, either letting her sympathetic vibe soothe me or waiting to see if I would freak out some more. "It'll blow over," she added. "Just wait."

I huffed. I didn't have time to wait. I needed to gather people on my side right now. The gossip would probably escalate overnight and be worse tomorrow. Would they alienate me when we passed out the candy tomorrow? And poor Melanie. She would face the gossip all day long in every class. What a nightmare!

I must have been thinking too long because Patty asked, "You alright?"

Not really; my anger had shifted to self-pity. "I'll be okay." I didn't want to be a downer so I perked up my voice. Drama practice came in handy sometimes. "I'll see you in the morning for the candy handout and we'll solve this thing."

"It'll be good. Wait and see. Bye."

More waiting. Lovely.

Well, what did I expect? That I could buy the whole student body off with chocolate to instantly forget anything bad about me they might have heard? For them to agree with my message and flood the next school board meeting with their support? To have Mr. Morgrin think of my presence at school today as showing initiative and perseverance?

That I could actually make a difference?

I rubbed my hands over my face and sighed. I stood, about to go to bed early, hoping my problems would disappear overnight, when the phone rang. It made me jump. I picked up the receiver. "Hello?"

"Charlotte Rogers, please." A man's solemn voice. A school board member? Mr. Morgrin? The phone started to feel slippery in my hand, and I cursed my sweaty palms.

"This is Charlotte."

"Hi. This is Mr. Dodd. I've been trying to reach you all evening but your line has been busy." He sounded formal over the phone. My heart pounded.

"I checked into it and I'm afraid there's no way you can be in the play without being a student at Oakmont. I'm sorry, Charlotte. It's disappointing for us both. I do hope you'll come watch it."

"Uh…thanks." I thanked him for the terrible news?

"Goodbye." I heard a click.

I hadn't really counted on that slim chance, but now that it was final, the slash in my dreams reopened to evaporate any drop of hope left inside me. The vessel now empty and dried up. Only my tear ducts could produce anything. I went to my room, shut the door, and sobbed into my pillow until there was nothing left to cry out.

CHAPTER TWENTY-NINE

I HADN'T SET MY ALARM, but a thump from Mark's room woke me. I stretched and quickly sat up, remembering my plan with the candy bars. Was I ready for this? Would it be worth it? I stepped into my slippers. The police would certainly be there. But so would Scott. I had to go through with it.

Dad poked his head in my partially open door. "Better skedaddle. It's a big day, and your friends will be waiting for you."

Gran hummed from somewhere down the hall. I pictured her wrapping candy bars and telling me and Melanie stories of the olden days. Those wrappers were meant to convey the idea of one race, whether or not they got me back into Oakmont. I had a mission.

I dressed in a white blouse and red plaid skirt and put on some mascara. At breakfast, Dad said, "I'll drive you. Your mom and I talked it over. I'll watch from my car to make sure nothing gets out of hand."

The butter knife in my hand hovered over my toast. "Do you think something will happen?"

"Not if you stay off school property. Those officers will be looking for trouble, but there's no law against handing out candy. Folks do it all the time at Halloween. Make sure you stay on the sidewalk and off school and personal property. No trespassing."

I nodded. "I'll remind my friends."

"I can help for fifteen minutes before I have to go," Mark offered.

I narrowed my eyes. "Just don't eat any. We worked hard on those."

He splayed his hands, shrinking back like I'd hurt his feelings. Mediocre acting at best.

"I'm right proud of you, Charlotte," Gran said. "Tell me all about it when you come home."

I cracked a smile. "You got it."

Without a ride from Dad, I would have been late to my own party. Grabbing the bags of candy, Mark and I piled into the car and headed toward the school.

I could see two cop cars parked at the school-side curb. No lights, no noise. Scott paced the sidewalk across the street with his camera hanging from his neck. Brad stood nearby. Patty's family car approached from the opposite direction. Jake would arrive on one of the earliest buses and Melanie, Ellen, and Gina should be here any minute. We could really make an impact today. A thrill tingled my spine.

Dad dropped us off and parked.

"Good morning," Scott said. His lips pursed in amusement. "What's black and white and red all over?"

If he was trying to loosen us up with a joke, he should have picked a better one. "I know that one. A newspaper. Hopefully the article you write for tonight's paper will be read all over the county."

"That too, but no. It's you!" He laughed at the confusion on my face.

Mark and Brad took in my black shoes, white blouse, and red skirt and chuckled.

I rolled my eyes. "Ha, ha." A deeper meaning about my skin color came to mind and I wondered if he'd meant that too. Surely not offensively. Not from Scott. If you asked me, I was pale—not black or white, not checkerboard or striped. We all had red blood running through our veins, even the so-called blue-bloods with money. One race—the human race. I quickly handed a bag to Brad and Mark, my thoughts circling back to our purpose.

Patty arrived with a homemade sign reading, "Candy for a Cause."

"Clever girl." I handed her a sack with candy. It looked like her sister had done her hair—teased to rounded perfection. I guessed Patty had prepared to appear in the newspaper.

Time for instructions. "Remember that we can't trespass. Students must come to us for their candy. You can shout anything to encourage them in a peaceful way. No arrests. Got it?"

212

They all nodded. A couple of cars entered the half-filled employee parking lot, and one car pulled up close to us. Melanie and her entourage got out of the back seat. "This is so exciting!" Melanie gushed.

Principal Morgrin came out of the front doors and glared at our gathering group on the sidewalk across the street. Maybe he thought our army would grow past this handful. He approached the nearest cop car, motioned the officer out of his car and pointed at us. We couldn't hear the discussion but the officer glanced right at me.

I held my bag forward. "We've got chocolate, sir, if you'd like some."

Patty elbowed me. "Good one."

"Was that meant for the cop or the principal?" Brad asked.

Patty answered for me. "Doesn't matter. We're an equal opportunity establishment." She laughed.

"Hey," Mark said. "That's a good idea. We should do this at Pennfields too."

I patted his head. "Such a smart boy. He takes after me." I got a couple chuckles from it.

Mark's lips buzzed as he gave me an eye-roll. "No, I got all the brains."

"Here comes the first bus," Gina said, pointing. It pulled into the front semi-circular turn around. Another yellow bus could be seen down the street. The other cop got out of his car.

"Candy for a cause!" I yelled. My helpers followed suit.

We didn't have to convince the students too hard. Jake led the pack our way, saying, "See? I told you trick-or-treat had arrived."

Apparently Jake had talked it up on the bus. I should pat him on the head too. No, I should kiss him. What great friends I had!

Scott started snapping photos.

Mr. Morgrin pointed at him. "You there! Go home. There's nothing newsworthy here."

Scott pointed the camera at the principal, and then must have thought better of it. Mr. Morgrin shot him a murderous look.

"Get back," Mr. Morgrin yelled at the students clamoring for candy, his arm furiously motioning them toward the school. "Let the cops handle it." This deterred a handful, but when they saw that others could get a small candy bar and then return without interference, they opted to ignore the principal.

The second bus began unloading. "What's going on?" someone said. "What's with the cops?"

Charlotte and her friends called, "C'mon over. Get your free candy bar."

The students were curious and could see that the first busload came back with something edible. Many crossed the street, careful to avoid the increasing traffic.

"Get away from them! You'll get hit by a car." Mr. Morgrin shouted. He turned toward one officer. "Do something!"

The officer stepped out into the street and began directing traffic in favor of the cars. A bunch of students piled up on the school-side curb, waiting to cross. The buildup with Mr. Morgrin and the police there seemed to make the students' desire to participate stronger than it might have been.

"Hey. No fair!"

"Yeah. It's our turn."

"We want chocolate!"

The officer ignored the student protests and continued waving the cars on. The other cop stepped onto the street and held his hands out to discourage students.

"What are we going to do?" Brad asked.

He was about twenty feet away from me but I could hear him over the crowd. "Keep cool," I shouted back. I didn't have a plan beyond that. We only had ten or twelve minutes before the first bell rang, and three-fourths of my share still sat in the bag.

Mark came over to give me the rest of his. "I have to go. See ya. Hope you don't die."

"Thanks, Mark." I said it sarcastically but his support had actually touched me. "I won't," I called after him. "See you later."

A chant started within the group at the curb. "Chocolate! Chocolate!"

Students pushed onto the street. They swarmed past the closest officer, who blew his whistle repeatedly. Cars in the street honked and had to stop. They also kept the last bus from turning into the circular drive.

The officer in the middle of the street found he'd lost control of directing traffic. Out of safety, he switched to hold up a hand to the vehicles and waved the students across. Mr. Morgrin started yelling again.

Groups flocked to one or the other of my little army. Nature had taken her course. We didn't have to do anything except hand out candy and repeat the message. "One race. The Human race. Stop segregation. One race…"

A few of the students picked up the chant. One girl came up close, called me a name, and shook a fist at me. I drew back, holding in an extra-long breath before another girl asked for chocolate. I kept offering candy but *man* her vibe affected me. I wanted to keep my head down but I forced myself to be outwardly pleasant. Would anyone else do something like that?

The last bus made its way into the unloading zone, and along with those arriving from the parking lot or getting dropped off, the last of the students came over to check out the commotion. My paper bag felt light, but I supposed that was a good thing. We didn't need any leftovers. I held one above my head. "Candy bars for a cause. Get 'em 'til they're gone."

Scott was right there with his camera in my face. He'd crouched down and got the shot looking up. "Far out. What a quote." He stood up and I didn't hear any more flashes pop. He must have used a whole roll of film already, hopefully getting some good ones.

Mr. Morgrin kept shouting, this time about the candy bar wrappers littering the school grounds.

My last chocolate bar went to a guy who snatched it out from under a girl's reach. "Hey, ladies first," she complained.

I pointed to Patty. "She's still got some."

The first bell rang and the students that were outside headed in. Mr. Morgrin held the door open, his mouth in a tight line. For a second, I almost felt sorry for him. He suffered some humiliation too. This wasn't personal against him. It hit me how much bigger my cause was. Could I really make a dent with things like handing out slogans on candy? Were students really my target audience?

Jake came over and gave me a quick kiss—this time on the mouth. Technically we weren't at school. "That was far out," he said. "I'll call you later after I see the newspaper."

The paper. That's where we would really reached people.

I waved as he skipped backward and then turned. "Bye," I said to his back. I watched everyone leave me standing there. Such a weird feeling—stuck between success and loneliness.

Scott suddenly appeared at my side. "That went well. You walking home?"

"No. That's my dad's car," I said, pointing. "But thanks. Thanks for coming. Your article will reach a lot of locals."

"My pleasure. You got a next step yet?"

I nodded. "I got on the agenda to speak at the school board meeting next week."

"Fab. I'll be there."

I started picking up a few torn wrappers in the street and stuffing them into my empty bag as dad started his engine. As I reached the middle of the street, one of the cops said, "You don't want to get any closer. We have orders to arrest you if you set one foot onto school property."

"Oh." I backed up.

"You're lucky we don't cite you for the litter," the other cop said. He had his thumbs hooked through his belt loop. A holster sat on one hip and a nightstick on the other. I opened my mouth, ready to say something about me not doing any of the littering but decided I better keep it peaceful.

Dad pulled up beside me. My knight in shining four-wheeled armor. I was never so glad to get into his car.

The day dragged on as I waited for the newspaper to come. I couldn't wait to see the article and judge the reaction we might get from it. I would base my next course of action on what it inspired me to do. Gran had given me something to think about, and I lay on my bed pondering it.

"Why not go to Pennfields for a while 'til this thing clears up?" she'd said. "Or at least get an education if it doesn't. Do some comparing. Arm yourself with facts. See how the other students deal with it. Then you'll sound like you know what you're talking about at that school board meeting." I found it good counsel.

Gran poked her head into my room. "Did you call in and get yourself on the agenda?"

"Yes, I did that yesterday. They had to call me back with their answer. They're going to give me five minutes next Tuesday night. It makes me wonder if they hope to make an example out of me for the future."

"Maybe. You can do a lot with five minutes. Use it well."

Good advice. I should think more positively like Gran does. I needed to write up a speech but I wasn't sure what to say yet. Maybe I needed a few days at Pennfields first. The sooner the better.

Granny's point made sense. I needed to stay on track and graduate with my class, even if I wouldn't be able to get a drama scholarship. Besides, I'd been bored skipping school today without my friends. I hated the idea of starting a new school twice within two months almost as much as I hated not being in the play. Ugh. *Quit being a baby.* Nothing would change in time for me to be in the fall play. I may as well continue at Pennfields and have something to compare against Oakmont.

My mind had won the fight with my heart.

After school had let out, I put on a sweater and sat in the rocker on the front porch out of the drizzling rain to watch for the newspaper boy. After a while, Gran came out to claim the other rocker. We sat in companionable silence until I saw a boy across the street on his bicycle with a canvas pack hanging on his shoulders. "Here he comes!"

It took five agonizing minutes for him to get to my house. At least his aim was good; I didn't have to fetch it in the rain. I picked up the paper and sat down. Gran leaned toward me. "It's not on the front page," I said to myself as much as her. I turned each page and scanned the contents. "There it is! Front page of the Education section."

"Well, look at you!" Granny chuckled.

Scott had used that last photo he shot—the one looking up at me with a candy bar raised in the air. "Candy for a Cause," the bolded caption read. "Sophomore Charlotte Rogers treats students at Oakmont to candy in hopes that they will read her message: One Race: the HUMAN Race. Stop Segregation."

We read the article together. It matter-of-factly stated that I was on suspension and ordered to attend Pennfields High for breaking Oakmont policy. The next paragraph mentioned my crusade to be reinstated at Oakmont, beginning with this morning's 'Candy for a Cause' campaign, along with seven helpers. "Rogers says it shouldn't matter what percent of her blood is white; segregation is illegal, and she should be accepted at any school she chooses." I read that line proudly.

"Uh-huh," Gran agreed, bobbing her head. "That goes for anyone. If he hadn't put that, I would call him up myself and tell him he should have."

There were probably a lot of should haves throughout Gran's life.

"Gran, I'm sorry if anything I did has made you feel bad. I wish I'd invited you to the school to see my history project. I wish I hadn't been worried about you sitting with us in church. I wish things could be different."

She reached over, patted my hand, and kept it warm for a moment. "I wish they could too, honey. We all have to feel our way through new situations and we make a few choices along the way that we might regret, but that don't mean we love one another any less. Child, you should know that I'm right proud of you." She pointed to the newspaper. "Look at all you've done, making a stand and going up against the school board. That takes some guts, that does."

My lips pressed tightly to minimize my smile. "Thanks, Gran. I love you."

"I know." She set the rocker back into motion.

I took my cue, picking up reading where we left off. "Rogers was informed that her school records have been sent to Pennfields High."

"Principal Morgrin did not return calls from *Palmetto Peaks Press*. Our previous quote from him after the Homecoming Dance partially states, 'We strive to uphold the preferences of the parents who send us their students.'"

The article ended with giving the time and date of the next school board meeting—a not-so-subtle plug that this could be a hot topic next Tuesday.

"Fabulous publicity," Gran said. "You'll be speaking to a full house."

CHAPTER THIRTY

THURSDAY MORNING I DRESSED FOR school and pulled my hair into a pony tail. Halloween. Such an awful day to start at a new school, but I needed these two days at Pennfields before writing my speech this weekend.

The first difference between the two schools was riding the graffiti-marked yellow bus that stopped a block from my house. I stepped onto the bus and walked down the aisle, looking for a seat to myself and found one with a torn seat cover midway. Nobody really talked to me but lots of eyes gave me the once over before ignoring me. One boy across the aisle said, "Hey new girl." When I glanced his way, he licked his lips hungrily, making his friends laugh. I took it as teasing rather than interest in me, and watched out the window as the normal chatter resumed. Half the pretty fall leaves were gone. The stuff that looked like Spanish moss but I learned wasn't, draped from the branches in intriguing patterns, almost making me forget those annoying boys.

The second difference was my light skin being obviously in the minority as I walked into the school. Not wanting to get stuck in that new-girl rut that started on the bus, I walked tall. The multiple shades of skin color were a refreshing change, making me smile. I'd say twenty percent of the student body was light-skinned. How nice that nobody here had to blend in.

The third difference was me heading to the office instead of meeting Jake at my locker for a kiss. I hated being away from him more than a day without Mom's baking. It simply wasn't the same.

The secretary gave me my schedule. I thanked her and walked away, stopping short when I gazed at it. Starting the day with math would not be something I'd look forward to. I easily found the classroom and entered. I swallowed, spoke to the teacher, and then straightened my spine as I picked an empty seat, hoping it didn't belong to someone. I didn't care to repeat the experience I'd had sitting in Melanie's chair before we became friends. Maybe all it took was time and getting to know these people. I didn't want to be here long enough to make friends though; I wanted my old friends. I bit my bottom lip to stop its quivering, and listened to the announcements over the intercom. Then I focused hard on the lesson. At least the teacher explained quadratic equations to the point where I got it.

The kids in second hour for Health were talkative. Maybe in first hour they needed time to wake up. The room already buzzed when I walked in, but I created more of a stir.

"We got a new girl." The boy who said it sounded enthusiastic. "My, my. What's your name, new girl?"

No hungry looks this time. Much better. "Charlotte."

"You got a friend named Wilbur?" He snorted at his own joke and slapped his knee. "Nah, you don't look like no spider. Have a seat." He pointed diagonally across from him to a desk with a gouge on the side. "I'm Lawrence."

Lawrence gave me a toothy smile. He had friendly eyes and a golden hue to his brown skin that complimented his sunny disposition. His slacks had faded at the knees and his button-down shirt missed a button. The book on his graffitied desk was covered in brown paper, like a grocery bag from the store. I noticed several books covered the same way. The girl in front of me turned around and squinted. "Are you that girl who was in the paper last night?"

Someone else who read more than the comics. Great. I gave a small nod.

"What? We got us a celebrity?" Lawrence asked.

"She's the girl who got kicked out of Oakmont for not being all white."

She blushed when she looked at me again. The girl looked mixed race herself, like Gran. I gave her a half-smile.

She returned it. "I'm Vanessa. Welcome to Pennfields in all its glory." She swept her arm out.

"Thanks." I sat tall.

"Don't expect all the students to make you feel welcome," she added. "There's a few who don't take to white chicks."

I arched an eyebrow, my shoulders slumping. At Oakmont I wasn't white enough. Here I wasn't black enough. What couldn't people get into their heads about only one race?

"You can hang with me, though."

I smiled in appreciation. A friend—or at least an ally.

"It ain't that bad," Lawrence said. "There's only a couple bad apples."

I leaned toward him. "Oakmont has their bad apples too."

"Speaking of…" Lawrence pointed his head toward a girl coming through the door. "Don't get on her bad side."

The girl went to her seat on the far side of the room. No light-skinned students sat near her. In fact, only now could I tell that there was a division of sorts. I wondered if it was just her or it the next class would be the same. So much to observe.

I glanced around the room. Students talked to one another and joked around like they did at Oakmont. There were more students per teacher—like there had been in my math class. I didn't know what equipment they had in the science rooms, the gym, or how well-stocked the library was, but I had a guess by the old chalkboard, books, and desks that Pennfields got the short end of the stick when it came to the school board doling out money. I didn't know how their Homecoming dance had gone or if one had existed. Did the school offer clubs or anything extracurricular? How could I understand what made these kids tick in a couple days?

The start bell rang, and I looked up at the teacher. She sported one of those new natural styles that my hair wasn't frizzy enough to wear. It looked good on her. She took a long pointer stick off the chalkboard ledge and tapped it twice on her desk. She demanded respect and quiet. Some things you can count on being the same.

I walked up the front porch and through the doorway, leaving the stress of a first day behind and sniffing the air. Mm. Hot biscuits. With butter and molasses. Mom, Gran, and Mark waited at the table, expecting to hear about my first day, no doubt. Mark had beat me home, not having to wait for a bus with several stops. He set down his empty glass of milk and took his last bite of a sticky biscuit.

Mom asked the inevitable question. "How was your day?"

"Not bad." I spread butter and molasses over a large biscuit and picked up a fork, cutting into the flaky crust and enjoying Mom's Southern food experiments. "I had lunch with a girl named Vanessa and nobody picked a fight with me all day." Especially not what's-her-name that Lawrence warned me about. I popped the bite into my mouth and chewed slowly. "Mm. Thanks, Mom." Her eyes had widened as I glanced at her. It's probably a good thing I hadn't said that nobody killed me, like I almost did. She wouldn't have known it for a joke.

Mark grabbed a banana and began peeling it. "I'll bet you hated taking the bus."

That was a given. I shrugged.

"Tell me about Vanessa," Gran said.

"She's in my Health class. She waved me over to sit with her group at lunch when I stood there holding my tray and looking around like a stupid idiot. Vanessa's a real nice girl. Smart too."

"Um-hum," Gran said, smiling. "And drama class?"

I had to hand it to Gran. She sure got down to business. "That was probably my biggest disappointment. It's a general level class. There isn't an advanced one for next year either." I chewed another bite, figuring out how to explain it. "The teacher was okay but the students bugged me. Most of them treated it like a free class—you know, an easy A. They were bored or too embarrassed to give their best in the role playing she had us do."

"They need your example," Mom suggested. "Show them how it's done."

"It ain't that easy."

Mom sent me a sharp look.

"I mean, it isn't that easy. I don't want to come across as stuck-up because I came from Oakmont. I need to break into it gradually."

"Fitting in don't mean lowering your standards," Gran said.

Mom set a fist on her hip. "You're at a crossroads, so let me tell you something. There are always people who want to keep you from your dreams, because your success might shed greater light on their own failings. It's not for them to decide. It's *your* choice what to do with your life. One day you'll give an accounting before God about what you did with what He gave you. He's the one you'll want to please over everybody else. That's how you decide what to do."

Wow. I blinked at her. I'd forgotten how hard Mom had worked at fitting into the white world to give me and Mark a better life, especially here in the South, where it made more of a difference.

"Yes, ma'am."

With my comparisons and fact-finding, I'd have to decide things to adopt or reject as I tried to fit in at Pennfields. Wait, I wasn't trying to fit in. My goal was to get back to Oakmont.

CHAPTER THIRTY-ONE

PATTY'S DOORBELL CHIMED AGAIN. "MY turn," I called, grabbing the bowl of candy. We both got up from the card table with the jigsaw puzzle after each ring to see what costumes kids wore. More ghoulish monsters. I gave them each a treat.

At the next doorbell, we found an especially clever papier maché Charlie Brown head staring up at us. "Fab costume!" I said.

His mother looked so proud. She had to help him down the porch steps and steer him in the right direction. The poor kid looked like a drunk.

We closed the door and giggled until the next doorbell, where two adorable little princesses made us both drawl, "Aww". It felt good being with Patty, and I was glad I had turned down a date to a scary movie with Jake to spend time with her. We both needed this. In fact, it sounded like she was more lost today than I was at the new school.

"Lunch was so weird without you," she said. "Melanie was getting all chummy with me. She did so much talking, most of it to me. Gina and Ellen hung on her every word. I almost gagged."

I laughed. "Melanie's not so bad. Give her a chance." It struck me that everyone needed to fit in somewhere. "Just don't let her replace me."

"Never!"

I'd only fit one puzzle piece into place when the doorbell interrupted us again. We knew it would be this way, but it made it hard to answer all of Patty's concerns and her questions about my first day at Pennfields. She grabbed the bowl of candy.

"Trick or treat."

These were two really big kids in masks. With deep voices. If I'd had the candy bowl I might have told them they were too old for trick or treating. Oddly, they didn't have a paper bag or anything to put candy in. Then I recognized the canvas tennis shoes.

"Brad! Jake!" Patty pulled Brad inside by the arm. "What are you guys doing?"

"We came to trick you," Brad said. "Or maybe treat you." He pulled off his mask and wrapped his arms around Patty.

Jake removed his mask, making a patch of hair stand up on top. "I sure missed you today." He grabbed me and silenced my laugh with a long, desperate kiss that left me with the sensation of seeing him off on an airplane for a long trip. Strange that it felt more like goodbye than hello.

☆ ☆ ☆ ☆

On Sunday after church, I sat down to write the five-minute speech I would deliver to the school board on Tuesday night. I crossed out my fourth opening line and tapped my pencil against the notebook paper. What did I really want to say? How big a reach should I make?

The unequal conditions I'd seen at Pennfields in two short days bothered me. How could I work that in without sounding like a rehash of Brown vs. Board of Education? There was the non-compliant segregation issue too. The elementary and middle schools had complied so that local elected officials could show they were working on it, though not necessarily "with all deliberate speed". However, I still believed they would stall at the high school level—where students developed romantic relationships—for as long as possible.

I shouldn't risk the school board drumming up images of armed escorts to get to school, like the Little Rock Nine. Not yet, anyway. With only five minutes, this was about me getting back to Oakmont, not saving the world.

I listed a few reasons why the board should allow me back into Oakmont, and looked them over. None of them addressed racial qualifications. I had skills and talents I could share, but the board could argue I could do that at either school. My goal to qualify for a drama scholarship wasn't their responsibility. Getting the best education could depend on what I put into it, not necessarily the school. They had provided quality teachers at both schools. My purpose and reasons, though well-meaning, sounded selfish, desperate, or trivial. Everything I wanted they could dismiss or turn the other way around, and nobody wanted to hear me whine.

My best reason for them to consider my case came back to whether or not I was truly white, which I was if the only categories were white or colored. In most places around the world, anything beyond three generations or less than one-eighth of an ethnic group was considered insignificant in categorizing a person. Would a majority be open to believing that here? If only it were as simple as me swearing to what I believed.

I tapped my pencil for a moment and shifted my thoughts to the board's motivations. There were obvious racial influences, but what else? Political? Who had a secret agenda? I shook my head. I hadn't lived here long enough to figure those things out.

Maybe I should expand on Mom's advice. I could tell them my dreams and get them to feel hopeful for me so they would want to be on my side. Then I'd suggest that the best opportunity for me to fulfill these dreams would be by attending Oakmont.

In half an hour I had some good thoughts down on paper. Some of them inspired me, but then they were my dreams. I wasn't quite settled on everything but I felt better having something. I should call Patty or Jake and run my draft by them. A little feedback wouldn't hurt.

On Monday I marched into drama class at Pennfields, ready to give it my all. Mom was right that I could be an example, but more than that, I should be true to myself and my dreams. Even if a few people got the wrong impression. I'd be a hypocrite telling the town my dreams tomorrow night if I would only work on them at Oakmont.

I sat on the front row of chairs. Miss Shepler, a young, slender black woman talked about the emotion that could come through a solo performance. "It's intimate," she told us. "Just you and the audience. You can use a chair for a prop, but that's it. It's gotta come from you and through you. Are y'all up to the challenge?"

A dare. I curved one corner of my mouth up. I looked around and saw maybe two nodding heads out of thirty. I admired Miss Shepler for continuously trying.

She handed out sheets of paper in yellowed plastic sleeves. "The first paragraph sets the scene. The rest is dialogue for y'all to use or adlib if you like. I'll assign by pairs so y'all only have to perform for one person. Take five minutes to read through it and figure out the primary emotion to get across. Then spread out, give a performance to your partner, and switch. Even numbers will go first." She began to number us down the row of chairs as one, two, one, two. I was a two.

I glanced at my partner, a heavy girl who slumped in her seat without yet looking at me or her paper. I silently read mine.

"C'mon, Lucinda," the teacher prompted, looking at my partner. "You too Jim."

My scene was set in a restaurant, where the waiter spilled soup on my suit/dress. Hm. Was I embarrassed? Angry? Indifferent? I kept reading. The dialogue suggested I tell the waiter off. My character seemed snooty, my clothing expensive. I pictured myself in one of those fancy restaurants I'd seen in a recent movie. I wore a hat that matched my gown. I touched the pearls at my throat, imagining their smooth feel. My boyfriend sat across from me, sending me adoring looks. I turned to Lucinda sitting next to me, "Ready?"

She wrinkled her nose. "Go right ahead." She didn't move. Okay, the restaurant was right here.

I scooted my chair to face her, sat up straight, and leaned forward to pat my lips with my imaginary cloth napkin. "George, that caviar was absolutely delicious. I can't wait to taste the soup." I pictured myself as a young, Southern woman from the last decade. A self-assured smile and the small, refined movements of my head and upper body guided me to become that adored girlfriend.

"Oh look. Here it comes now." I lifted my gaze to the waiter as he set his tray down and picked up my plate. My eyes widened. My pleasant smile became a high-pitched inhale as my mouth opened and I shrank back, my arms rising from my lap. The pose held for half a beat before my arms flopped down. "You fool! Look at my dress. That soup will *never* come out." I looked at Lucinda, ignoring her twitching lips, and pleaded, "George, do something!"

I frowned at the faceless waiter and chewed him out. "Your apology, sir, will not pay the cleaning bill. Nor will it change my mood back to what it was. You have ruined our entire evening." I set a fist on my hip, rolled my chin away from him, and huffed.

The partners to our left clapped. "Wow. You're good," one girl said.

Lucinda narrowed her eyes at me. "You trying to show us up, white girl?"

Ignoring the hint of a threat in favor of the deep, slightly husky quality to her voice that I found unique, I took a breath, then looked her in the eye. "One race, sister. The Human race. Now you show *me* whatcha got." I scooted my chair back and folded my arms.

She scoffed and looked at her paper. "Mine's stupid. I ain't doing it."

"Why not? You have such a fascinating voice." I reached out my hand. "Here, let me see. I can give you some suggestions."

She tossed the paper to the floor. "I don't want no suggestions." She folded her arms and raised her chin, staring off in the distance.

Miss Shepler stepped toward us. "Everything going alright?"

"Sure." I kept my voice pleasant. "Lucinda's a great actress. Why just look at her. She's mastered the scenario of the indifferent reception a housewife gives to a salesman at the door."

Lucinda squinted at me, her head tilted, and then looked up at the teacher with the look I'd described.

"Good," Miss Shepler said. "Two minutes, everybody."

Lucinda was silent for those two minutes. I watched a few groups still performing for their partner, but I caught her glancing at me a couple times.

Miss Shepler clapped twice. "Okay. Anybody want to do theirs for the class?" She looked around the hushed room. "Lucinda?"

Lucinda shook her head and pointed her thumb at me.

"Yeah, ask her," the girl who had complimented me agreed.

"Charlotte?"

"Okay." I stood.

The teacher looked relieved. I spent a few seconds re-picturing my character.

I dragged my chair out in front of the first row of chairs. "I'm at a fancy restaurant." I sat down, real lady-like, pretended to eat something delicate, and repeated the rest of my earlier performance. The class clapped and a murmur of approval rippled over the two rows of chairs. I gave a slight curtsey and returned to my seat.

Lucinda gave me a light punch on my bicep. "Good job." Then she folded her arms and slouched in her seat, never looking my way for the rest of class.

I'd take whatever small victories I could.

CHAPTER THIRTY-TWO

GRAN CALLED DOWN THE HALL toward my bedroom. "Charlotte, honey, time for supper."

I wasn't sure if I could eat, but I came out to join the family, which I'd have to do eventually.

"Can I call you honey?" Gran asked with a twinkle in her eye when I appeared. "As long as I don't call you late for supper?"

I cracked a smile.

"That's my girl," she said. "Oh, now I'm calling you my girl." She chuckled to herself when she saw that her familiar joke wouldn't work twice.

Dad asked Gran to say grace, and she added a plea for me to settle my nerves. I stared at my plate for a really long time, rolling peas around with my fork and hoping the prayer would kick in. I couldn't concentrate on the conversation around the table. My speech didn't feel ready. I felt sick to my stomach. It wasn't like stage fright. I didn't mind delivering the speech so much. It was the uncertainty of my own future, the finality of their verdict that soured my stomach.

We all got into the car. I sat with my hands folded in my lap on the nicest Sunday dress I had, a pastel green, modestly cut. Gran broke the silence first. "Just say what's in your heart, child. Nobody can argue your feelings away. It might soften a heart or two."

I squeezed Granny's hand. "Thanks, Gran."

Mom nodded at me from the front seat. "You'll do fine."

"Yeah. Break a leg," Mark said with a chuckle.

My stomach rumbled, reminding me I hadn't eaten, though I still wasn't interested in food.

We slowly pulled up to the school district office twenty minutes early and stared out the car windows. Cars already lined the curbs. Three cops stood on the sidewalk near twenty or thirty people who marched around in an oval off to one side of the steps, picket signs on wooden slats waving in their hands. Were the signs for me or against? All adults. All whites. I swallowed hard. Some of the signs had a wolf head symbol, whatever that meant. I read the word *Fraud,* and felt my stomach convulse. It was just as well I hadn't eaten.

There were several spots in the parking lot and Dad claimed one. We bunched together behind Dad as we followed the sidewalk toward the front steps. I saw a bright flash and spotted Scott on the street. He headed over, putting himself as a barrier between us and the picketers, though they continued making their loop. One cop stood between us and them, and waved us through.

Someone howled like a wolf and the protesters got noisy. A chant picked up. "Keep our School Pure."

I looked at my mother and grandmother, sure they hadn't told me all they'd dealt with through the years. Was this a small taste of their suffering? My great-great-grandmother, Mary, had suffered much more. Yet, she would probably be the first to remind me that Jesus had suffered all things. Compared to those, this was nothing. Still, I trudged into the building with dread.

"You ready? How are you feeling?"

"Huh?" I lifted my head to see Scott's excited expression. "I just want it to be over."

Scott laughed, the sound brightening my mood. "I've seen what you can do. You'll be fab."

I perked up. "Thanks."

A sign with a large red arrow directed us to what must be the largest room the building had. Two room partitions were drawn back and secured and a hundred or so folding chairs had been set up. A couple dozen of them had already been claimed.

I spotted Pastor Jensen in one of the seats, and my feet wouldn't move. Was he behind those protestors out front? He dipped his head to me in acknowledgement of my presence, like he wanted me to know he was there and that I better watch out. I couldn't respond and looked away. I saw Brother Mike too, and my throat tightened at my awareness that he would be loyal to the pastor.

"It won't be enough room," Dad said, leading us into a row near the front. "They should have held this at the school auditorium."

Scott quickened his step to get ahead and capture the whole family in a shot. He responded after no one else had. "But then it wouldn't be neutral ground. Those who have to stand in the hallway will have to read the paper instead."

I bit my bottom lip. Jake, Patty, and all my friends better not be late. I needed some friendly fa— "Mrs. B!" I stood and gave her a hug when she came over. "And Mr. Dodd!" He followed right behind her. I shook his hand with both of mine. "Thank y'all for coming."

"We wouldn't miss it," Mrs. Burkhart said. "Good luck."

I introduced them to my family. Then in walked Principal Morgrin, Vanessa from my new school, and various adults—some white, some not. The seats filled quickly now. I clamped my teeth down on a fingernail, something I hadn't done since grade school. John appeared in the doorway, giving me a big smile and a thumbs up. I perked up and waved. Seeing him at church on Sunday wasn't enough. I missed not having drama with him. I could use one of his soothing neck rubs but I longed for a few minutes to ask about the play.

There! Patty, Melanie, Brad, and Jake walked in together. I heaved a sigh and waved.

At 6:55 the room had filled beyond capacity. People stood in the back. The school board president closed the door to a roar of protests in the hall. He made a few people move out of the aisles and let them stand behind the tables with name plates that reserved seats for board members. The board took their seats—four at each of three long, narrow tables facing the audience. I knew from the list I'd picked up at the district office that three of them would be women, but now I could see that all twelve were white. Even the name Roland Jensen hadn't meant much until I stared at him. He looked a lot like a younger version of the pastor. Not a good sign.

The silver-haired president spoke into a small table microphone, calling the meeting to order. "Welcome y'all. We will begin with the pledge of allegiance. Please excuse the lack of Boy Scouts for this meeting. We expected there wouldn't be room for them and so the flag is already posted, as you can see. Please stand and repeat the pledge with me."

We all did so. "…with Liberty and Justice for all."

When the audience sat and quieted again, the president put on his glasses, picked up the piece of paper on the table in front of him, and stated that they had a few minutes of regular business to take care of before moving on to the scheduled agenda. "Everyone must be quiet and patient. Only myself and whomever has the floor may speak. If you cannot abide by those rules, I will have this officer clear the room except for those names listed on the agenda." He looked over his glasses at the audience. "There are restrooms down the hall, but if you leave, I can guarantee your seat will not be waiting for you." The people standing behind the tables chuckled.

I glanced over the packed room as the board raised their hands to vote yea or nay three times on other business. Jake caught my eye. He made an exaggerated terrified face, shaking his head and arms like he was scared, and then give the surfer's Shaka sign for me to hang loose. Finally, he winked at me. My smile came easily. I mouthed, "Thank you." I wouldn't say I'd gotten comfortable, but it took the pressure off for a bit.

The president continued leading the meeting. "We will now proceed with the case of Charlotte Rogers, who has petitioned to be reinstated at Oakmont High School."

A light murmur surged through the room. My heart pounded at the mention of my name. Mom put her hand on my back and smoothed it over my shoulder blades.

The president continued. "Miss Rogers may speak for five minutes. After which, we have opened ten thirty-second slots for public comment—all of which have been filled."

I heard my dad whisper to my mom, "When did they decide that?" She shrugged.

"There will be no other comments at this venue. The board will then take a five-minute recess to discuss if they are ready to vote tonight."

Vote tonight? I could know my fate this very hour. My heart raced and I licked my dry lips.

"Miss Rogers?" The president gestured to the microphone and gave up his seat for me.

I stood on shaky legs and made my way to the table mic, glad that I could sit. I unfolded my speech paper. A blur of movement distracted me as Scott moved in and flashed his camera at me. I blinked a few times. "Thanks, Scott. Now I can't see what I've written." It got me a few laughs and soothed my nerves. I cleared my throat.

"Like all of you, I have a dream." I paused to let it ring familiar. "Like Dr. Martin Luther King, my grandest dream would be for us to see one another as one race. The human race. Tonight's vote is about me as one person attending the high school of my choice, but my dream is for anyone and everyone to have the same privilege. It will take all of us. I hope every one of us will become a part of making those changes.

"For the last four school days, I have attended Pennfields High. I have made some new friends there and the teachers do a good job with the challenges they face. I can't help but notice the older desks and text books, and over-crowded rooms. The comparison between schools is truly unfair, though that is not why I want to go to Oakmont.

"Today I will speak of a personal dream. I came to Oakmont to pursue my passion for the theater. I dream of going to college on a drama scholarship. I dream of being a mentor to younger kids who would love the opportunity to perform and express themselves.

"I swore before a notary that I am white, and I am. That is where I fit best. No one has questioned that fact until last week. My origin and the culture I grew up in have not changed in the past two months or ever. I shouldn't have to hide the one-sixteenths of my blood that isn't white. It doesn't change anything."

I looked at Gran. She held her palm to her chest, a tender look in her shining eyes. My chest heaved and I stopped reading. *Speak from your heart, like Gran said.*

"My father goes to work, earning a living to support his family. We go to church and have supper together. We own a car and shop at the supermarket like most Americans. I like to wear jeans when I can. We sit on the front porch and watch the people go by. Sometimes we get to a concert or the art gallery. We ride bikes and hike in the great outdoors. We are involved in the same things other white people do.

"I was cast with a major part in the school play, fulfilling a dream for this sophomore." I tapped my chest bone twice. "I'd been deemed worthy because of my talent, and then stripped of the honor. My heart broken. Unless this board does the right thing for at least one person tonight, I will not be in that school play, the drama club, or attending the regional drama festival. My opportunities will be limited. It's not only me that you'll be hurting. I'm merely one step on a stairway to following what the Supreme Court has judged as the legal, American thing to do, with fair treatment for all."

Had I said too much? They couldn't deny me my feelings but I don't think I'd softened any hearts. They were Southerners first and Americans second. According to the timer next to the mic, I still had half my time. Now what? I couldn't get the play out of my mind.

"In *The Music Man,* the female lead is a lot like me. Marian the Librarian is a kind, gentle soul with a talent for music. My talent is drama, and I consider myself a good Christian. Marian's only fault is falling in love with the con man who comes to town, because she sees the good in him when he gives hope to her little brother with a stuttering problem. The mayor's wife gets all her lady friends to pick at and gossip about Marian because she is a spinster and keeps to herself. They are prejudiced against her for no good reason. The ladies prolonged this injustice against Marian because they didn't know her."

My hands came out from under the table as if they had a life of their own, motioning toward them with open palms to emphasize my next words. "That's what is happening here." I tucked my hands back on my lap. "We need to stop finding little things about others to pick at." My gaze found Vanessa. "We need to give equal opportunities to all schools and all people."

Instead of the audience, I looked at the board members on either side of me. "My motto is: one race—the human race. What harm would it do for someone like me to attend Oakmont? I humbly ask you to consider what is right. Thank you."

Half the room applauded for me, Patty the loudest. A small smile creased my lips. I got up, anxious to leave the microphone, yet knowing I could be proud.

The clapping ceased by the time I returned to my row. My family patted my back, whispered "good job," or other positives as I filed past them. I sat down, feeling good about myself. I'd done my best.

"Thank you, Miss Rogers. We will now have the first five to give comments line up behind me." He read the names of four men and one woman. Pastor Jensen would be first. My confidence plummeted.

"You will each have only thirty seconds." The president rose from his chair.

Pastor Jensen, dressed in a nice suit, sat at the microphone. "Miss Rogers is a clever girl. She knew her only chance was to focus on herself." He threw up his hands and made a skeptical face. "Come on now. Are we supposed to let all students who want to be white attend Oakmont?" A chuckle floated through the room. "But that is the kind of girl she is: clever but selfish. She wants the best for herself, but she doesn't deserve it. She is not white like the rest of us whites. She is a deceiver—a wolf in sheep's clothing."

My jaw dropped. So that's where the wolf symbol figured in. He had set up a whole campaign against me. Had he signed up people for all ten slots too? I felt gut-punched.

"Miss Rogers swore to being white but she has also said that she has one-sixteenth Negro blood. Deception. Make no mistake about it. Rules are in place to avoid this very problem. If one wolf gets in, it will only be the beginning." The pastor quickly stood before they could mention that his time was up. Someone here was clever alright. My teeth ground together. A rumble of whispers buzzed in the room. Could they be believing these outrageous accusations?

The next in line had already taken his seat. A man about Dad's age that I didn't recognize. He set his hat on the table.

"Hi there. I agree with Pastor Jensen. The Rogers's came to our church ev'ry Sund'y, gitting our congregation used to them and such. Then one day they show up with that grandmother lady over there," he said, pointing, "and spring the truth on us. Maybe Miss Rogers figures she can weasel into the school like her family did at church. Like a wolf trying to git at a flock of lambs."

I heard someone nearby click their tongue in disgust. I prayed the board wasn't falling for all this hogwash.

"Don't let her do it. Don't let her in." He stood, dipped his head, and put his hat back on.

The next three had similar hooey to tell, leaving an unfavorable impression about me with nothing I could say in rebuttal. I added it up. These ten people would speak for the same amount of time that I spoke, except with the getting up and down from the chair, it would take longer than their combined five minutes. It also had the feel of ten against one. How could I come out ahead with odds like that? I put my elbows on my knees and propped up my head with my hands. Dad barely shook his head at me and motioned for me to sit up. He was right. I had to continue to look the part of confidence even if I didn't feel it. Still, the way this was going, I didn't stand a chance.

CHAPTER THIRTY-THREE

THE SCHOOL BOARD PRESIDENT ANNOUNCED the next five names. The second one was Brother Mike. I felt sick to my stomach. My own Sunday school teacher was here to testify against me. He would have to lie. I hoped he couldn't sleep tonight.

First, a lady from Pastor Jensen's church used the school setting this time. Her daughter had history class with me and told her how I kissed up to the teacher so she would let me do my history project on my relative who was a dark-skinned slave. If that wasn't proof that I didn't belong at Oakmont, she didn't know what was. Mrs. Burkhart stared down the lady, her arms folded and a sour look on her face that I never would have imagined she could make. I wished Mrs. B could get up there and speak for me.

Something else about this meeting wasn't right. I was certain it had to do with Pastor Jensen's son. How else could they have filled ten slots to testify against me and nobody else had a chance?

Brother Mike smoothed his hair and took his place at the microphone. I couldn't breathe. Tears welled up in my eyes and my throat choked off. I made an awful jagged sound trying to get air. Luckily he said hello into the microphone at the very same time.

"I was Charlotte Rogers's Sunday school teacher and youth leader, so I believe I know her the best out of all who have spoken. Charlotte is a good Christian girl, like she said."

What? I waited for the catch.

"Pastor Jensen does a lot of good in this community—for the white population. He means well and he knows how to deliver a sermon, but he's stuck in the traditions of the past. Like a lot of us stubborn

Southerners. I'm probably the only one you'll hear tonight with anything good to say about Charlotte, besides herself of course."

He smiled at me then, showing his dimple like Dad's, and I don't think I've ever felt such love fill me from anyone outside my family. An answer to my prayers. Tears streamed down my face, but I was smiling back.

"I may lose my Sunday job over it, but I would be remiss if I didn't stand up for this fine young lady."

"Amen."

The president scowled out at the audience in my general direction. I knew Gran's voice but he couldn't pinpoint her by only one word.

I wiped my cheeks and glanced back at Pastor Jensen. He did his best to keep a blank face, but his eyes smoldered.

Mike continued. "Charlotte is a friendly, talented, loyal, and trustworthy young lady. She is kind to others and works hard. I have no doubt she would be an asset to Oakmont's drama program. I say let's give her a shot at her dreams and see how far she can go. Oakmont should be thrilled to enroll this girl. Imagine her as a senior in the drama program! Whatever the vote, Charlotte, you find a way to make your dreams come true because that is the kind of young lady you are. Thank you."

I could have run up there and hugged him.

A light, brief applause sounded before the president scowled.

The last three public comments were like the first six. They all threw me to the wolves.

The president excused himself and the rest of the board into another room, leaving the cop at the door to maintain things. I knotted my fingers on my lap. Some people smiled at me or said something but I couldn't recall their words. An eternal ten minutes ticked by before the board retook their seats.

The president spoke into the microphone. "Ladies and gentlemen, we are prepared to vote on the petition to restore Charlotte Rogers's records to Oakmont High School with her as a student there. I will ask for the board's vote by hand with "yea" being her acceptance and "nay" being denial. We will go with the majority, and should there be a tie, I become the tie-breaker. Any questions first?"

Not a soul moved and I could bet they all could hear my pounding heart.

Scott moved to the end of the row of tables, where he could get a shot of the voting. The president called for yea votes. Two hands raised. I gulped. A tiny spark of happiness that anyone at all voted for me was quickly dashed because I knew what the vote meant. Something like numbness created a barrier between the results and my emotions, so that I couldn't identify or display how I felt. Shock, perhaps?

"Nay votes raise your hands." Ten hands stabbed the air, blasting away my numbness. They may as well have stabbed my heart.

"Thanks for coming. Meeting adjourned."

I hurried to the car, not wanting to talk to anyone. Mark and Dad kept up with me, but Gran couldn't walk that fast so Mom stayed with her. The protesters were outside with their signs, bobbing them up and down and cheering. I had to get away from the noise.

Once we were in the car together, I started bawling like a baby dipped in cold water. I couldn't help it. The verdict had come in but the stress wasn't over. Now I'd have to face kids at Pennfields who knew I didn't want to be there. I'd have to sit through a basic drama class with students who couldn't care less about my passion. People would expect me to follow through with my One Race campaign, and right now I didn't have the heart for it. Patty needed me. What would happen to me and Jake if we hardly saw one another? So many bad things came from that one decision.

I started hearing things like, "It's not the end of the world," and "You did such a good job," and how the Jensen's had played dirty. None of it soothed me. They hadn't said anything I didn't know. It wouldn't change what I now faced. A good cry couldn't fix it, but that's all I could do. I feared I had a long road ahead that wouldn't get me over this either. My high school life was ruined forever.

CHAPTER THIRTY-FOUR

I SHUFFLED INTO HEALTH CLASS on Wednesday, hoping for the same lack of attention I'd had in math. I'd been sentenced to shuffle through the next three years.

"You did a fine job last night," Vanessa said as soon as I sat at my desk. "You can be proud of that."

"Thanks." I examined the cuticles on my hand. I should thank her for coming but I didn't feel like engaging in conversation.

"Cat got your tongue?"

Yeah, and its claws were digging into my heart. I shrugged. She wouldn't understand.

"Oh, don't be a sourpuss. Don't you know about making lemonade? Being stuck at Pennfields ain't so bad. You got us." She pointed her chin at Lawrence, who was coming down the aisle.

"Who's got us?" he asked.

"Charlotte. The board voted last night that we get to keep her."

"Right on." Lawrence beamed at me. "Gimme some skin." He held his hand out for me to slap.

My lips twitched. I appreciated they'd made an effort to cheer me. Budding friendships were fragile. Their kindness still didn't change the fact that the next three years of my life were ruined.

He stretched his hand a little closer. "Don't leave me hangin'."

I played along because I knew he would keep at it until I complied. Just as our palms would have connected, he jerked his hand back.

"Gotcha." He grinned at me. "Oh, c'mon. Don't I get a smile?"

Vanessa spoke to Lawrence as if I wasn't there. "There was foul play with some church-going cats bombarding her, but she did a real good job. She put in a plea for the board to help out Pennfields High too."

"Yeah?" Lawrence kept his gaze on Vanessa. "That might make us want to help her."

"I agree. The thing Miss Sourpuss don't realize is that she should pursue her dream right here. She's had it too easy in life and don't know about squeezing the lemons she been handed. There's more opportunity here than she realizes."

I blinked hard. "What opportunities?"

They continued to ignore me. "What she wanna do?" Lawrence asked.

"She got this dream about drama and being a mentor—said so in her speech."

"She ought to do something about that instead of moping. She can't replace Miss Shepler though. Who she gonna teach?"

Vanessa tapped her lip. "That's a good question. All I know is she's got three years to do some good here, maybe stuff that she wouldn't be able to do at Oakmont."

"I could mentor students here—if they'd let me. Maybe after school." I leaned forward, taking a big breath in my growing excitement. "What if I started a drama club?"

Lawrence put a finger up. "Hey, what if she started a drama club? Kids are always looking for something to do after school. I might be interested in joining a club like that—if she can get some chicks to show up."

I felt my heart lift. "Really?" I looked from one face to the other but they still didn't acknowledge me. "Guys?" They'd better not be messing with me, because ideas already blossomed in my head.

"All she has to do is get one of them forms at the office and apply." Vanessa kept her face straight, and I believed she could get into acting too.

"But I don't know if this Miss Sourpuss, whoever she is, would do all that. Hey, maybe we should tell Charlotte about it. Charlotte?" He looked around the room above my head.

I punched his arm. "I'm right here."

Vanessa pointed at me. "You could run the club and be the president too. As a sophomore. That don't look too shabby on a scholarship application."

Lawrence shook his head. "Uh-uh. No it don't."

I laughed, but they were right. "You know y'all acted out a mini scene, with adlib dialogue and everything?"

Lawrence chuckled. "Imagine that."

I stared him in the eye. "Did you mean it—about participating?"

"Yeah. I'll give it a shot as long as that Miss Sourpuss don't show up."

I leaned over my desk and threw my arms around him and then Vanessa. The teacher tapped her pointing-stick twice on her desk. I didn't care one bit that it was directed at me; Vanessa and Lawrence had given me hope. As soon as class let out, I would go to the office and ask for one of those forms.

☆ ☆ ☆

I hustled to drama class, hoping the teacher would have a minute for me. She sat at her desk and it looked like she was marking grades in her roll book. Ideal timing or not, the sooner I got this off my chest, the better. "Miss Shepler? I've got a question for you."

She looked up. "Yes, Charlotte?"

"I want to start a drama club, and it says I need a teacher advisor for that. Would you be willing to be the advisor? You don't have to do anything but supervise. The group will decide what we do and I'll run it."

"I'm impressed with your ambition, but do you really think there's enough interest to form a club?"

"I hope so, ma'am. It might start small, but we'll grow."

She nodded. "What would be the club's purpose? How will this be different from class time? There needs to be something to motivate your members."

I pursed my lips. "I haven't got it all figured out yet, but we'll want to perform. I want to look into ways we can perform for the community at different events—an Elks Club Christmas party or a Founder's Day program. That kind of stuff."

She tilted her head at me. "I can see the club doing something at a school assembly, but do you really think the whites in the community would be anxious to see our diverse group perform?"

"I…I don't know. I didn't think about that." We shouldn't *have* to think about that. Maybe a drama club wouldn't work at Pennfields. I could feel my eyes sting but fought it, knowing a few students had entered the classroom.

"Think about it some more and we'll talk again. Okay?"

"Okay." I forced a smile.

"Then if you still want a drama club, I'd be happy to be the advisor. I can squeeze in an hour after school on Tuesdays."

I grasped at the proffered straw. "Thank you, Miss Shepler."

"You're welcome."

Thinking about the drama club some more turned out to be quite time consuming. I couldn't get it off my mind. First, I worried that Miss Shepler was right and we wouldn't have any venues outside the school to perform. Then I remembered the band that Oakmont hired for the Homecoming dance. If you were good at what you did, you'd have an audience. I started seeing ideas everywhere.

I peered out the school bus window at the community center sign which read, "Give Thanks." My mind jumped to the churches—except for Pastor Jensen's congregation. Three of the four would probably let us do a little something at one of their meet-and-greets. We passed a little market where a banner proclaimed: "Apple Festival—An Apple a Day." If we had something ready for their next marketing promotion, we could put on a live commercial in front of the store or on the airwaves at the local radio station—like a mini reader's theater. A small club could do something like that, and we could whip it into shape in no time. Who wouldn't want free performers for their advertising? I could see our club being sought after before long.

As soon as I got home from school, I took a couple of Gran's warm molasses cookies into the den for some privacy, and nibbled the first one as I dialed Jake's number. His mom answered on the second ring and soon his soothing voice came over the line.

"Charlotte? You left so fast last night I didn't get a chance to tell you how fab you were. Too bad about the board's vote. I could have punched all those dumb speakers. I miss you like crazy at school."

"I miss you too. Hey, guess what? I'm starting a drama club at Pennfields."

"Doesn't their drama program stink?"

"Pretty much. They put on one play per year for the parents, not the community. And it's in the gym. There's no auditorium. They don't really have costumes either. As a club we can perform at outside events wherever they'll let us. I have several ideas going already."

"That's cool. Hey, when will I see you again?"

"Soon. Don't you want to know about my ideas?"

"Sure. I'd rather talk about it in person though. I miss you."

His last three words oozed loneliness. It kind of turned me off. I missed him too, but not in a mushy be-with-you-or-die kind of way. "Well, that's why I called as soon as I got home. So we could talk."

"Yeah, but it's not the same. I want to see the cute way you wrinkle your nose and stare into your gorgeous eyes."

I paused. Didn't what was in my mind hold more attraction than me crinkling my nose? But he was right; talking in person was more fun. "Okay. What about Friday night?"

He grunted. "I've got the football game and I'm helping out with this sign thing for it. What about Saturday?"

Sign thing? Why didn't he invite me to help with it too? "We're moving Granny back to her house Saturday. I'll be gone all day and into the evening."

"Sunday?"

"That's family day. Unless you want to hang with us and come to church or Sunday supper?"

"I'll get back to you on that one. What I really want is some time alone with you."

But not like talking on the phone? Because he can't stare into my eyes? He used to be okay with me sharing my ideas and concerns by phone.

I exhaled with a muttered, "Hm. We'll figure it out. Well, I wanted to tell you about my idea for a drama club."

"That's great. You'll be good at it. I only wish it was something we could do together."

His voice lacked conviction, and I pressed my lips together. Together was sounding more and more difficult. "Yeah. It won't be the same, will it." I didn't say it as a question.

"No. I'll call you though. Soon."

CHAPTER THIRTY-FIVE

I SAT IN CHURCH AND craned my neck to look for John. He saw me and winked, and I sent a wave back. I settled into the pew and picked at my fingernails, half-listening to the sermon. Not having Gran here didn't feel right, but I supposed she must be happy to be back with her congregation. She would head back here for Thanksgiving weekend, which really wasn't so far away on the calendar. I'd gotten used to seeing her every day and hearing her advice and stories. I missed Jake too. He'd left a hole in my heart, but not as big as Gran's.

I went to the youth Sunday school class expecting to sit by John when I saw Brad. "What are you doing here?"

He grinned. "I told my dad what happened at the board meeting with Pastor Jensen and his so-called public speakers. Dad didn't like what happened. We're trying out this church today. He might be opening up to some changes around here."

"That's wonderful! I guess there was some good that came out of that awful night."

Brad nodded. "There might be others opening up to change. You know what else? Dad heard that Roland Jensen is looking to run for mayor in the next election."

I wrinkled my nose. "Ugh. Don't say that."

Brad didn't seem phased. He kept his expression bright. "What it means is that we have our work cut out for us."

"We do?"

"Yep. We have to keep making noise for the One Race campaign."

I came up on my toes. "Really? And you'll help me?"

"Me and Patty and Melanie and lots of us. Plus anyone you want from Pennfields too."

"What about Jake?" I bit my bottom lip.

Brad's expression fell a notch. "I don't know. Maybe. He's gotten a little…distracted."

My breath hitched. "Distracted?"

Brad paused, figuring out his words. "Since you've been gone, there's a cheerleader after him." He put up one hand to keep me from speaking as I narrowed my eyes at him. "He didn't go seeking her, and he's resisting, but I'm afraid she's drawing him in with you not around. Sorry to tell you."

The stab went in sharp and fast, but hadn't twisted. While I fumed inside, I managed to thank Brad for telling me. It explained a lot.

So Jake was a look-you-in-the-eyes, hands-on, lips-on kind of guy. Now I knew. And maybe that was okay. Between the drama club and the campaign, I had better things to do with my time than hang onto a shallow guy. That's what I told myself, but the news still left a wound.

"So, did you know I'm starting a drama club at Pennfields?"

Butterflies took over my stomach, but more from excitement than nervousness. I knew that drama club wouldn't be a total wash because Lawrence and one of his buddies had promised to show up. Since Friday, Miss Shepler had seen to it that drama club got mentioned on the morning announcements, and she announced it in both her drama class periods. I walked into the drama room Tuesday afternoon with curiosity and hope. To my astonishment, Lucinda sat in a chair near the teacher's desk.

"Lucinda! Are you joining the drama club?"

She snorted. "You don't want me. I'm barely passing the class. I'm here for an extra-credit assignment."

"Oh but I do want you. Wait 'til you hear what we're going to do. You have the perfect voice for it."

"I ain't no actress."

Miss Shepler returned from the file cabinet at the back of the room with a paper in her hand. "That's not a bad idea, Lucinda. I also like the deep, throaty quality of your voice. You can decide if you'd rather give the drama club a try for two weeks or do the written assignment on an actor or actress."

She snatched the paper and shuffled out of the room. I hoped everyone didn't have the same opinion.

It took a couple minutes longer for anyone to show up. I was relieved when Lawrence and his friend walked in. He introduced me to Joe and then a short, pretty girl from my drama class joined us.

I directed them to pull their chairs into a circle. "Okay, let's get started. Thanks for coming."

"Is this all there's going to be?" Julia asked. She didn't sound or look very happy.

"Unless someone walks in soon." I smiled at her. "Don't worry. We'll spread the word and more will join us."

"My friend said she would come if you'll join her club—the math club. They're preparing for the Scholastic Bowl."

I winced. "We'll have to get members another way." My positive vibe resurfaced. "Just wait 'til you hear what I have planned. You'll be glad you came. First, we have to make the club official. We need to see if you want any bylaws and hold an election."

Lawrence spoke up. "Buy whats? Not with my money. Just kiddin'. We gotta have rules?"

"Let's not worry about rules yet, but we need a club officer or two."

Lawrence gave me a toothy grin. "I nominate Charlotte as president." He elbowed his friend.

"I second it." Joe said with the same grin.

Miss Shepler, who had been listening from her desk, asked, "Julia, are you in agreement?"

"Yes." Julia's slight frame sat up taller.

Miss Shepler nodded. "Then you now have an official club with Charlotte as president. Anybody else want to become an officer?"

We looked at one another. Lawrence shrugged. I took charge again. "We can do that later. Let me tell you about our first gig."

Miss Shepler raised her brow.

"We got a gig?" Lawrence slapped his thigh. "Ooo-whee!"

I appreciated his enthusiasm. I might have had everyone running for the door instead. "We're doing a short spot for Kesley's Market on the local radio station." Joe squinted at me. "Radio? I thought we were acting."

I nodded. "We'll get more visible but one thing at a time. This will give us a chance to practice enunciation, voice inflection, and projection." Julia already knew about that, but I explained it for the boys.

"What are we supposed to say?" Julia asked.

"We get to decide and have Kesley's approve it." I gave them my best excited face. "The theme is: Let's Talk Turkey. We want something like, 'My moist turkey will be talked about for years to come because I got it at Kesley's,' or 'I'm the perfect turkey. You can find me at Kesley's.'"

Julia looked horrified, Lawrence laughed and flapped his wings, and Joe asked, "Can I do a turkey gobble?" He gave a demonstration, which actually sounded pretty good.

"Sure, as long as you're not silly about it. We can even be turkeys talking to one another about Thanksgiving dinner as long as we do it professionally. You okay, Julia?"

"Uh...I guess."

I believed she would get used to the idea. It sounded like the boys were on board. I had Miss Shepler's full attention. She walked over and said, "Charlotte, you've gone to some effort here. I'm impressed. Now each of you must know that if y'all say you're going to do this, you show up and do it. Understand?" She looked the other three in the eyes and got nods from them. "Charlotte, do you have an appointment to record this?"

"Yes, ma'am." I gave the details.

She nodded and went back to her desk.

"About the script...here's an idea. Since there's four of us, we're like a barbershop quartet." *The Music Man* had crept into my mind.

"Or the Beatles," Julia said with a giggle.

I waved my hand. "Yeah. Okay. So maybe the first one," I pointed to Lawrence, "says, 'Let's', the next 'talk'," I pointed to Julia, "'tur-' will be Joe, and 'key'", where I pointed to myself. Then everyone together says, "at Kesley's."

"Then I gobble?" Joe asked.

"Yeah." I gave him a thumbs up. "Let's try that much."

252

We ran through it a few times with me giving specific directions each time, until the line was nice and smooth. The noticeable progress jazzed them up.

"What y'all think, Ms. Shepler," Joe asked. I liked the confidence in his tone.

"I'm proud as a peacock…or turkey," she said, smiling.

I nodded my approval to the group. "You're doing great. We have about twenty minutes to come up with the rest and run through it. Ideas?"

Julia spoke first, and I was glad she was no longer terrified by doing something different. "I'm trying to imagine what turkey friends might say to one another."

Joe laughed and added to that idea. As a small group, the brainstorming worked well and quickly. It wasn't long before we had 30 seconds of what Miss Shepler thought was good material. The members didn't mind doing a Thanksgiving commercial talking about turkeys. They liked being creative, included, and doing something none of their friends had ever done. I would definitely thank God for a positive outcome tonight. The first meeting had been a success.

Patty called that evening, asking how drama club went. I took the call in the den, sitting at Dad's desk. I told her all about the small but cooperative drama club. She chuckled when I told her about our little gig. "It's not *The Music Man*, but I still loved doing it."

"Way to go, Madame President."

I snorted and pushed on to my big question. "What do you know about Jake and some cheerleader?"

"Not much, but something's going on. He hasn't eaten lunch with us for the last two days."

It didn't sound like Jake resisting the cheerleader; it sounded serious. "What does Brad say?"

"I've tried to put him on the spot but he doesn't want to betray his friend. He tells me to go to the source. I didn't like doing that to Brad though, so I won't push it."

"Okay. Did you see Jake at the football game?"

"I didn't go. I had a headache."

"Huh." I sorted through the information. It seemed like something changed right around that football game. Mom said he called while I was at the club meeting, but he didn't ask for me to call him back. The last I talked to him was Wednesday. Wow, it's been a week. It took a second before I closed my mouth. I hadn't been gone two weeks and he's spending time with another girl. "Do you think Jake is shallow?"

"You want the truth?"

My response was automatic. "Of course."

"It's time to move on."

The stab this time was more of a pin prick. "You're right. I'll miss him but he's not worth crying over. I hope he has the decency to tell me himself."

"You okay? You don't seem too broken up."

"I know. What's with that? Going to Pennfields has been an eye opener in so many ways—not only about the school and the students but about me."

"Hm. Any interesting guys at school?"

"Not really, but I haven't been looking. There's a guy named Lawrence who is becoming a good friend. If he asked me out, I'd go. I like how happy-go-lucky he is and his sense of humor. He joined the drama club to support me."

"How sweet. Could be a keeper."

"I don't know if he's interested in me that way. Guess I'll find out when I find out."

Patty was quiet for a minute. "Charlotte?" Her voice was soft.

"Yeah?"

"We'll continue to be friends, right?"

"Of course!" Poor Patty, worrying like that. "Just because Jake and I are drifting apart doesn't mean we are going to. Neither of us is shallow. It'll take some extra effort. But you're worth it. I promise."

I heard Patty exhale. "And it'll get easier once I get my license. Melanie gets hers first so maybe the three of us can do stuff."

"Without her groupies? Are you kidding?" We both laughed. "I'll have to see if I can borrow my dad's car more. Gran's car isn't here to borrow. She moved back home."

"Perfect. I'm glad she's well enough to do that," Patty said, "and I'm glad she doesn't have to stay alone at your house Friday night. I wouldn't have been able to get her a play ticket."

"I know." Gran would love going. So unfair.

"You can pick the tickets up from a will-call table in the lobby."

"Thanks."

"Brad and I are going Friday too. I got all our seats together. John will be happy to know it all worked out. He's been bugging me about making sure your family got tickets for Friday night."

"John's been bugging you? That's weird. He's only the constable but I told him I wouldn't miss it for anything." I sighed. "I miss not having drama with John. He always made it fun. At least I get to see him most Sundays at church."

"Maybe he gets to do something bigger than that constable part. There's a rumor going around school that there's something in addition to the play—like a special warmup act. I thought the rumor was spreading to help ticket sales but maybe it's real and John has a part in it."

"Groovy. If there's a bonus, even better." I wouldn't put it past Mr. Dodd to come up with something extra.

"Yep. We'll see."

"I better get to my homework. Thanks for calling and for reserving our tickets."

"No problem. I have to go too, but let me run something past you."

I cocked an eyebrow. "Okay."

"It seems like you're adjusting to Pennfields, and I'm glad. I hate that you can't be at Oakmont, but I'm glad you can start a club and continue working on your dreams."

It was sweet but I couldn't help rolling my eyes. I had a good day today but knew that progress would inch along like a snail. "Some big dream. Three other members. That's not worth putting on a scholarship application, but thanks. I'm trying." Only time would tell if the club would grow or dissolve.

"What I mean to say is that though you're working on making improvements to the drama department, would it be alright if we continue with the One Race campaign? Melanie and I have an idea."

"Are you kidding? Sure! What's the idea?"

"We checked the city's regulations. The sidewalk near the auditorium is public property and we want to hand out flyers as people come to the play—this time without candy bars."

I laughed. "I'll help you."

CHAPTER THIRTY-SIX

MOM DROPPED ME OFF AT Oakmont early enough for me to hand out flyers to the earliest attenders at the play. Early-arrivers would come along soon. Melanie squealed when she saw me and I gave a hug to her and Patty.

I looked at the half-sheet of mimeographed purplish text encompassed by a hand-drawn peace sign. The words *One Race: The Human Race* stood out. Below that read *Support Peace and Brotherhood*. The tiny print at the bottom read *The One Race Campaign*.

"Do you like it?" Melanie asked. "I drew the peace sign but Patty had the idea for it."

I grinned. "It looks fab. Sounds like a real organization too."

"Yeah," Patty said. "We should look into registering it or something." She handed me a third of the flyers.

I looked to Melanie. "No Gina or Ellen?"

She shook her head. "We didn't want to overwhelm the ticket holders. This will be a quiet effort. No shouting or pouncing on anyone. We hold it out to them and see if they'll take it."

"And no reason to call the cops," Patty added. "The goal isn't to make anyone mad but to gently keep pushing. We do it over and over and over again until they make the choice for equality and freedom."

Freedom. Mary would love this idea. I put on my sweater against the growing chill, now that the sun was setting. "Do you think the majority will accept freedom for all in our lifetime?"

"I do. The Supreme Court backs it up, and we'll do our part."

I liked the confidence in Patty's voice. Our little efforts could matter. A few people walked toward us on their way to the auditorium. I smiled and offered a flyer.

Over the next twenty minutes, we handed out all the flyers that Patty made. Some were crumpled up and tossed into the garbage can up by the building, but most would have glanced at it first.

As soon as my family arrived, Melanie said, "I have to go." She backed away toward the door. "You guys better get to your seats too."

Patty looked at me and shrugged. Did she think we didn't know that? Melanie rushed ahead and we followed her inside.

I picked up my ticket and found my row in the rather full auditorium. I sat by Mark. Patty and Brad filed in, and I grinned at them. "Great seats. Right smack in the middle." Patty agreed with a nod.

I looked around and waved at some friends I hadn't seen in nearly two weeks. The chatter went on around me as I examined the program until the house lights dimmed and brightened again. A moment later, Mr. Dodd came out in front of the curtain and a spotlight shown on him. The noise died down.

"Ladies and gentlemen, we welcome you to this evening's performance of *The Music Man*. The students have worked hard and I know you will enjoy it. Before that, however, I have a special surprise."

Patty and I exchanged a glance. I imagined John was in on it.

"We wish to feature the work of two outstanding students, one tonight and one tomorrow night. These students have developed their drama skills in extraordinary ways. Tonight we will present a short historical reader's theater written by the student herself, which she performed in her history class."

My heart skipped a beat and then made up for it by double timing. Did he mean me? Mark glanced at me. Patty grabbed my arm. They had to be wondering the same thing. Brad remained in his seat, so I relaxed the tiniest bit. He should be back stage if he was involved.

"Without her prior knowledge, we now present a historical short work written by Miss Charlotte Rogers."

I gasped as the curtain opened to reveal three people sitting on stools: Melanie, John, and…Gran? Granny found me instantly, having known where to look. I clasped my hands to my chest and felt a quiver in my chin. How perfect that Gran could play Mary. How did they know to do that?

A murmur rose through the room but quickly died down as the lights came up on the actors. I supposed the audience found it alright for a colored woman to perform on stage as long as she didn't sit in a seat that was meant for white people.

John began the narration and sucked me into the time period with his deep voice and the gold pocket watch chain trailing from his vest pocket. It didn't matter that I practically knew the script by heart. I was seeing it as an audience member for the first time.

John, of course, did a fabulous job, and Melanie sounded the finest I'd ever heard from her, but Gran? Gran touched my heart. A true master story-teller, with all the right voice inflections that conveyed Mary's emotions. She looked so cute in her white apron and kerchief head wrap, I wanted to hug her.

I found myself leaning forward, fully engaged—not only through my eyes and ears but with my heart. I sensed the early connection between Sue and Mary as childhood friends, and then their growing distance as life's realities forced them apart. I felt the heartache of Mary's defilement and the exciting horror of the battle and being trapped in the cellar. The ending was sad—where Mary dies of consumption, but not too sad. An air of hopefulness would live on with Mary's dream of freedom implanted in her children. Those children would walk in the ways their mother had taught from the pages of her first true possession, and later from a Bible their father had purchased. They would make further strides toward the cause of freedom with each generation. I was a part of that. No one could tell me my one-sixteenth wasn't important, and I would never try to hide it again. I am what I am, and I'm happy with that.

When the three of them slipped from their stools and bowed in unison, I bounded to my feet, applauding with tears in my eyes. Several others stood to applaud as well. When I sat back down, Gran remained on stage, still holding her microphone.

"I'd like y'all to know that I'm so proud of Charlotte. Her friend, John, wanted to give her this gift so she could list it in her scholarship portfolio. You see, her dream to perform in the play tonight was taken from her. Some of you know that—for better or worse—the school board voted to send her to Pennfields High. I am the granddaughter of Mary the slave, and Charlotte is my granddaughter. We have a rich history. Let us learn from it. Thank you."

A growing murmur filled the room. Patty started clapping vigorously and a smattering joined her. She whispered to me, "This will do so much more than handing out those pieces of paper ever could."

I didn't have a response. I sat there, trying to process everything. John did this for me—with the approval and help of Mr. Dodd? When had Gran gotten involved? Would it really make a difference like Patty thought?

Three-fourths of the audience had given a standing ovation. Some of that would be for the performers, some likely wanted to recognize my effort, but some must have applauded a story that possessed the power to make them feel. Right? There was more to the message than something historical. Would as many have applauded if they knew ahead what Gran had revealed? Doubtful. But it made them think. It created emotion within. It forced them to choose.

I should use Mary's story more. Yeah, get the full version published in black and white. It was good to make people think and feel and choose.

The curtain had closed, the murmuring vanished, and Mr. Dodd stood in the spotlight. He looked unconcerned that Gran might have caused any discomfort. "I hope you enjoyed that. Without further ado, the drama department of Oakmont High now presents," his arm swept across the stage, "*The Music Man.*"

EPILOGUE

Charlotte, June 1966, South Carolina

I STOOD IN LINE WITH a hundred plus students in the Pennfields High gymnasium, waiting to march to my seat. With the last name of Rogers, I was about two-thirds the way back.

The girl next to me made small talk as we waited. "Your hair looks nice, Charlotte."

"Thanks." There were benefits to knowing Patty's sister. "You look nice too." The conversation took my thoughts off myself—the best remedy for those stomach flutters that showed up at big events like this and on opening night of a play. "What are your plans after graduation?"

She took in a breath and stood a little taller; her chest seemed to puff out. "I'll be attending Boxwood County Community College—first girl in my family to go." Her expression lifted, though I could tell she tried to contain her smile.

"Groovy. I'll be at Boxwood too. We'll probably see one another." I visualized us crossing paths on the magnolia-lined sidewalks between buildings that suddenly shrank to a friendly size. The idea of seeing someone from Pennfields in my next stage of life felt comforting, though I didn't know her well. Her parents had to be so proud.

I couldn't help reminiscing over the last three years. So much had happened. Back then, I never thought this day would come, but I made it.

The line ahead started moving. For the most part, I ached to move on from high school. John and I both received full drama scholarships to the community college. Mine was the first a drama student from Pennfields High would receive. We would be working together again, and I couldn't wait.

I marched past John, sitting next to Gran and the rest of my family in the audience section. I gave them all a tiny wave. It wasn't the time for cheering yet, but Gran showed me two thumbs up. Mom and Dad looked gratified but Mark twirled a finger silently in the air in a sarcastic whoopee, already anxious to go home. John met my eyes and returned my smile, which sent a flutter to my heart. On his lap sat a bouquet of pink roses like the ones he'd given me last month when Pennfields put on their second play of the year, the one where Miss Shepler let me work as assistant director.

Marching in alphabetically, Lawrence wasn't far from me, and he inclined his chin to me as I filed in behind his row. I grinned at him. He and Vanessa had been my lifesavers, remaining rare friends while too many saw me as a threat with big ideas my sophomore year.

Part of me held some fondness for the struggles I endured, now that they were behind me. It took a while for students to see my true colors. I fought to get six club members before that first Christmas, and now we had twenty-seven. Many more were taking drama classes. Miss Shepler had added an advanced class this year, and she said it was because of me. I pressed my hand against my chest and I exhaled long and slow. Funny how good for me Pennfields turned out to be.

I sat in my seat in the graduate section, feeling a measure of pride as I fingered the tassel on my cap. I'd earned every inch of my diploma through sweat and tears. Tomorrow night I would sit with the audience at Oakmont High and watch those friends feel as proud as I do now. Then I'd attend Patty's graduation party. We'd celebrate our accomplishment and new freedom.

Patty, Melanie, and I kept tight that first year, when I needed their friendship so badly. We wrote letters to the newspaper editor, handed out more flyers, and staged a protest with picket signs in front of Pastor Jensen's church. I'd like to say we remained tight, but relationships rarely flourish when you're separated and busy. Patty and I may not talk on the phone as often now, but we'll always be friends.

I had a wrapped gift for her sitting on the desk in my room, and one for Melanie, Brad, Mr. Dodd, and Mrs. Burkhart. Miss Shepler already had hers. Gran had paid a printer to make copies into a thin paperback of Mary's story. When Scott heard, he got the newspaper to publish sections in installments, becoming one of its more popular features and giving me some extra spending money after paying Gran back for the books. The book would always remind my friends and mentors of our time together. I had no doubt Patty and I would stay in touch after she left for South Carolina State.

I guess we'll never know how much of an impact our campaign efforts made. Certainly some good came from it. We opened a few eyes to the change that was coming. The real good came from the government, and next fall there would be total integration and more fiscal equity between the two county high schools. Mark will have two years to see those improvements, and I count on hearing his feedback. If things don't go as I expect, I'll be writing more letters to the editor.

My thoughts continued to drift as I listened to speeches from the boy and girl valedictorians. It felt momentous again when my row lined up to have our names called, shake the principal's hand, and get our diplomas. All at once I was in the front, hearing my name: "Miss Charlotte Ann Rogers." A certain group whooped and hollered along with the general clapping. I heard a cowbell clanging that Mark must have brought. I held onto the diploma and waved with my free hand, grinning like a toothpaste commercial star.

When all the names had been read and everyone had returned to their seats, the principal stood again at the microphone. "Congratulations Pennfields High Class of 1966!" I threw my tasseled cap into the air and shouted along with the rest of the students. We did it!

I made my way to my family. John hung back to let them congratulate me first, the bouquet of roses now hiding behind his back. Gran stepped up to me first. I hugged her middle, pressing my cheek against hers. "I did it, Gran. I graduated!"

"Of course you did, child. We had no doubt." She laughed. "I 'spose I best quit calling you child now that you've graduated."

"You can call me whatever you want, as long as you—"

Gran finished the sentence with me, "—don't call me late for supper."

ABOUT THE AUTHOR:

Renae Weight Mackley is a mother to six, grandmother to more. She lived during one of the story time periods, though too young to remember much, and has visited the battlefield area of the other. Her desire is to put a touch of faith into her novels, because hey—we can all use a little inspiration. She's a bicycle rider; a former substitute teacher; creator of music, fiber arts, good food, and the written word.

Please visit her website www.renaeweightmackley.com and her author Facebook page at www.facebook.com/RenaeWMackley/

OTHER BOOKS BY RENAE WEIGHT MACKLEY:

Secrets of the King's Daughter, 2016, Covenant Communications, Inc.
Survival of the King's Daughter, 2017, Covenant Communication, Inc.
Samuel's Sword: A Stripling Warrior Romance, 2018, Renae Weight Mackley
Coming Soon: *A Brush with Danger: An American Historical Romance*

Made in the USA
Las Vegas, NV
02 February 2021